"Who do you think you are, ordering me about?

"If I'm such a burden to you, why don't you just leave me here?"

Alec's voice was low and tight with anger. "Because if I leave you here I will only have to come and get you out of a whorehouse, or rescue you from a pack of Gypsies, or fish you out of the blessed bay—at midnight in a thunderstorm, no doubt! No, you're going with me to Grass Valley, where I can leave you safe and sound!"

"I shan't be carted off and dumped like some unwanted parcel! And I won't travel without a proper chaperon."

Alec grasped her upper arm, and Rowan felt the unbreakable strength of his hold. "Don't worry about chaperons. Believe me, the last thing I want on this green earth is to take liberties with the likes of you!"

Dear Reader,

There is a lot to look for this month from Harlequin Historicals.

Sweet Seduction by Julie Tetel is the first of two intriguing stories set in Maryland during the early 1800s. Heroine Jane Shaw was raised as a Southern belle, but she is more than a match for the British soldiers who sequester her family's home. And don't miss the sequel, *Sweet Sensations,* coming in July.

Readers following the TAGGARTS OF TEXAS! series by Ruth Jean Dale will be delighted to discover the prequel to the earlier books in this month's lineup. *Legend!* is the story of Boone, the Taggart who started it all by turning the little town of Jones, Texas, on its ear.

Captured Moment by Coral Smith Saxe is set during the California mining days. Straight off the boat from the old country, the impish Rowen Trelarken stumbles into an immediate series of misadventures, dragging an unwilling Alec McKenzie along for the ride.

Frenchwoman Elise de Vire marries Sir Adam Saker as an act of revenge, but the force of the attraction between them places them both in mortal danger in *Beloved Deceiver,* a medieval tale from Laurie Grant.

Four new romances from Harlequin Historicals. We hope you enjoy them.

Sincerely,

Tracy Farrell
Senior Editor

Captured Moment

CORAL SMITH SAXE

Harlequin Books

TORONTO • NEW YORK • LONDON
AMSTERDAM • PARIS • SYDNEY • HAMBURG
STOCKHOLM • ATHENS • TOKYO • MILAN
MADRID • WARSAW • BUDAPEST • AUCKLAND

Harlequin Historicals first edition April 1993

ISBN 0-373-28769-0

CAPTURED MOMENT

CORAL SMITH SAXE

could never study in the library while she was in school—there were too many tempting books around to distract her. One day when she was in graduate school, a book about Henry V beckoned to her and she never did get her doctoral thesis finished. She now creates her own romantic distractions at her home in central Texas, where she lives with her physicist husband, her co-ed mother-in-law, twin sons and twin cats.

To all those who helped,
but most especially to Dorothy Saxe,
who gave me the best gift of all: the time to write.

Chapter One

San Francisco, 1867

"Look there! Didn't I tell you? The streets of San Francisco *are* paved with gold!"

Rowan Trelarken looked up from the canvas sack she was tying, and pushed a fog-dampened lock of red hair from her forehead. She narrowed her eyes and peered down the rough, weathered planks of the wharf to the street, where one of her shipmates, a girl named Mary, was pointing.

"Surely you're mistaken—" she began.

She got no further. A narrow shaft of early-morning sunlight beamed through the mist and glinted off the surface of the wet, muddy thoroughfare that fronted the wharf. The girl beside her drew a sharp breath. "See? It's true! Gold! We didn't come all this way for nothing!"

Before Rowan could move or speak, Mary was off at a run, her heavy valise banging over the planks as she went. "Wait!" Rowan called, fumbling with the knot on her bundle. All the possessions she had brought from Cornwall were tied up inside the large oiled-canvas sack, but the rope that drew it closed was fickle—too tight for Rowan's slender fingers one moment, coming loose and flapping the next. "Wait. I'll come with you—uh!—as soon as I can get this tied!"

Shouts filled the air around her, drowning out her words, as well as the screeches of the gulls that wheeled overhead. The other steerage passengers from off the *Southern Star* had sighted the bright yellow specks by now, and they stormed past Rowan, eager to grab up the prize they'd dreamed of ever since the ship left the docks at Liverpool.

Rowan hesitated, though her knot was now secure. This couldn't be true, she thought, coming to her feet. Stories of gold in the streets were just that—stories. She'd heard many such tales back home in the village of Carn Rose, but she'd always been skeptical. One didn't find copper in the streets at home; why would there be gold in the streets here?

Yet lack of gold—money—was part of what had driven her family from their home, and almost broken the proud Trelarken spirit. It had left her mother beggared and bewildered, her brother, Gil, without a future, and had bound Rowan, the highborn Trelarken heiress, in marriage to Luke Syms, a common miner in a foreign country—a man she hardly knew. If she could gather enough of this gold, she thought, she might solve most of her problems in a single morning!

The clamor grew around her, and she was drawn into the onrush. Hefting her bundle, she hurried to the street, half under her own power, half carried by the shouting, struggling passengers.

"'Tes gold, all right! The real thing!" shouted a man next to her. He bent to the ground and scraped up more flakes from the muddy street.

"Are you sure?" Rowan asked, tugging at his sleeve.

"Just 'e look at that," the man said, extending a grimy paw. Yellow flecks decorated the mud in his hardened palm. "'E'll not find the like of this at the bottom of Wheal Glennys back in Cornwall, that's a bet. I were a tinner there, before it all went bust. But I'll not be diggin' no more!"

"Yes, but how—?" Rowan was shoved ahead by the mob, and was unable to finish her question. She'd lost sight of Mary and was fast being swept away from the miner from home. She had to clamp her hand tightly around her bundle to keep from losing it altogether.

Rowan stooped to pick up some of the gold-speckled dirt. Holding her ground as the raucous crowd flowed past her, she pushed at the dirt in her palm and saw how delicate bits of the debris caught the light and shone.

"It can't be," she breathed. And yet here it was. Real gold, in the streets of this strange new city.

She carefully brushed the dirt into the pocket of her plain black wool dress and hauled on the knot that bound her sack. She needed a plan, she thought. If she could just find somewhere to set her sack down, she could get both hands on the wealth that lay before her. Excitement surged up in her. She had to get out into the street and claim a share of the gold for herself.

Everywhere, passengers from the ship were scrambling in the mud, many on their hands and knees, scraping and fighting like wild things over the golden specks. One woman used a carpetbag to scoop up the mud; two boys had found a bottle and were forcing handfuls down its narrow neck. Mud covered their faces, their clothes, but it was clear that they didn't care. Rowan felt a twinge of pity and disgust at the sight, though she knew her own need was as great as theirs.

A woman holding a wailing baby rushed past, jostling her, and she was bumped up against a tarred wooden piling. Quickly she caught up a rope that dangled from an iron loop fastened to the wood. Here was a way to get her hands free to dig. All she lacked was a container for her gold, and there was bound to be something around the wharf she could use. She was running the rope through the knot on her bundle when she heard laughter floating down from overhead.

A high-pitched male voice was heard over the racket of the gold-seekers. "Look at them, Durrell! Look at the tall skinny one banging the short one over the head with his boot!"

"This beats the burlesque," another man cried. "You've surpassed yourself this time, Carson. Salting the street with gold dust—it's inspired! Look, just look at that one with the coffeepot!"

Rowan stepped back from her bundle and peered up at the speakers. She saw three well-heeled-looking young men lounging on the balcony of a two-story warehouse, laughing and pointing at the crowd below.

Oblivious of Rowan's gaze, they leaned on the railing and watched the spectacle with relish.

The light-haired man, the one named Durrell, nudged the tall, brown-haired man in the middle. "Look there, Alec, now there's a picture for you. And you without your camera, eh?" Durrell shook with mirth, but his friend Alec said nothing, only watched as the other two continued to point and bray their amusement.

Stunned, Rowan turned to look at the crowd of her shipmates, still grubbing in the street. No one in that crowd was half so well-dressed as the men on the balcony. Indeed, the cost of one of those men's waistcoats alone would pay a Cornish miner's rent for half a year, perhaps longer.

She'd been right. It was too good to be true. They were making fools of themselves, all for the entertainment of these—these jackasses!

At home, the quicksilver Trelarken temper was famed throughout the county. Rowan was no exception to the family rule. She flung down the rope she held and marched into the street. Shouldering people aside, she reached into the wettest, dirtiest pothole in sight and scooped up a huge handful of mud, heedless of her clothes and of the treasure sprinkled on top of the mess. She pushed her way back through the crowd and climbed up the back of a flatbed wagon that stood waiting to be loaded. The sight of the tall, slender young woman with murder in her bright blue eyes and an enormous mudball in one hand distracted people nearby and they stopped to watch as she took a stance in the bed of the wagon.

"You!" she shouted upward. "You three ill-bred, shameless tyrants up there!"

The three men fell silent, surprised by the vehemence of her words. The watchers fell silent, as well.

"Here," Rowan called, taking careful aim. "I believe you gentlemen dropped something!" She drew back her arm and let fly with every ounce of strength she possessed.

The mud hit its mark with soul-satisfying accuracy. It struck Alec, the man in the middle, square on the chest and spattered in all directions, effectively covering his friends in the process. He was nearly a head taller than the other two, so they caught most of the spray full in the face.

The people clustered around the wagon gasped. Rowan stared up at the three men, who were frozen in surprise.

"What the hell . . ." the fair-haired one spluttered.

"Look at them!" Rowan shouted over the noise of the crowd. "Look at the men who tried to make fools of us all. There's no gold here. Only a few pitiful flakes!"

"Oh, no, girl. That can't be. Look what all I've got!" A woman thrust her fist upward to show Rowan her findings.

Rowan pointed at the men on the balcony. "Show it to them! These fine fellows salted this street with gold dust just for the sport of seeing a lot of stupid immigrants grovel in the dirt! Isn't that right?" she demanded of the three.

None of them spoke. Word was spreading through the crowd. More people turned to look at the men, and at Rowan, who was still perched on the flatbed, hands on her hips, head tilted back to meet their gaze with defiance.

The man named Carson was the first to speak. "It was only a joke..." he began.

"Oh, yes, and a funny one at that," Rowan cried. "If that's what passes for humor in your San Francisco, then heaven help the people who cannot afford to laugh!"

Carson reddened in fury and leapt toward the steps. His companion, Alec, was on his heels in an instant.

"Quick, girl, get down from there!" One of the men from the crowd tugged at the hem of Rowan's skirt as the third man, Durrell, went after his partners. "Get out of here before there's trouble."

Rowan hesitated a moment, then saw the look of pure rage on Carson's face as he hurried down the many steps to the street. She was suddenly aware of the danger in her position. She hopped off the wagon and grabbed up her sack.

"Here, over here!" A woman threw a wooly shawl over Rowan's head and pulled her into the depths of the crowd. "Keep covered, or that copper hair of yours will give you away in a fast tick."

Rowan found herself surrounded by people, all of them pressing close in around her. Dimly she heard shouting from the edge of the crowd and knew that the men from the warehouse had reached the street. Step by step, keeping her head down, she was ushered toward the opposite side of the street, handed to one stranger after another, each time moving farther away from the pranksters and closer to safety.

"Stay here till it's over," a boy told her, helping her with her bundle. "They'll give up lookin' soon, I guess. There's too many of us."

"Thank you," she managed to stammer.

The boy grinned, eyes bright in his dirty face. "Didn't you just give it to 'em good, though! I wished I'd o' done it, too. Them sneakin' cowards."

Rowan stared at him and realized what she'd done. "Don't say that! I did a very stupid thing. I could have hurt everyone here by angering those men."

The boy wasn't much daunted. "Maybe. But I'd o' fought for ya. It's a ruddy mean thing to do to folks just 'cause they're poor and from a dif'rent place."

He darted off into the street before Rowan could speak again. The noise was dying down, and the crowd was dispersing, many people going back to the wharf where they'd abandoned their belongings in the first rush for gold. Rowan caught sight of a policeman's uniform and shrank back into the shadow of the building behind her. The last thing she needed now was to land in jail for muddying up the local gentry. Only an hour before, government officials had checked everyone in steerage aboard the *Southern Star,* and some passengers had been detained on the ship. Could she be held back from entering the United States if she assaulted someone the moment she stepped off the ship?

"Why did you do that, Rowan Trelarken?" she moaned to herself, leaning back against the wall. "The Trelarken Luck and your foolish temper, same as always."

"You can say amen to that," a deep voice beside her said.

She started in terror. The man grabbed her elbow before she had gone two steps. "No, you don't. If you go back there now, you'll only be in deeper trouble. Stay here until the police have cleared the place."

Rowan swallowed hard, looking up at the man who towered over her. Mud covered his expensive suit and his silk waistcoat. Bits of mud—speckled with gold, of course—clung to his thick brown hair and even decorated the dark brows that glowered over his snapping brown eyes. It was Alec, the man in the middle. He'd received the lion's share of the mud she'd thrown, and it was even now drying into hard evidence against her.

Dear God! she thought. She hadn't been in this country half an hour, and already she'd committed a crime! Her mind whirled. What did Americans do with foreign criminals? She was fairly certain they had courts and jails. But what did they do with those they convicted? Her vivid imagination quickly conjured up a panorama of horrifying punishments. Was it possible they took the law into their own hands here in California? She glanced down at the hand that encircled her upper arm. It looked and felt powerful, with a broad palm and long, tapered fingers.

She swallowed quickly as her eyes traced the line of Alec's arm to his shoulder. He had either the cleverest tailor in America, she thought distractedly, or the strongest, leanest shoulders she'd ever seen. Miners in Carn Rose weren't weaklings, not by a long stretch. What set this man apart from the men at home, besides his fine clothing and his longish hair, was his height. To have a tall son in Carn Rose was a misfortune in most men's eyes. How could a tall man ever hope to find work in the cramped tunnels of the mines? This Alec would have been given up for a soldier or a sailor before he was sixteen.

The man's voice broke into her scattered thoughts. "There. I think we can go now."

Rowan hung back. "Go where?"

"Away from here. Someplace where you can't get into any more trouble. Somewhere I can get out of these clothes and get cleaned up." He turned to start up the street.

Rowan pulled her arm out of his grip. "Oh, no, we are not," she said, standing firm in her place. "I'm to wait here, at the wharf. Someone is to come and meet me." She thought it best to leave Luke's name out of this. He might not appreciate being dragged into one of her scrapes.

"Do you see them now?" he asked.

Rowan stole a glance behind her. "N-no."

"Well, if you stay here, Tom Durrell and Whit Carson will have you arrested, I can guarantee it. You can come back and meet your friend later." He took her arm again.

"Let me go!" she cried, temper flaring. "Let me go, or I'll dirty the rest of you ... you great bully!"

He stared at her, obviously taken aback.

"Only a bully makes sport of people who can't defend themselves—"

He took a step back and slowly surveyed her, from the tips of her muddy boots to the top of her head, with its soft crown of deep red braids. His smile was slow. "I don't know where you come from, miss, but I think you're going to fit in just fine in San Francisco."

His amused tone and his measuring glance annoyed Rowan. "I'm not going to be in your San Francisco for long," she retorted. "I'm here to go to an even better place."

"Oh? And where might that be?"

"The Grass Valley. Not that it's any of your affair."

He threw back his head and laughed aloud at this. Rowan realized, in some small part of her mind, that she had not heard his laughter coming from the balcony earlier. She would have recalled such a rich, rolling sound. But that was no matter now.

"What is so amusing about Grass Valley?" she demanded.

His laughter subsided to a chuckle. "*The* Grass Valley, remember? And I think I'll leave it to you to discover why it's so amusing. Right now, you're going to have to move fast before Carson and Durrell spot you. See?"

She looked where he pointed and saw that the other mud-spattered men were conversing with the police officer she'd spied earlier. If they turned around, they'd surely see her.

Without a word, she yanked her bundle off the ground and started up the street, away from the wharf. The heavy load of her possessions banged against her shins as she sought to lengthen her strides.

"Here, at least let me take that." He came alongside her and reached for the bundle. A tug-of-war commenced as they continued moving down the street.

After the long journey around Cape Horn in the pinched, stifling quarters of the *Southern Star,* after impoverishment and loss, after being sent on a fool's hunt for gold, Rowan had had enough. She jerked the bundle away, dropped it onto the wooden sidewalk at her feet and whirled to face her adversary.

"All right, come on, you sniveling Yankee!" she said between clenched teeth. "Do your worst! It's nothing to what I've withstood so far and no worse than what's coming to me, I fancy, so do what you will! You'll not take a Trelarken very easily, I can tell you that bloody much right now, so come on you, just you come on, let's get on with it!"

He caught her fist in midswing, just scant inches before it would have connected with his jaw. She froze, staring up into the nearly black depths of his eyes. A long moment passed as they seemed to struggle with their wills, rather than their bodies. It was a close contest, but Alec came out ahead. "Don't tempt me," he whispered. "You're the one who started this, remember?"

"I started?" she said, gasping. "Of all the insufferable cheek—"

"Look, I give up." He held up his hands in a gesture of surrender. "If you don't want my help, I'll clear off. I think it's a mistake, but it's your funeral, Miss Trelarken."

"That's right," she retorted. "It is my...my funeral," she finished lamely, realizing how ridiculous she sounded.

He gave a short bow and turned away from her. He was walking back to the wharf, toward his friends. She watched, frozen, waiting for him to hail them and point out where she stood, only half-hidden by a stack of crates.

The moment never came. He threw his arms around their shoulders and walked down the street with them without a backward glance. The policeman waved off some men who were still prospecting in the street and cleared the way for oncoming traffic. Then he, too, walked away without looking in her direction.

Rowan breathed again. She counted herself fortunate to have escaped from both the law and that Alec. She waited until the officer was out of sight and then headed back to the wharf that served the *Southern Star*. She hauled her bundle to a spot near the street so that she could watch the carts and wagons and buggies rolling past. Luke would be here soon, she guessed. Hoisting herself up on a barrel that looked to have served as a bench many times before, she settled in to wait.

It wasn't a very pretty place, this San Francisco, she thought, gazing about. Everything seemed to be new and raw, and somewhat unfinished. It smelled of every odor under the sun, and looked as if its builders had no idea what a proper city should look like.

It was near the sea, like most of Cornwall, and some of the smaller fishing boats tied up at the docks looked like the boats at home. But the resemblance ended there. Here there were no tall mine chimneys or engine houses perched on cliffs above the water's edge, and there were no snug, square miner's cottages, their stonework freshly whitewashed, dotting the landscape.

Instead, through the clearing fog, she saw a crowd of buildings, most of them evidently scrabbled up hastily to house impatient owners. Closer by, the noise and bustle on the docks were rivaled only by the pungent smells of animals, plants and spices emanating from the holds of ships and from warehouses. Paddle wheelers steamed across the bay, and tall ships sailed in from the Pacific.

Rowan sighed. She saw nothing and no one she recognized. She was alone in this new country, far from family and friends. She recalled the late winter day when the merchant Henry Syms had appeared at their cottage door, taken her aside and proposed a marriage arrangement between Rowan and his brother, Luke. It wasn't a prospect she relished, but the debts her family owed to Syms were higher than she or her brother Gil could ever hope to repay. The shame of her father's theft of mine funds and his abandonment of his family still stung. It was the only way she could see to preserve the honor she'd always felt was synonymous with the Trelarken name.

"It's a good offer, Mother," she had said. "No one has offered better." She gave a wry laugh. "Truth to tell, no one else has offered anything."

"That's no reason to settle for Luke Syms."

Louisa Trelarken had been seated by the east window of their cottage, as she sat each day, just as if it were the sunny morning room of Nanstowe, the Trelarkens' former estate. She had deeded to her daughter her dark red hair, her wide, luminous blue eyes, and the sensitive nature that had served her well in good times, when the family had lived at Nanstowe and Louisa's every need had been met without question. But Louisa had never recovered from the shock of learning that her husband was both a profligate gambler and a thief, and that his conduct had robbed her of her mate, her station in life, her house, her lands, and her children's future. She'd retreated into a gentle fog of forgetfulness and fantasy, from which she was seldom roused. As for Gil and Rowan's father, Francis Trelarken, when he had fled the duchy under cover of night, all he had bequeathed to his children was his peppery temper, a love of life and nature, and an unconquerable will to survive.

"There simply are few men of your station in Carn Rose," Louisa had continued. "It must be a viscount for my daughter, or at least a baronet. If we were to go to Devon, perhaps, or even to London..."

Rowan cut her off gently. "No, Mother. There can't be a trip to anywhere to meet eligible gentlemen. I'm nineteen. Too old and too close to gentry to marry a working man in Carn Rose. Too young and too poor to marry into one of the old families of the county, let alone Devon or London. We owe Henry Syms more than we can ever hope to repay. He's prepared to cancel our debts when Luke and I are married."

"But America..." Louisa said, slender hands to her cheeks. "How will you live in that wild place? New York might be acceptable, but California? We hear nothing from there except news of mines and murders."

"I'll be marrying a Cornishman," Rowan said. "And we know that people from here have gone to the mines in Wisconsin State and in California."

"That may be true. But you are neither a Polgreeb nor a Tolbathy."

"No, I'm a Trelarken," Rowan replied. "A penniless, homeless, fatherless Trelarken."

"Rowan!"

"I don't mean to be harsh, Mother." Rowan paced before the hearth, trying to summon up the right words to convince her mother that her plan was the best hope they had of breaking free of charity. "I only want to make you see the truth of things. I'm a Trelarken now. But when I get to America, I'll become a Syms. Everything is different there. Merchants and miners are quite acceptable."

Louisa's shoulders slumped just a bit. "Well, I suppose Luke might do. He was a nice enough young man, sober and quiet. And I've seen him looking at you when he comes around. He does harbor feelings for you. Though you're too young, of course," she mused.

Rowan didn't bother to shake her mother from her lapse into the past. She had closed off that part of her mind that shouted objections much stronger than her mother's. Luke was a nice enough man, she insisted, at least what she remembered of him. He'd gone to California more than five years before. He was clean. Honest. And if he was close to forty while Rowan was nearer twenty, well, that only meant he'd be more stable, less apt to wander. Rowan wanted no part of a drifter.

As she sat on the sunny San Francisco wharf and watched passengers come and go, she smiled at the memory of her younger brother, Gil, waving from the train station at Plymouth. Only eleven months separated them in age; both were tall and slim, with fair skin that ran to freckles in summer, and the trademark

Trelarken red hair—Rowan's a deep red, like Louisa's, Gil's penny-bright, like their father's. Gil and Rowan had fought through their childhood, scrabbled for an education, and brought each other up in the chaos of their parent's affairs. As they grew older, they'd formed a tight alliance that often excluded all others. It had been their anchor when their father disappeared and his misdeeds came to light.

Later that day, after she'd left Louisa by the window with her needlework, Rowan had dragged Gil to their special spot, a soft rise that overlooked Nanstowe and all its lands. When they were settled on the ground beneath a lone beech tree, she had turned to Gil, her eyes bright with purpose.

"This was to be yours, Gil," she began.

"Oh, do give it up, Row," he had groaned. He stretched his lanky form out over the grass. "It's never going to be mine, and you know it."

"Perhaps it never will," she retorted. "But that doesn't mean that we have to live like paupers!"

"Well, we're not exactly sagging at the pockets and purses, are we?" Gil asked.

"Never mind that now, just listen to me. You know the vicar said that you could read law if only you could go to London— No, don't interrupt me," she said quickly, as she saw that he was about to protest. "I have a way to do it. I've accepted Henry's offer of marriage to Luke."

Gil's Trelarken temper flamed white-hot at that. "I cannot have it, Rowan!" he shouted, jumping to his feet. "I will not have it!" In seconds, their easy camaraderie vanished and Gil stormed off, repeating his vow to see Henry in hell before he'd let his sister marry a Syms. He was gone more than two hours, and when he found Rowan again, his face was cold with rage and frustration.

"You're serious?" he asked her, his gaze keen upon her.

"I am."

"Damn the man," Gil muttered. "If I could just— And what do you get in this bargain?" he asked abruptly. "A miner's lot is the same, in Cornwall or in California. Black dirt, cold pasties, and the lungs gone before he's fifty. Not to mention how you'd listen to every bell that rang, every day, fearing that it would sound the alarm for an accident below. If anything happened to Luke, you'd be left alone in a strange place, perhaps with children to care for all by yourself. Have you thought of that? Or do you imagine that things will suddenly change, that the Trelarken Luck will run with us instead of against us?" He slammed a fist against his thigh. "It's no good. I can't accept such an offer, Row. I won't!"

"Yes, you will," she said with sudden fierceness. "I know about the mines. Haven't I lived here all my life? My part of the bargain is the peace of knowing that the Trelarkens aren't beaten. That I can take care of my own. That I won't leave my family to scrape for themselves."

There was a brief silence. "You mean as Father did?" Gil's voice was husky.

Rowan didn't speak.

"That is what you mean, isn't it? You don't have to prove yourself to me. Or to Mother. Forget what all the gossips around here say. Father's gone, and that's that.''

"No," she said. "I don't have to prove myself. But this is my plan. It's what I want. It's a way out of our debt to Henry for the rent on the cottage and the coal to heat it, and the water in the well, and the earth in the garden, and—and the very air we breathe each day! He never says anything, but I see the satisfaction in his eyes when he and his wife come to visit, that look that says, 'So, the mighty Trelarkens are flesh and blood like the rest of us.' He won't hurt us by a word, but he just may kill us with his kindness.'' Her hands were clenched tight on her knees. "I want to do this, Gil. I have to. Please help me.''

Gil, already a man of strong persuasive powers, argued long and hard. When Louisa grew ill over the next few weeks, he argued that Rowan must stay for her sake. But Rowan's resolve was of steel. They needed her protection even more now, she insisted. There was no one else to turn to. If her mother died in poverty, she would never forgive herself.

In the end, she won out, and after seeing their mother improved and comfortably settled under her maiden aunt Morwenna's care, she and Gil parted in the spring, amid tears and teasing, at the Plymouth station. Using the last of their money, Gil took the train to London, while Rowan went north to Liverpool and boarded the ship that sailed through the long weeks to San Francisco.

"And now that I'm here," she murmured to a watchful pelican perched on a nearby piling, "where is Luke Syms?''

Chapter Two

Ten hours of waiting, and still no sign of Luke.

Dark had come on faster than Rowan had antici-
pated. The wind was blowing off the water, and she
shivered beneath the shawl she'd wrapped about her
head and shoulders. Fearing she'd mistaken Luke's
instructions, she'd checked and rechecked the brief
letter she'd carried in her pocket all the way from
Cornwall. But there was no error. She was to wait at the
wharf, and he would come to where the *Southern Star*
lay at anchor. She'd even cabled him on the last leg of
their journey, saying that all conditions were right for
the *Star* to arrive as scheduled. Correct date, correct
ship, correct city and country, she recited to herself. So
why was she still sitting all alone at the evening tide?

It was quieter on the docks, now, but noisier in the
saloons and gambling houses that lined the opposite
side of the street. From time to time, Rowan jumped at
the sound of gunfire or breaking glass, but no one disturbed her.

Luke had been delayed, she'd told herself all day. It
was probably a long trip from the Grass Valley. He'd

arrive at any moment. But the hour had grown late for those comforting thoughts. It was too dangerous to stay at the docks. She'd have to find a place to stay the night. But where could she go?

She slipped off the barrelhead, hoisted her sack and headed up the street. The sidewalks were less deserted here, and carriages and wagons rattled past, their wheels swishing in the muddy ruts of the street. Every few yards, streetlamps marked the way. She kept within their glow as much as she could. She estimated that she had enough money for a room for the night, if only she could find an inexpensive lodging house, or an inn that would be safe for a single woman. But was there such a place in San Francisco?

She passed a restaurant and breathed in the scent of roasting meat and strong coffee. Her stomach growled, reminding her that she hadn't eaten since she and her fellow passenger Mary had shared a dried apple and a cup of broth at dawn aboard ship. She moved on quickly. She could ignore hunger—she'd done so before. But she was tired and cold, and this strange city seemed unsafe, as well as unfamiliar.

At last she decided she'd best ask for help. Trying to get by on her own was just getting her colder and wearier. She paused at a streetlamp and waited for someone who looked kindly and safe to come along.

She rejected the man with the pistol stuffed in his belt. Likewise, the impressive black-hatted Spaniard whose footsteps rang with the music from his silver spurs. An old woman came by, wearing a sunbonnet and carrying a basket. Rowan started forward, then withdrew when she heard the woman muttering angrily to herself in some foreign tongue.

Rowan scolded herself for not knowing better. She could just hear Gil's good-natured teasing. "Trust our Rowan to go looking for an honest soul at a liar's tea party," he would say. How many good, compassionate souls could she expect to find in this wild place, especially at an hour when honest, hardworking folk were home in bed?

"Here, girl!" A woman's voice broke into her thoughts. "You looking for a room?"

Rowan whirled about. A short woman of fifty or so was beckoning to her, just two doors up the street. Warm, cheery light poured out of the doorway behind her, silhouetting her comfortably plump form and her frizzy gray hair. Rowan lifted her burden and hurried over to her.

"Looking for a room, dearie?"

"Yes, I am," Rowan said, relieved. "I was supposed to meet someone at the wharf—I've just come in on a ship—and no one has arrived, so I thought, as I'm new here . . ."

"Slow down, slow down, dearie! You can stay here tonight." The woman reached out for Rowan's canvas sack and brought it inside. "Just come in and get warm, girl, there's a good fire in the stove there."

Rowan stepped into the heated room and pulled the door shut behind her. "I don't know what the cost is," she said, following the woman over to the stove. "I'm afraid I can't— That is . . ."

The woman waved a plump hand, and a number of gaudy rings caught the light. "Don't you fret yourself about it, dearie, we'll find a way to meet the bill. Irish, are you? I mean, with that accent, and all that red hair."

Rowan knotted her shawl about her waist and held her hands out to the glowing warmth of the potbellied stove. "I'm English. Cornish, actually." She smiled. "I'm Rowan Trelarken."

"Rowan? Nice name! Got a real pretty ring to it. Folks around here'll like that. I'm Letty Brown."

She offered her hand, and Rowan shook it vigorously. "I can't tell you what it means to have found your inn, Mrs. Brown. I've never been in San Francisco before, I must confess."

"No! Why, I never would've guessed it!" Letty exclaimed. "Naw, I'm only teasing. This town's full of newcomers, and we make 'em welcome as best we can."

A man came down the stairs, buttoning his waistcoat and straightening his spectacles. "See you when I get back next week, Letty," he called to Rowan's hostess.

"Sure thing, Ted," she said, bustling to open the front door for him. "It's always good to see ya. Now mind you don't fall down one of them holes you work in. We want you back soon."

When he had gone, Letty bustled back to where Rowan was standing and took her chin in one plump hand. "You're a pretty thing, for all your skin and bones," she said. "Pretty blue eyes, an' that white Irish skin."

"Cornish," Rowan murmured, not liking to contradict her benefactress.

"Cornish, that's right," Letty said with a laugh. "Well, wherever you come from, they didn't have a lot of meat and potatoes, that's clear. Could you eat a bite?"

Rowan nodded, eyes wide. "But I must tell you, I can't pay much. Perhaps a little tea and a bit of toasted bread?"

Letty burst into a cackling laugh. "Tea and toast? You're a caution, girl. Come on into the kitchen and we'll see about some real supper, not bird feed."

Another man came down the stairs, brushing his hair back with both hands. Letty showed him to the door, as she had the other, exchanging a few cheery words with him as he departed.

Rowan smiled to herself. She'd found more than she could ever have hoped. A nice, warm, friendly place to spend the night, and a hostess who was like someone's grandmother. If only it didn't cost too dearly, she told herself, she'd be able to sleep soundly her first night in America. In the morning, she could make a plan to find Luke.

She followed Letty to the kitchen at the back of the establishment, and permitted herself to relax for the first time since she had arrived in this strange new place.

"A moment, Alec, old man. That's all I ask. She's probably completely smitten and utterly loyal to the man. Ten minutes and I'll be back down here to join you in a bottle of cheer."

Those had been Daniel Taggart's words to him half an hour before, and Alec was still cooling his heels in the plush lobby of the Montgomery Hotel. His friend Taggart had set off in pursuit of the lovely Miss Saranne Ringlander as she left Whit Carson's mansion on Nob Hill, and he'd dragged the protesting Alec along with him.

"I may not succeed. Her heart may belong to Carson's millions already," Taggart had said on the carriage ride to the hotel. "Come along, and if I fail to win her heart, you can bear me and my tattered soul to Billings's for some cold, bubbly comfort."

Taggart had accepted no arguments, and Alec had felt he couldn't refuse, what with all the doors Taggart had opened for him that evening. He'd been a true benefactor to Alec, introducing him to his many rich friends, and doing it gracefully, allowing them to discover that Alec made his living as a photographer, rather than seeming to force him on them. Taggart had also treated Alec, as he always did, as if he were one of that glittering, carefree crowd, and not an immigrant's son who still worked hard at his trade. Alec owed Taggart for this night.

But there was no way to repay him now, and Alec wanted to go home. It was evident that Taggart's winning smile and mischievous humor had once more stood him in good stead with a lady. He shook his head in grudging admiration, even as he hoped Taggart would heed the word of caution he'd offered. The aristocratic Whit Carson was not only rich and powerful, he was known to have a hot head with his foes and a cool hand with a gun or a knife. It was unlikely that he would take kindly to anyone entertaining his beautiful fiancée behind his back.

Still, Taggart was a grown man, and he possessed an uncanny knack for landing on his feet. Alec couldn't protect him from his own follies.

His mind made up, Alec rose from the deep chair among the potted palms and strolled toward the front doors, buttoning his topcoat as he went. The doorman sprang to pull the door open for him.

"Shall I get you a cab, sir?" he asked.

"No, thanks. I've only a short way to go."

As he walked, Alec gratefully lifted his face to the cooling breezes. Carson's champagne had gone a bit to his head, and the Montgomery's lobby, with its steam heat, had been almost tropical. The brisk night air was a welcome change, invigorating him and setting his feet to moving at a quickstep pace. At the corner, he had to go out of his way to avoid a puddle that had formed a minor lake between the wheel ruts and the sidewalk.

More mud was the last thing he needed today, he thought wryly. One suit making an untimely trip to the launderer's was quite enough for Alec's thrifty Scots soul. Miss Rowan Trelarken had managed to muddy everything from his forehead to his knees. Impressive work for one slim girl.

He couldn't say that he blamed her much. Carson and his buddy Durrell had played a very dirty trick—literally—on those hapless steerage passengers. Seeing through their game, the girl had dared to serve them up a taste of their own medicine. Alec wished she'd chosen one of the perpetrators as her target, but as he'd done nothing to prevent the prank, he supposed he was as guilty as they.

He reflected for a moment on the picture she'd made, standing on that wagon, eyes ablaze with fury, ready to take on all comers for the sake of justice. He couldn't think of a single woman he knew who would dare as much.

He also couldn't think of a single woman he knew who was as striking to look at. Rowan Trelarken wasn't a beauty, not in the traditional sense; the golden-haired, curvaceous Saranne Ringlander fit that bill much more closely. But there was about that red-haired mud-flinger an air of loveliness and freshness, a touch of royalty, even, that appealed to him. Even her lips didn't conform to the accepted fashion of a pink, neat bow, he recalled. Instead, her mouth was generous and curving and upturned at the corners, giving a tantalizing hint of a smile, even when she was serious. Her eyes were blue—not the usual deep blue, but a clear, light blue, circled with rings of indigo at the outside and nearly black at the pupils. How could he ever capture that strange combination? he wondered. He'd need to light the picture very carefully, and then perhaps tint the print—

He drew up abruptly. What was he thinking? He'd never see the girl again, let alone make a photograph of her. Besides, if he was any judge, Rowan Trelarken had been trouble from the day she first drew breath. Residents of "the Grass Valley" would be well advised not to cross her, if they valued their heads. He, for one, wasn't about to get involved with any woman, let alone a lass who wielded mud and words with such alarming results.

He glanced up at the soft gray-blue fog that was rolling in over the city, muffling sounds and shrouding the streetlamps. He thrust his hands into the pockets of his coat and turned his thoughts to his favorite subject: his long-awaited photographic expedition into the Southwest Territories. He walked on, dreaming, and soon he began to whistle.

"I'll just take them shoes down and get 'em cleaned."

Letty huffed as she bent her bulk to pick up Rowan's muddy boots, but her cheery smile never left her face. "Now, you get settled in. Some of the others will stop in to chat tomorrow mornin', I'm sure. We're a real friendly place here."

"You've been so very kind," Rowan said. "But I'm terribly afraid I shan't be able to pay my bill. If you could just tell me how much this room costs—"

Letty waved away Rowan's protests. "Don't you worry about that tonight. Just you make yourself at home and we can have a nice talk after breakfast."

"I don't see how you can do it, but please know that I'm ever so grateful."

"Darn me, but you Englanders can sure speak pretty. You're gonna give this old house some real tone!" Letty laughed and sailed out the door.

After she'd gone, Rowan got up to examine her new quarters, pulling the pins from her hair as she went. In addition to the bed and rocker, there was a squat chest of drawers that backed against one wall, and a marble-topped table that held a chipped white basin and pitcher. On the wall over the bed there hung a brightly embroidered shawl with a foot-long fringe, evidently someone's small attempt at decoration.

There was a knock at the door, and a young woman of about Rowan's age stuck her head inside. "Are you alone?" she asked in a soft, childlike voice.

"Yes, I am. But do come in, please." Delighted to have someone to talk to, Rowan hurried to move her bundle closer to the dresser so that there would be room for her to sit on the edge of the bed. She motioned to the rocker. "Please sit down. I'm Rowan Trelarken."

"They call me Molly. Molly Jenkins." She perched on the rocking chair. "I heard you and Letty talking and I thought there might be somebody new here in number 3."

Rowan was startled to see that Molly was dressed in a thin cambric nightgown, worn black stockings and a cheap cotton shawl. Her soft brown hair was braided down her back and tied with a faded pink ribbon. Was this the way Americans dressed at home?

Molly smiled at Rowan, her thin face brightening. "You just come tonight?" she asked, wriggling back in the rocker.

"Yes. In fact, I came to San Francisco just this morning. I was to meet someone at the wharf, but they must have been delayed. I was looking for a night's lodgings, and Mrs. Brown was kind enough to take me in."

"Yeah, Letty, she's good at that."

"Yes, very. Will you be stopping here long?"

Molly wrinkled her forehead. "Stopping here?"

"I'm sorry, I'm from England—"

"That much I figured." Her forehead smoothed out again. "Oh, I know what you mean.... How long have I been at Letty's? That'd be two years now."

"Two years?" It was Rowan's turn to look puzzled. "That seems quite a long time. But I'm sure that's none of my affair," she added hastily.

"No, it's all right." Molly pulled her feet up beneath her gown and wrapped the thin shawl closer about her shoulders. "Maybe it's none of my business, but are you serious about only staying one night? I find that kind of hard to believe."

"Oh, yes. I'm sure that Luke is coming for me tomorrow morning. He's traveling all the way from the Grass Valley."

Molly's forehead wrinkled again. "Did you tell that to Letty?"

"Not in so many words. I thought she understood. I did tell her that I hadn't much money to pay for food and lodging. She said we could talk about it in the morning." Rowan caught the note of concern in Molly's voice. "Why do you ask?"

"Sweetie, did you say some fellow was going to come calling for you tomorrow?"

"Yes, at the wharf."

"Who is this fellow?"

"My...my fiancé."

"Sweet suffering saints!" Molly quickly unfolded herself from the rocker. "Where're your shoes?" she asked, pointing to Rowan's stockinged feet.

"Mrs. Brown has them—"

She got no further. Molly grabbed Rowan's bundle and thrust it into her arms. "Come on, we've got to get you out of here, quick."

"But why? I must have my shoes!"

Molly seized her by the arms. "Letty's got 'em, and you're not going to get 'em back. Don't you see? That's how she keeps her girls here. Nobody's going to run out into the night in their bare feet, and by the time they've been here one night, she's got 'em workin' for her."

"Working?" Rowan echoed. "You mean like your black slaves? I thought the war—"

"Working!" Molly said, giving her a shake. "For men, sweetie, see what I mean?" She stepped back and held out the skirt of her nightgown.

Dawn broke. "You can't mean it! That lovely Mrs. Brown is a—?"

"That's right, sweetie. I don't suppose you've ever—?"

Rowan felt warmth rush to her cheeks. She shook her head. Molly nodded. "I kind of figured." She ran to the door and opened it a crack. "The hall's clear. Grab your sack and come on." Molly darted back into the room, yanked the top sheet off the bed and ran back to the door.

"But wait!" Rowan said. "I don't understand. How could Mrs. Brown make me . . . if I didn't want to . . . work for her?"

"Trust me, she has her ways. Some of 'em aren't nice. I ought to know." She slipped out the door and beckoned to Rowan.

Stunned into silence, Rowan followed Molly's lithe figure out into the hall, taking care to go on tiptoe.

They crept along the threadbare carpeting until they came to the door marked 7.

"Be real quiet," Molly whispered. "My boy's asleep."

Still speechless, Rowan slipped in behind her companion. Molly pressed the door shut, wincing at the barely audible click of the latch sliding home. She turned to Rowan and beckoned her toward the bed. With one quick motion, she ripped away the quilt that covered it.

"Start tying the sheets together," she ordered, tossing the top sheet she carried onto the bedding. "I'll give a listen for Her Nibs."

Rowan set down her bundle and did as she was told. How could this have happened to her? she wondered. What was she doing in a—*a brothel,* in the middle of the night, with no shoes and nowhere to hide?

She heard a soft gurgle and looked behind her. In the dim lamplight, she saw a basket resting on the chest of drawers. Inside, a round little body stirred in sleep.

A baby! In this dreadful place? How could Molly—?

"He's all mine," Molly whispered fiercely, as if she had read her thoughts. "And I care for him as good as any other mother, and we're going to be just fine."

Rowan opened her mouth to speak, but closed it again when she saw the fire in Molly's gray eyes, saw her thin fists clenched in defiance. She turned around and finished tying the knots.

"Get your things out first," Molly hissed, motioning to the window. "Then you go. Hurry, I hear her down in the front room!"

It seemed that Rowan's fingers had never worked so slowly. She managed to fumble a loop around the neck of her sack and make it secure, then held her breath as she eased open the grimy window, which faced onto a narrow alley. Hauling the bundle over the ledge, she lowered it past the darkened windows on the first floor.

"She's coming up! Get moving!"

Rowan could hear the telltale creaking of the stairs now. Feeding the tied sheets over the ledge as fast as she could, she gave a soft cry of joy when the bundle touched the ground. She ran the free end through the footrail of the heavy iron bed and knotted it tight.

The noises on the stairs were growing louder. Rowan looked at Molly as she tucked her hem up into the waistband of her skirt. "Thank you. I—"

"Never mind! Go!"

Footsteps sounded in the hall, down by room 3. They heard voices, Letty's and a man's. A door slammed.

Rowan hesitated a second, then untied the warm, wooly shawl that was wrapped at her waist. She tossed it to Molly and slung one leg over the ledge.

"Go on, go on, go on," Molly was chanting at her. "She's got Tiny with her. I can't hold the door against them two!"

Rowan was lowering herself down the sheet rope when she heard the door burst open and angry voices filling the room. The baby promptly woke and began to wail. Surprisingly, Molly's girlish voice rose over all, berating the others for waking her child.

"There she goes!" Rowan glanced up to see Letty and an enormous, burly-armed man grab hold of the rope and begin to pull. Glancing down, Rowan guessed she had less than ten feet more to go. She closed her eyes and let herself slip downward as the rope was hauled up. Her hands burned like fire as the rope ripped its way up through her grasp.

She crashed to the alley below, going limp enough to save her feet and legs from the punishing impact. As she scrambled to her feet, Letty leaned over to screech out the window. "Stop, thief! Help! Help, somebody! Get that girl!"

Windows shot up all along the alley. "What's the noise?" a man bellowed.

"Stop that girl! She robbed me! Stop her!" Letty shrieked.

Rowan ripped her sack free of the sheet rope, and threw it over her shoulder. The wet, cold ground was soaking her stockinged feet, and the alley was filling with fog. She raced for the streetlamp ahead, whose light was dimly haloed in the mists.

"Ow!" Tears came to her eyes as her foot came down hard on something jagged. Still, she ran on, hearing more voices shouting in the alley, feeling her heart speeding faster than her feet. She was running at full tilt when she reached the end of the alley and ran headlong into a warm, solid mass.

"What the—" The man's cry was cut off as they both toppled into a mud puddle.

Rowan struggled to her feet, ready to run. "I'm sorry," she gasped, turning to flee.

He had hold of her in a split second, with an iron grip that pulled her up into the light of the streetlamp.

She blinked and started in fear, but she couldn't break free of his grip.

"Miss Trelarken," Alec groaned. "I might've known it was you. I recognize your calling card."

He raised his hand and dabbed a smear of mud down the length of her nose.

Chapter Three

"Please let me go," Rowan begged. "Please, they're after me!"

Alec held her fast. "Who's after you? Whose suit have you ruined this time?"

"Don't be an idiot," she snapped. How dare he laugh at her when she was in such danger? "Just let me go, please! I'll pay for your suit! Here!"

She began to struggle with the knot in her sack, but a shriek from Letty carried up the alley to where she stood. She made ready to bolt once more.

"No, you don't." Alec caught hold of her again. He saw that she was trembling, and her eyes were wide with fright. He glanced down the length of her and saw not only that her clothes were muddy, but also that she wore no coat or shawl, and her stockings were in shreds on her shoeless feet. Her hair had come undone from its neat, soft braid of that morning, and it now hung in heavy, dew-moistened waves to her waist. The streak of mud painted on her nose added the crowning touch to her dishevelment.

"Tell me who's after you," he said, more gently this time. "Maybe I can help."

Rowan eyed him cautiously. The ruckus in the alley was dying down. "It's nothing," she said. "I can take care of myself."

"Like hell you can," Alec said, a bit of a smile playing about his lips. "If you could take care of yourself, you wouldn't be out here at half-past midnight looking like the mud flats at low tide. But if you don't want to tell me, fine. Just tell me this—do you have a place to stay?"

"Oh, yes," she said, glancing away. She pointed vaguely toward the wharves. "A friend of mine lives only a few houses from here."

Alec chuckled. "Never play poker, Miss Trelarken. You're the worst liar I've ever met. Your face is so transparent, everyone would know what cards you held." He nodded in the direction she had pointed. "There are no houses down that way, only shops and warehouses."

Rowan glowered. "I don't play at cards, Mr.... Mr...."

"MacKenzie."

"I don't play at cards, Mr. MacKenzie, not that it's any concern of yours. Now, if you will excuse me, I must embark."

She drew away from his grasp and lifted her muddy, tattered bundle. Pulling up tall, she extended a slender, albeit somewhat grubby, hand to him. Yet her cool, regal smile all but erased the effects of her dirty clothes and disheveled hair. Alec's well-trained eyes caught the impression of refinement once again and stored it away for later consideration. Right now, all he cared about was getting home without diving into the mire a third time. The safest way to accomplish that was to take this lovely urchin with him. That way, he could keep an eye on her, and on the muddy hazards of the San Francisco streets.

"You don't have anywhere to stay, Miss Trelarken," he said flatly, refusing her hand. "And what's more, the fog is coming in so thick, you'll most likely lose your way, no matter where you try to go. I can't in all good conscience let a young lady roam the streets at night, so there's only one thing for it. You're 'embarking' home with me."

"I am not."

"Yes, you are," he said, taking her elbow. "You'll take my bed, and I'll sleep downstairs, in my office. Behind a locked door. Where are your shoes?"

"It isn't proper—"

"Neither is throwing mud or knocking people into puddles. Where are your shoes?"

Rowan was silent. Alec looked at her quizzically. "I know you had shoes this morning."

"I lost them."

"How?"

"Playing poker!" she snapped. "Does that satisfy you?"

He laughed. "It'll do for a start. Let's go."

Rowan hung back. "I don't think I can trust you. Everyone in this San Francisco is either a drunk, a scoundrel or a ne'er-do-well."

"Or a shameless tyrant, as you so charmingly put it this morning," he said. "And you're probably right. But I'm from New York. Does that satisfy you?"

Rowan peered at him. His face was expressionless, and his dark eyes held no malice in them that she could see. But then, Letty's eyes hadn't, either, and look where trusting Letty had got her.

She couldn't think what to do. He was right. She had no place to stay, she knew no one, and who knew if Letty and her friend Tiny would come looking for her? At least she'd be in the company of a tall, strong man for a few blocks, she reasoned. That would get her out of Letty's neighborhood. Then she could slip away and go into a stable or some other warm place to sleep.

"Very well," she said, pleased to have worked out a plan for herself. "I'll go with you."

Alec wordlessly took her bundle from her and started off down the street. Rowan followed him, taking care not to step down too hard on her injured foot, which was beginning to throb.

"Do you live far from here?" she asked, trying to sound casual, as they rounded the corner and headed toward Letty's "hotel."

"Just three blocks ahead."

They were drawing closer to Letty's. Rowan moved around Alec to take the outside of the sidewalk, away from the storefronts that lined the streets.

"Is this where they are, the people you were running from?" Alec asked.

He had stopped directly in front of Letty's. Rowan wanted to run, out of fear and shame. "Yes," she whispered.

Alec glanced up to the second floor. A red-paned lantern hung out over the street, its glow cutting through the fog. "You didn't want to go in there, did you?"

"No." Rowan was inching away from the door, seeking the shadows. "I had no idea what sort of place it was."

To her horror, Alec raised a hand and rapped loudly on the door. After a long moment, Letty came to open it. She caught sight of Rowan in the shadows right away.

"That girl's a thief, Mac," she cried. "I wouldn't doubt but that she's got all my silver spoons in that there sack!"

"Your spoons are tin, Letty, and I'd say that you're the thief who stole her shoes." Alec's hands were in his pocket and he rocked back easily on his heels. His tone was genial, but firm. "Suppose you go get them, and we'll call it even."

Letty opened her mouth to protest, then snapped it shut. She shook a finger at Rowan. "You're just lucky you got a man like Mac on your side, girl. Eatin' up peoples' victuals and usin' their heat without payin'! It's criminal. Criminal!"

She turned around and went to fetch the boots. When she returned, she handed them to Alec, who returned them to Rowan, his eyes never leaving Letty's.

"We're much obliged, Letty," he said, touching the brim of his hat.

"Hmph!"

Rowan stood there in wonderment. Was she in even more trouble than before? This Alec MacKenzie was on a first-name basis with that awful woman! What sort of man was he? Her thoughts flew to the second floor. Were Molly and her little boy safe in such a place?

Alec brushed past her, his long strides outstripping hers by a considerable measure. Rowan hurried after him, but not before she'd cast a fearful backward glance at the bright doorway and the bulky figure standing there.

He was still going at a great rate when she caught up to him. Pain shot up her leg from the cut on her foot. She couldn't walk straight any longer. She lifted the foot gingerly and placed her full weight on the other one as she struggled to match Alec's speed.

Alec noticed the change in her gait. "What's the matter?" he asked, stopping again.

"It's nothing." Rowan kept walking, setting her feet down as naturally as she could. The result was so excruciating that she cried out. She halted, head down, biting her lower lip.

Alec shoved the sack into her arms. "Take this," he ordered.

"I can walk—" Rowan began, but Alec was already sweeping her up into his arms, bundle and all, and carrying her off.

She kept still, unable to think of a word to say, as Alec strode down the sidewalk, passing curious strangers and darkened shopfronts. He carried her with perfect ease, though Rowan knew well that she and her bundle were not feather-light. She felt his face close to hers, and she kept her eyes averted, making a vain effort to pretend that there was nothing unusual about her position, and that the heat from his body wasn't penetrating the wool of her dress, warming her chilled skin.

He turned a corner and stopped at last in front of a shop door. "Here, lean on me" was all he said as he lowered her down. She leaned as lightly as she could while he fished a key out of his waistcoat pocket and fitted it to the door. The gold lettering on the glass read MacKenzie Studio. What did that mean? she wondered.

When the door was open, he swept her up again before she could protest. He carried her in and set her down on a bench in the darkened room. "Wait here," he ordered, shedding his muddy topcoat.

Rowan didn't move as he fetched a lighted lantern from a back room and returned to help her up from the bench.

"There are stairs," he said. "Can you manage if you lean on me?"

"I believe so. This is very kind of you, Mr. Mac-Kenzie, but I shan't be staying long. If I could just freshen up and perhaps—"

"Miss Trelarken?"

"Yes?"

"Hush up."

She did so. He led the way to the stairs at the back of the room and then went behind as Rowan made her painful way up, curling the toes of her injured foot under to avoid coming down hard on the sole. At the top, they stepped into a small apartment, sparsely furnished, but clean, and pin-neat. The room held a cast-iron cookstove, a sink, a scrubbed pine table with two chairs, and a small cupboard that hung on the wall. At the far end of the room, a red calico curtain was stretched across the space, dividing the room in two. Overall, Rowan had the impression that, neat as it was, everything in this place could be packed up and moved at a moment's notice.

Alec set the lantern down on the table and turned up the gas lamp that hung overhead. Rowan limped to a chair under his supervision and sat down with a grateful sigh.

"Did you cut this in the alley?" Alec knelt before her. He took her ankle in one hand, bent her foot back with the other and studied the cut, which ran across half the width of the ball.

Rowan stared down at the top of his head, conscious only of the gentle touch of his strong hands on her foot and ankle. She knew it wasn't ladylike for a young woman to show her ankles to a man, but somehow, that rule didn't seem terribly relevant in this crazy city or on this extraordinary day. "Uh-hmm..." she murmured at last.

Without a word, Alec slid his hand up her leg and beneath her dress and petticoat, found her garter and deftly undid her stockingtop. She gasped in surprise as he rolled the stocking quickly down over her thigh and calf, his hand smoothing her bared skin and easing the tattered garment over her wound.

"There," he said, oblivious to her shock. "It's a good thing you didn't have this exposed to the dirt any longer. It's already begun to swell." He dragged the other chair around and laid her foot on the seat.

Rowan watched as he went to the stove and lifted the teakettle to pour warm water into a basin. He found a clean cloth, a bar of soap and a bandage roll and carried them all, with the basin, to her side.

"This will smart a little," he said, taking up her foot again. "Tell me if it hurts too much."

Rowan was so astonished and mesmerized by his actions that she couldn't have spoken if it had hurt. But his touch was so gentle as he bathed the foot and bound the wound that she sat still, half hoping that his soothing ministrations would go on for another week or two.

He tied off the bandage and glanced up at her at last. She met his gaze and was held there, startled at the sudden surge of anticipation and excitement that caught in her chest. For one moment, she thought she knew what he was saying with his eyes. Was he going to touch her again?

The moment passed, and she lost the sense of connection between them. He frowned, took the washcloth and solemnly wiped the streak of mud from her nose.

"Thank you." Her voice sounded distant in her ears. She was utterly unaware of anything but the nearness of him and her disappointment that whatever had passed between them had been so abruptly lost.

"You're welcome." He stood, rolling the bandage into a neat ball. "I saw a lot of injuries like that in the war. If they got treated right away, it was nothing. But if the fellow had to drag it through the fields to get back to his camp, it was as bad as a gunshot wound."

He picked up the basin and went to empty it in the sink. The quiet in the room felt awkward to Rowan. What was she supposed to do now?

"Were you in the war?" she blurted, then immediately wanted to retract the question. Of course he was in the war! Hadn't he just said as much?

"I served in the engineers for a while. Making maps, mostly. I rode with the cavalry for almost a year. Then I worked for Mathew Brady, taking photographs."

"Photographs? Oh, do you mean daguerreotypes?"

"Yes, although I use a newer method than daguerreotyping."

"I see."

Silence fell once more. Alec went about replacing the items he'd taken out to treat Rowan's injury. She watched, fascinated, as he placed each item in a space that appeared to be exactly designed for it—the bandage roll in a tin box, the bar of soap on a small dish by the water pump, the cloth neatly wrung out and hung on a peg under the cupboard. She'd never met a man who was so meticulous about his things. Gil, for one, was a tornado; he came and went in their cottage, strewing coats and books, papers and boots, in his wake. She had to admit that she wasn't much better.

"Is this your home?"

"This is it." He got the kettle from the stove, carried it to the sink and added water to the kettle to replace what he'd used in the basin. "It's not much, but then, I don't need much."

"It's quite nice."

"Thank you."

Rowan felt like a fool again, making polite chat with a man she'd so far pelted with mud, knocked into a puddle, berated, lied to and permitted to carry and even undress her after less than half an hour's acquaintance. Many times on the long voyage from England, she'd tried to picture her life in America. If anyone had told her that her first day in her new country would begin with a mudfight and end in a strange man's apartment, she would have strongly advised that person to see a physician.

But she had indeed been planning to be in a strange man's company this night, she recalled. Not Alec MacKenzie's, but Luke Syms's. She was an engaged woman, and the fates of at least two other people depended on her marriage to Luke. What would Luke say if he knew that she was in some other man's home at such an hour? Might he refuse to marry her? She couldn't take that chance.

She lowered her foot and began to push herself up from her seat. Alec, who was still at the sink, turned at the sound of the chair scraping back. He seemed about to go to her, but then he leaned back against the sink and watched her with a calm, amused stare.

Rowan flashed him a smile. "I really mustn't take up any more of your time, Mr. MacKenzie. I fear I've made a dreadful nuisance of myself. I'll just be off now."

"Whatever you wish, Miss Trelarken."

She managed to get out of the chair and stand on one foot. She hopped to her bundle and stood over it, one hand on the wall to brace herself. Gritting her teeth, she lifted the heavy load with one hand and dragged it toward the chair, hopping all the way.

She felt Alec's eyes on her and flushed with embarrassment and anger. He was enjoying her struggles! She got to the chair and sat down with a thump, the bundle before her on the floor.

It took some doing, but she managed to force a carpet slipper on over the toe of her injured foot. She buttoned up her other shoe, shrugged into a wool jacket and retied the bundle, still prickling at the awareness that Alec's sharp brown eyes were following her every move. Coming to her feet—or, rather, foot—she took up the bundle and prepared to be off.

"Mr. MacKenzie," she said politely, offering her hand as if he hadn't just witnessed her embarrassingly inept efforts to dress herself. "Thank you so very much for your help."

"Think nothing of it," he said smoothly. "It was the least I could do."

Rowan cast him a suspicious glance and then hobbled around to face the stairs. She crossed the room, keeping her weight on her good side and coming down on only the heel of her injured foot. The bundle slid jerkily along behind her, balking every couple of feet, like a protesting child being dragged to his bath. She got to the top of the stairwell and faced pitch blackness.

She swiveled clumsily. "Mr. MacKenzie. Would you—would you be so kind as to light my way down?"

Wordlessly he took the lantern from the table and carried it to the stairs. He moved past her and nimbly descended to the bottom. Hooking the handle of the lantern over a peg on the wall, he waited for Rowan to follow him.

Getting down the stairs was like waltzing with a dead-drunk partner in high seas, Rowan thought grimly. She managed four steps, counted eight more to go. Her lower lip caught up under her front teeth, she hopped, thumped and dragged her way down four more.

On the ninth step, disaster struck.

The slipper shook loose in midair and landed under her bootheel. Both feet shot out from under her. She skied down the remaining steps on her bottom, crying aloud. Her voice seemed to trail along behind her as she fell.

Strong arms stopped her descent before she crashed to the floor. Alec effectively absorbed the shock of her flying body with his own, but he was bowled over. He sat down abruptly, Rowan cradled in his lap, her legs on either side of his hips.

Silence reigned for a full minute.

Rowan finally stole a look at Alec's face. His eyes were closed, and his face was unreadable. She could feel the solid warmth of him around and beneath her, and could feel the way his breath stirred the loose curls at her temple. Unreasonably, she felt quite at home in his arms, as if her body had been created to fit against his in just this way. She felt a momentary impulse to slip her arms around the broad, flat chest that supported her with such ease.

Confused and embarrassed by her wayward actions and thoughts, Rowan moved, trying to rise. For a second, almost imperceptibly, his arms tightened around her, keeping her close in his embrace. Then he let go of her with a groan.

"Miss Trelarken..." he began.

"I know, I know," she said miserably, scrambling to her knees. "I did it again. I do assure you, Mr. MacKenzie, I am not always this accident-prone, but it's just that I'm new here and—"

"Yes, I see." Alec brought an abrupt end to Rowan's ramblings. "Now, it's late, Miss Trelarken—"

"Rowan."

"What?"

"Please call me Rowan. I think we're better acquainted now."

He tried again. "It's late, Miss Trelarken. Rowan. You have nowhere to go. I can't send you out into the streets to endanger other innocent people. Please, please, stay here tonight. You may have my bed. I will sleep down here, in my office, a considerable distance out of harm's way."

Rowan chewed on her lower lip, debating with herself. It didn't seem proper to stay alone in a man's home. She glanced at him, noting the firm set of his jaw and the piercing brightness of his eyes. He had helped her a great deal already. And he seemed to be set on having her stay. Besides, she'd just proven beyond question that she couldn't get around with any sort of ease. Did she really have a choice?

"Very well. I will stay." She hugged her bundle against her chest.

"Oh, thank you so much," he said with a sigh. "I'll rest easier, I know, and so will the fair city of San Francisco."

He rose, swept her up into his arms and carried her upstairs, bundle and all, a look of mingled resolution and relief on his face. He crossed the room to the curtain and shouldered through the opening in the middle. Setting Rowan down on the neatly made iron cot, he went to light the lamp on the chest. When it was glowing softly, he stood back, hands on his hips.

"There's water in the bowl," he said, nodding at the ewer and basin set on the chest at the foot of the bed. "And there's a cloth and some soap. Call if you need anything."

"Thank you."

Rowan sat still after Alec went out. She listened to his quiet movements as he went about some task in the kitchen area. She wanted to call out to him, to summon him back, but she couldn't think of a valid reason to do so. At last, she undressed, bracing herself against the lamp table and laying out her nightgown on the clean red-and-white pieced quilt. A quick search of her bundle located her hairbrush, and she sat down to brush out her tangled mane.

As she relaxed in the quiet, she felt her weariness take hold. What a long day it had been, she thought. How could so much happen in one day? After the long, tedious journey by ship around the Horn, she wasn't used to things happening so quickly. As she brushed her hair out into a shining wave, she recounted the day's events to herself, imagining how she would write about them in her next letter to Gil.

Caught up in her nightly ritual, she was unconscious of the figure on the other side of the curtain, seated on one of the pine chairs, sipping good Scotch whiskey from a plain tin cup. He sat in near-darkness and watched the lovely shadow play behind the thin calico drape.

Alec shook his head. How could such a beautiful creature be such a hazard? he mused. And she was indeed beautiful, he decided, though unconventional. Unconventional! That was a good one. Rowan Trelarken defined the word *unconventional*. What was more, she seemed to manage it with charming innocence and not the slightest bit of guile or coquettishness.

But it would be absolute folly to pursue her. Not just because he would likely fall victim to the avalanches and flying carpet slippers that no doubt accompanied her wherever she went; he'd dodged enough missiles at Bull Run and Gettysburg to last him a good long time. But if he let himself become attached to another person, he would be letting them both in for an enormous hurt.

Taggart, as close a friend as he'd ever had, understood. Alec was solitary by nature and a risk-taker by trade. His dream of being the first man to photograph the new country in the Southwest was a dream that was his alone. If he had wanted to be a part of a group, he would have accepted the post of field photographer for one of the government geological expeditions. He'd had several offers, and while the money would have been good, he would have been forced to meet the captain's schedule, photograph when he had a chance, and develop his negatives in haste. He loved the ease and freedom of working alone, answering to no one. And now, more than ever, he needed it for his very soul.

That was why he chafed so at being kept here in San Francisco, just so that he could earn money by taking portraits of rich, celebrated, and often eccentric San Franciscans. It had taken all his meager soldier's pay, and the little he had left from his time with the Brady studios in New York and Washington just to finance his trip west, and his pride and the interest of friendship prevented him from borrowing from the wealthy Taggart. He'd had enough setbacks, and he'd had enough of polite chat and refined poses. He wanted to be off and away, in wild places, with the promise of something new just over the next rise.

An affair with any woman at this time would be sheer folly, and Alec was not a foolish man. It would just be another delay. He'd make sure that the charming, hazardous Rowan Trelarken was whisked out of his life tomorrow morning. For her sake, as well as his.

But tonight—tonight he would sit and enjoy the enchanting silhouette behind the curtain. His eyes were his life and his livelihood, and using them would be satisfaction enough. There in the dark, he noted the delicate curve of her throat and the way she lifted her arm to gather up the profusion of curls at her neck as she splashed water in the basin to wash her face. As she bathed, he gloried in the perfect line of her long, slender torso, and the soft outline of her small, high breasts.

She pleasured him, all unawares, as she slipped the nightgown over her head and let it fall over her slim hips. He smiled when she gave an inelegant rub to her bruised backside for good measure. He watched as she lifted the brush once more and stroked it through the luxuriance of her hair. He watched until she rose, stretched, and extinguished the light. And he watched long after he heard her soft, even breathing in the darkness of his silent room.

Chapter Four

Rowan woke to the sound of whistling, and suffered a wave of embarrassment as visions of red lights, mud puddles and stairways passed before her mind's eye. She rose quickly, dressed, and packed her bag, eager to get away from the site of so many awkward and unsettling events.

"Good morning," she said, coming to stand by the table in the kitchen area.

Alec turned and smiled. "Good morning."

Rowan felt a queer stirring within her at the sight of his slow-spreading smile. In shirtsleeves and braces, his collar open at the throat, he looked less like the very proper gentleman of last night. He appeared more relaxed, certainly, but it was also clear that his broad shoulders and powerful arms could not be attributed to any tailor's skill. Taut muscles were clearly revealed through the cream-colored muslin of his shirt. She found herself still staring as he turned back and poured a pitcherful of clear rinse water over the dishes in the sink.

He picked up a towel and dried a blue enamel plate as he spoke. "How is your foot this morning?"

"Much better, thank you," said Rowan, coming out of her reverie. "It can bear a little of my weight, at least."

"That's good to hear. I've just finished my breakfast," he said, facing her. "Would you like some?"

"Oh, no," Rowan said. "I mustn't put you to any more trouble. You've been so kind to me already."

"Whatever you say." He put the plate up in its place in the cupboard and reached for a tin cup. "Do you think your friend will come today?" he asked, putting away the dry cup.

"Oh, yes. I'm quite sure of it. There was just some simple delay, I imagine."

"You're probably right." He emptied the soapy water from the basin into the sink. "Well," he said as he dried his hands, "if you can wait a moment, I'll take you down to the wharf."

"No, that won't be necessary," she said quickly. "You must have work to do."

"Do you know the way?"

"No."

He looked at her slippered feet. "Do you think you can make it through the mud in those?"

Sheepishly she said, "I suppose not."

He spread his hands. "Then it's a matter of good sense. I'll take you there. My first customer won't be here until eleven o'clock, at the earliest."

"Very well, then, if you say it's no trouble," Rowan said. "The sooner I get there, the better. Someone may be waiting for me even now."

He buttoned up his shirt and put on a soft wool jacket and hat. They descended to the studio below, Rowan going along gingerly on her bandaged foot.

Alec went ahead and raised the heavy green shades that covered the tall windows at the front of the studio. Rowan gasped in surprise as brilliant sunlight flooded the room.

"This is your photograph studio!" she exclaimed. "Now I see what the words on your door meant." She turned where she stood, taking in the large, long room, and all the wonders in it. "Is that a camera?"

"Yes."

Alec held his breath as she crossed to take a closer look at the oak box mounted on a tripod near the center of the room. He let it out in silent wonder, and not a little relief, as Rowan approached the instrument, hands clasped behind her back, and studied it as if she were viewing a treasured porcelain statue in a museum.

"I've seen daguerreotypes," she said, peering into the darkened lens. "A man came to Carn Rose and made pictures of the church and the town hall and even the shops. He said they'd be shown in an exhibition in London." She lifted her head and met his eyes. "How does this work?"

Alec laughed. "You don't want to know much, do you?" He motioned for her to step behind the box. "Actually, it's not as complicated as some people would have you think." He lifted the black curtain that hung over the back. "You look into the lens from here," he said, pointing into the box. He twisted the lens cap off. "Can you see now?"

"Yes. I see that table on the platform straight ahead. Only it's upside down."

"That's right. That's how the camera sees the image with its lens. If you wanted to make a view of that table, you'd slip a glass plate in here." He tapped the side of the camera, indicating a slot in the side of the box.

"A glass plate? Why?"

"It's a special plate that's been coated with certain chemicals." Alec was warming to his subject. It wasn't often that anyone asked how he made his photographs. Most people asked only when they'd be finished and what they would cost. "When the plate and the chemicals are exposed to light, the image of whatever stands in front of the lens will be etched onto the coated glass."

Rowan ducked back under the black drape. "But how does the plate know to record only what's in front of the lens? Wouldn't it make a picture of whatever is in front of it before it gets into the camera?"

Alec grinned. "That's a good question. I wish I'd asked that myself the first time I was allowed to fool with a camera. I made several photos of my ears and fingers before I learned that the plates can't be exposed to light until they're slipped into the camera. You keep them in a frame that protects them from all light until they go into the slot. Then you uncover the lens—" he twisted off the cap again "—and voilà! The lens only lets in enough light to make an etching of what's in front of it."

Rowan popped up again, eyes bright with wonder. "But those pictures over there aren't made of glass," she said, pointing to the wall behind them, which was covered with portraits.

Alec hesitated. "You know, you don't have to be interested for the sake of politeness, Rowan. I'll understand."

"Understand what?"

"Most people's eyes begin to glaze over at about this point in my lecture," he said with a rueful laugh.

Rowan's look of was one of unfeigned surprise. "But I want to know. I've never seen a photographer's studio. You must think me very ignorant not to know all about cameras and such. I'm from rather a small village, I'm afraid."

In that moment, Alec wanted to put her in his pocket and keep her there forever. Rowan Trelarken was an original, the antithesis of all the simpering, coy or just plain world-weary women he'd known in New York and San Francisco.

In the next breath, he scolded himself. Truth was, his vanity had just been treated to a sweet dose of honey, that was all. He wasn't going to succumb to his own weakness. It was time to put a little distance between him and this lovely flatterer, even if she did flatter him unwittingly.

"It's a long process," he said, stepping back from the camera. "And we'd best be off to the wharf. You don't want to miss your friend." He motioned to the front door. "Why don't you wait on the sidewalk? I have to hitch up the wagon."

He did an about-face and headed for the back of the building, leaving a bewildered Rowan in the middle of the room, staring after him. He let himself out the back door and locked it behind him.

Rowan frowned. She'd obviously offended him, but she couldn't think how. Had he believed she was trying to make fun of his work by asking so many questions? She'd been fascinated by the chance to see such a magical device up close. Her gaze went to the portraits on the wall. Perhaps there was a clue there.

She crossed to the display and looked carefully at the stern businessmen seated in thronelike chairs and the demure women in fine gowns, their hands clasped around lace fans or clusters of roses. Was there a face here that held some significance for Alec? Or was there something hidden in the vast landscapes that he had so strikingly captured with his art?

A shadow in the corner of her eye drew her attention to the street, and she saw Alec climbing down from the seat of a small wagon. She took up her sack and hurried to meet him at the door.

"Thank you," she murmured as he helped her up to the seat behind a sturdy black mule. She studied Alec's face. He didn't seem to be angry, only very serious and determined.

Alec climbed up beside her and started the mule down the hill. They rode down into a low valley and then back up to the summit of the next rise. When they cleared the top, the entire bay lay before them, and Rowan couldn't suppress a soft cry of pleasure at the sight. The wind and fog overnight seemed to have washed the air itself, leaving the sky bright and the water a dancing, deep blue. White sails fluttered as tall ships rounded into the harbor from the open seas, passing in front of Alcatraz Island to find an anchoring spot. Even the wharves, with their clutter and their rough wooden planks, looked inviting on this shining morning.

Enchanted, Rowan turned to Alec and found him smiling at her. She looked away at once, suddenly shy. Still, a smile played on her lips. It felt good that he had shared her joy in the beautiful scene before them.

They rode down the hill and found the *Southern Star* still in her berth. Alec lifted Rowan down onto the dock and went to lift her sack out of the wagon. He set it down near the barrelhead where she'd waited the day before.

"Your friend will be here soon, I guess," he said, squinting up the hill. "Probably just got caught in some bad weather coming down out of the mountains."

"Undoubtedly," Rowan said. "I appreciate all you've done for me, Mr. MacKenzie. Thank—"

"Alec."

"I beg your pardon?"

"Call me Alec. I think we're better acquainted by now."

Rowan peered at him. Alec's mouth twitched at the corner, just the slightest bit. "I see. You're making sport of me. Well, I suppose I deserve it." She smiled and offered her hand. "Thank you very much, Alec. Goodbye."

"I'd better wait here with you until your friend arrives...."

"Oh, goodness no— I've troubled you far too much already! I came halfway round the world on my own. I believe I could manage a short wait here in the open."

Alec grinned, then opened his mouth as if to speak, but thought better of it. He took her hand. His smile faded from his face. "Well then. Goodbye, Rowan."

They shook hands, and Alec tipped his hat to her. Climbing up onto the wagon, he spoke to the mule and pulled away into the busy traffic along the docks.

Rowan felt terribly alone as she settled onto her barrel again. She tried to enjoy the fresh, sunny day, but she kept thinking of Alec MacKenzie, and his camera, and his meticulous ways, and the feel of his arms around her. She felt certain that he had wanted to go on holding her, as she had wished herself. She was glad she wasn't going to be staying in San Francisco, even today, when it seemed to be on its best behavior. Somehow, San Francisco would always be mixed up with Alec, and he was the last person she wanted to remember. Yet she couldn't help but think of him and imagine what it would be like to spend more than a few hectic hours in his company.

She pondered these odd new feelings as she sat and let the winds play with the stray curls that escaped from her coiled braids. By noon, she hadn't resolved those feelings in any way.

The afternoon dragged on. Stiff from sitting, Rowan got up and walked along the wharves, still favoring her injured foot and keeping an eye on the sack, which she'd tucked behind some crates. She looked out to sea, watching the whitecaps dancing in the sunlight and the quick sailboats darting about over the waves.

Living in Cornwall, she'd never been far from the sea, and so the voyage to California had held few terrors for her. Her only concern had been at night, when she was compelled to go below and crawl into her tiny berth. She'd always had a dread of being confined, but it had been most acute on board ship. Though only a curtain separated her from the relative freedom of the hold, where she could stand erect and walk about, she had felt gripping fear each night as she crawled into the cramped space and lay with scant inches between her face and the upper berth.

On those nights when the fear was too strong, she had crawled out of her berth, struggled into her coat and stolen up on deck. There, hidden behind some coiled rope or keeping in the shadows, she could breathe in the cold winds and feel the panic ease out of her as she exhaled the fresh salt air.

Today, she strolled about the docks in her carpet slippers, enjoying the sun's warmth and the rushing winds that fluttered flags and sails everywhere she looked. She'd never have to face the terror of confinement like that again. She was in a vast new country, where everything seemed wide open and fresh and possible.

Was that why she could entertain thoughts about Alec?

Lord, what a clumsy nuisance she'd been to him! She felt her cheeks flame at the thought of all she'd done yesterday. Alec wouldn't want a woman like her, of that she was sure. With his perfectly ordered home, his economy of motion, and his careful speech, Alec would fall in love with a princess, a paragon whose braids never came unpinned, who never threw mud, who always used the correct words, and who never, *never* had to be rescued from a brothel.

Rowan conjured up a picture of Alec's true love—a fragile blonde, whose skin wouldn't freckle up in summer, especially because she'd always remember to wear a hat and carry a parasol. An impeccable housekeeper and cook, she would no doubt arrange his shirts in alphabetical order, and serve her own petit fours and raspberry jam; Rowan couldn't boil water without supervision. Last of all, this princess most certainly would not be tall and arrow-straight, but small, and curving, and flower-petal dainty—with a bosom that would put a pouter pigeon to shame.

Rowan hated her already. She aimed a halfhearted kick at a scavenging gull, then continued to stroll the wharf, watching the ships and dreaming of someday.

As the afternoon shadows lengthened, she had to face the truth. No one was coming for her. She'd been sent halfway around the world and left here, alone.

It was a betrayal that stung her to the heart, recalling her confusion and shame when her father had ridden away, never to return. She'd taken careful steps since then to ensure that she was immune to this sort of pain. She had taught herself to be strong, self-reliant, and cautious with her heart. Or so she had thought.

Facing the bay, she looked across at the dark gray outline of Alcatraz and blinked back tears. She wasn't strong, and she certainly couldn't rely on herself—she'd proven that in the few hours she'd been in San Francisco. And some vague, disturbing thought at the back of her mind told her that, at least where tall, taciturn photographers were concerned, her heart was most definitely vulnerable.

She was still mulling over this disturbing turn of events and feelings when she looked up to see Alec storming toward her across the docks.

Dan Taggart had been waiting at Alec's studio when he returned from the docks.

"My governor's ordered me to take inventory at the warehouse, old friend," he announced. "Or else I can find another hapless, paternal soul to keep me in champagne. How about lending me a hand?"

"Can't. Sorry. The dreaded Miss Lavinia Foster is due for a sitting her within the hour."

Taggart whistled in sympathy. "That's a high price to pay for your art, old man. But perhaps I can entice you with news of something that just arrived yesterday. Something from Anthony and Company, Photographic Suppliers to Wandering Scotsmen?"

"My wagon?" Alec's face lighted up. "It's here?"

"Complete with every little potion and package you ordered. It's waiting at the docks. What do you say I stay and help entertain the dreaded Miss F., and in exchange you come along and jot down a few crates and barrels with me?"

"You've got a deal," Alec said.

The morning's photographic session passed with blessed swiftness, thanks to the blond, blue-eyed Taggart's very charming manner. When they arrived at the warehouse early in the afternoon, Alec went straight to his new photographic wagon and hitched up his team of mules. After a quick, tantalizing look over its build and its contents, they left the wagon and Taggart's buggy in front of the warehouse and went inside to oversee the rest of the shipment from the East.

To his credit, once they began, Taggart worked hard. When the sun sank below the windows, casting the big room into shadow, he dismissed the men who were assisting them. Tossing aside the ship's manifest, he stretched and yawned. "Work," he said with a shudder. "How do people tolerate it?"

"I don't know," Alec drawled. "It must be a real challenge to avoid work as often as you manage. You've got a real future ahead of you, my man."

"I believe you're right. But don't tell Taggart, Sr."

They stepped out onto the balcony and prepared to take the steps down to the street. Alec looked out over the darkening wharves and let out a short, colorful oath.

"What is it?" Taggart asked, following Alec's gaze.

"I can't believe it," Alec growled. "They've just left her here." He started down the steps.

"Her who?" Taggart asked, close behind him.

"A girl. Cornish lass. She's been waiting at that spot for two days, now."

"A girl, you say?" Taggart's eyebrows shot up in wonder. "Has the coolheaded MacKenzie fallen at last?" he intoned, addressing an invisible audience.

Alec ignored him. Reaching the bottom of the stairs, he headed straight for where he'd left Rowan that morning. She slid off the barrelhead when she saw him coming, and brushed a hand over her face and hair.

"Alec!"

"Alec?" Taggart echoed. "She calls him Alec?"

"Why are you still here?" Alec's tone was rough. "Don't you know it's dangerous to be on the docks after dark?"

Rowan's posture stiffened. "I'm not afraid. Besides, it isn't dark yet."

"Hasn't anyone come for you?"

"Obviously not, as I'm still where you left me this morning."

"This is madness. You can't wait down here alone every day."

"It is not madness! It is my plan to wait as I must. I haven't anywhere else to go, as you are well aware."

"I'm well aware that you can get into more trouble than any five people I know, and in half the time."

"And I suppose you are never at the mercy of luck or Providence, sir?"

"No one is at the mercy of anything, if she just takes the time to look about her!"

Taggart watched in wonder as Alec and the girl stood toe-to-toe, arguing incomprehensibly. He crossed his arms, leaned back against a post, and took in the scene with open curiosity.

"Would you prefer that I stay at Letty Brown's establishment?" Rowan demanded. "You seemed to be on very good terms with her last night."

Alec cursed under his breath. "Don't be a fool. Who's supposed to meet you? Are they here in San Francisco?"

Taggart grinned at his friend. Alec's Scots accent was coming out. Whatever he and this lovely young woman had done last night, it must have been significant for Alec to be this agitated.

"Ahem."

Alec and the girl looked at Taggart. Alec waved a hand as he made the introductions. "This is Miss Rowan Trelarken," he said gruffly. "Rowan, Mr. Daniel Taggart."

"How do you do?" Rowan offered her hand.

"Very well, thank you," Taggart said with a smile. "Is there some way that I can be of assistance? I'm afraid my friend Alec has misplaced his wits momentarily."

"You're very kind to offer, but I'm fine, really."

"Were you to meet friends here?"

"Yes. I fear that there has been some delay."

"And you have no place to stay."

"No, I'm afraid not. Circumstances have dictated that I wait here." Rowan glanced at Alec who was glaring about the wharf, avoiding her eyes.

"Well, that's easily remedied," Taggart said. "Please allow me to extend my hospitality to you—"

"No," Alec snapped.

Taggart went on as if Alec hadn't interrupted. "Allow me to extend my hospitality and secure a hotel room for you tonight. It would be no trouble at all."

"Oh, that's most kind of you, Mr. Taggart, but I can't accept such generosity."

"But you haven't anyplace else to go, and it would give me a great deal of pleasure to provide your lodging for the night. And Alec here would worry less, knowing that you are safely out of danger." He placed a hand on Alec's shoulder and grinned at him.

Alec answered him with a narrow-eyed scowl. Then his brow smoothed and he faced Rowan with a bland smile. "I think Taggart's offer is a good one, Rowan. It's in your best interests. You can begin contacting people tomorrow. Don't you agree, Taggart?"

Now Taggart looked suspicious. He stared intently at Alec, then turned back to Rowan. "Yes, ah . . . yes, I agree with Alec, Miss Trelarken. Please accept my offer. It would truly be my pleasure."

Rowan hesitated, glancing about at the fading light. "Very well. But you must permit me to repay you as soon as I am . . . situated."

"It's settled, then." Alec lifted her bundle and motioned for Taggart and Rowan to precede him. "Miss Trelarken will be more comfortable in your rig, Taggart. I'll follow along behind."

Taggart offered his arm to Rowan, and they led the way off the wharf to the warehouse. Alec helped Rowan up into the seat beside Taggart, and they started off into the hills.

Alec followed in his new wagon. Somehow it didn't interest him as much as he would have thought. His attention was concentrated on the neat black buggy ahead of him, and its two occupants. If all went as he hoped, Rowan would be in love by tomorrow morning. Taggart's charm had never failed him yet, and Rowan was lovely enough to attract any man. He just had to make certain that she stayed as close to Taggart as he could possibly arrange. Then she'd be off his hands, and his mind, forever.

A short while later, Rowan watched the door close behind the concierge and sat down in a brocade chair with a soft thump. Nanstowe, her old home, had been gracious and well furnished, but it was a cottage in the wilds compared to the Montgomery Hotel. Where Nanstowe was often drafty and damp in winter, this hotel suite was warm as toast—and not just in the spots nearest the fireplaces. It was as opulent as a rajah's den, with silk hangings, a multitude of flowers, and porcelain figurines gracing the mantelpiece.

Taggart must have a great deal of money to afford this suite. It was going to take a good long while for her to repay him for the cost of even one night here. She hoped that one night would be all she needed. Taggart had paid for her to send a telegram to Grass Valley, and perhaps that would yield quick results. It wasn't right for an unmarried woman to stay long in the care of any man. Besides, she'd had enough charity from Henry Syms; she wasn't about to become a kept woman, no matter how innocent the situation, and she wasn't going to expose herself to comparisons with her wastrel father.

Still, for just one night, she was in the lap of luxury. "If I'm going to pay for it," she told her reflection in the mirror, "I might as well enjoy it."

She frowned as she took in the splendor around her. The room was lovely, but silent and solitary. She needed to share all this with someone. Alec had made it plain that he did not wish to spend another moment with her. Taggart had left just as quickly. Even if they had wanted to stay, she couldn't properly have entertained two gentlemen in her hotel rooms. But who else did she know in San Francisco after just one day?

The events of yesterday came back to her in a rush, including her escapade at Letty Brown's. Molly Jenkins! She'd invite Molly to come and share some of this splendor with her. That way, she could also pay off the debt she owed her for helping her escape Letty's nets. It was a grand plan.

Smiling, she crossed to the desk by the windows and uncapped a bottle of ink. Taking a sheet of the stationery provided for guests, she dipped her pen and wrote out the invitation. She summoned a bellman and gave him directions as best she could.

Rowan danced to the bedroom to change. She was drawing a bath—from gilded taps, yet!—when she realized how odd it would seem to the hotel messenger that she should send for someone from Letty's establishment. Her eyes widened in horror for a moment as she stared at herself in the mirror.

Then she gave a laugh. This was San Francisco. She doubted if anything could shock these people. By the time a knock came at her door, she'd bathed and dressed, pinned roses in her hair and pulled two comfortable chairs up to the fireside, ready for the party to begin.

Alec scowled as he labored over the printing materials in his darkroom. A yellow lamp, the sole source of light for the room, burned dimly overhead, throwing his angular face into sharp contrasts of light and shadow, making him look like a glowering totem.

Nothing seemed to satisfy him tonight. When he'd left Taggart and Rowan at the hotel, he'd gone home with the intention of exploring his new wagon and all the supplies he'd ordered from New York. He'd ordered the wagon specially outfitted to his design, so that all the supplies for his trip would fit neatly into their own drawers, bins and shelves. It would be his rolling darkroom, as well as his home for the long months in the Southwest.

Despite his anticipation of the vehicle and all it signified, he'd only gone over half of it before becoming restless. He'd caught himself imagining Rowan and Taggart together, having dinner, talking, laughing. He'd realized that he knew very little about her. It had rankled, for some reason, to think of Taggart learning about her home, her family and her friends while he, Alec, was left with only the memory of her bewitching smile, her silken hair, and her remarkable gift for getting into trouble.

Irritated by those thoughts, he'd gone resolutely to his darkroom, determined to immerse himself in his craft and forget all about the couple who were spending the evening together in the lush, luxurious atmosphere of the Montgomery. He'd had little success.

He should be pleased that Rowan was safely away, he told himself. It was just a matter of time before she succumbed to the patented Taggart charm. Then she'd be taken care of, and out of his life and his thoughts.

Yet he grew more uneasy as the evening progressed. Taggart was a good fellow, but was he too worldly for a young woman who professed to be from a very small village? A woman who'd managed to get taken into a well-known bordello, utterly unaware of its purpose?

Alec tried to shake off his doubts as he carefully timed a chemical process, but it was no use. He'd put Rowan into this situation with Taggart, and it was his job to get her out of it. He owed her that much protection, at least.

He put away his supplies and hastily cleaned up the darkroom. Bounding up the stairs, he changed his shirt and grabbed his hat and coat, then hurried out to the street. He looked to the stable in back of his studio and decided it would be too much trouble to hitch up the wagon. He set off on foot for the Montgomery.

"Mr. Taggart? Is anything wrong?"

"Not a thing. I just wanted to see if you had everything you needed."

Rowan stepped back from the door, and Taggart came into the room. He made a point of opening the door wide and leaving it open as he stood in the entryway. Rowan smiled as she realized that he was trying to preserve her reputation. So there were some gentlemen in San Francisco, after all.

"I didn't expect to see you again tonight," she said.

"I had some business here in the hotel. Have you had dinner already?" He peered into the drawing room.

"No," Rowan said. "But this suite is so lovely I don't think I need to eat!"

Taggart grinned. "You look quite lovely yourself."

Rowan smiled shyly and touched the white rose buds in her hair. "Thank you. I robbed one of the bouquets, I confess."

"Good for you. They'll just throw them out tomorrow, anyway. But you must eat. I've ordered up one of Montgomery's special suppers. They'll bring it soon."

"You've been too good, Mr. Taggart." Rowan's eyes shone. "I feel like someone out of the Arabian Nights, and you're the magical djinn who grants me three wishes."

"I'm good with things like this, but for magic, you want Alec MacKenzie," Taggart said. "He's always cooking up some kind of alchemy in his studio."

"You're both modest and a loyal friend. I won't forget all you and Alec have done for me."

"You're more than welcome." Taggart stepped back into the hall. "I'll come by in the morning, and we'll set about getting you to your friends. How does ten o'clock sound?"

"It sounds quite fine. Though I can be ready earlier, if you wish."

"Lord, no," Taggart said with a laugh. "I'm constitutionally incapable of rising before nine o'clock." He tipped the brim of his hat. "Good night, then, Miss Trelarken. I'll call for you in the morning."

Rowan smiled, then leaned forward and impulsively kissed him on the cheek. "Thank you, Mr. Djinn."

Taggart's smile was broad as she closed the door quietly behind him. He swung down the hallway, humming.

"Hold it right there." Alec stepped out from around the corner and caught Taggart by the arm.

"MacKenzie! How's the wagon?"

"Don't try to charm me, Taggart. It won't take. I know you too well."

Taggart stared at his friend. "What's up?"

"You know damn well what's up, Rowan. I saw you coming out of her room."

"Yes?" Taggart drawled.

Alec's face flushed in anger, and a touch of his old accent emerged. "I saw you kissing. What the hell do you think you're doing? She's no Barbary Coast dolly. She's a country-born girl, a lady."

Taggart took a step back, freeing his arm with a scowl. He regarded his friend closely, and then a smile began to grow at his lips. "What do you think I was doing? I was paying a courtesy call on Miss Trelarken. She gave me a sisterly kiss on the cheek as I left, as thanks for helping her." His smile grew into a grin. "You'd best clean up your own conscience, old friend. Perhaps you were thinking more about what you wanted to do with her?"

Alec's face was still stony. "I don't want to do anything with her. But I don't intend that a young woman under my protection should come to any harm. She's an innocent, Taggart."

"I know that. She was when I went into that room, and she was when I left it." He grew serious. "Look, I came back to the Montgomery tonight with designs on a young woman, I admit. But that woman is not your pretty Miss Trelarken, delightful as she appears. I have designs on only one lady—Saranne Ringlander, who is staying in a suite on the next floor up."

"Saranne Ringlander?" Alec echoed.

"If you want proof, come have a listen at the keyhole. You seem compelled to do that sort of thing tonight, anyway."

Alec's expression softened. "Why didn't you tell me?"

"When could I have told you? When would you have listened?" Taggart tapped Alec on the lapel. "And while I may be a bounder and a cad now and again, I have never, never, been the sort who bandies a lady's name about. I've only told you about Saranne because you were making a prize jackass of yourself over your so-called 'ward,' Miss Trelarken!"

Alec's rigid posture relaxed. "Sorry, Taggart. I should've had more faith in you."

"It's all right—just don't make a habit of it." Taggart's eyes twinkled. "I just find your thinking is a bit skewed when it comes to blue-eyed redheads. With delicious English accents."

"Don't get carried away. Just because you're all in a ferment over some female doesn't mean that the rest of the world has the same problem."

"Not the rest of the world," Taggart said. "But I do know I'm not alone. *Adieu, mon frère.*"

He turned and headed up the stairs, taking them two at a time. Alec stared after him for a moment, as if he might still manage to have the last word. When Taggart's humming was lost in the upper reaches, he turned and strode down the hall to Rowan's room.

She opened the door at once, her skirts swirling around her, her face wreathed in smiles. His breath caught at the brightness in her eyes, though he couldn't think why.

He doffed his hat. "I just stopped here on my way to a friend's home," he said, amazed at the lie that was coming out of his mouth. "I wanted to see if you were settled comfortably."

"Yes, I am, thank you. Mr. Taggart has been so kind to me." She stood back from the door, and her hand made a graceful arc that took in the warm, lavish room. "I feel quite spoiled by all this luxury."

"Good. Good. That's good." Lord, he sounded like a fool! What had possessed him to come here? Still, he couldn't seem to make his feet move away from the door, couldn't tear his gaze from the slender form before him. He recalled the silhouette he'd seen the previous night. He knew what treasures were concealed beneath her neat black dress. The thought was enough to jolt him into action, before he was carried away entirely. "Well, I'll just say... good-night to you, then."

"Thank you. Good night to you, too." She held out her hand.

He took her hand and gently shook it, then stepped back into the corridor. "I hope that everything goes well for you," he said, gathering up his wits. "If I don't see you again, I wish you all the best of luck, Rowan."

"Alec, old man!"

They turned to see Taggart coming back along the hall, a self-satisfied, mischievous smile dancing at the corners of his mouth.

"Taggart." Alec regarded his friend with trepidation.

"You didn't tell me how you liked your new rig. Did my men get it here in one piece? All the powders and potions in their rightful places?" He halted before them and gave Rowan a short bow. "Miss Trelarken, did you know that MacKenzie here has just received a brand new wagon, all fitted out with the latest photographic gewgaws and feather dusters?"

"No, I— Yes, at least I saw a wagon—"

"Yes indeed," Taggart went on. "He plans to take a trip south with it, but he's never driven it before. I think he should take a shakedown journey with the thing before he goes off into the wilds of Arizona or someplace."

"You might be right," Alec said, but his eyes were watchful of his friend's cheery expression.

"The wilds of Arizona?" Rowan asked.

"Yes," Alec replied. "I plan to make an expedition into the Southwest Territories, to take photographs. I'll be far from civilization, so I want to carry everything I need with me."

Rowan caught the light of longing in Alec's eyes. "It sounds wonderful. And dangerous."

"Oh, it's sure to be dangerous," Taggart said. "The desert's a savage land, and MacKenzie is sure to be in the thick of things. Which brings me to my point," Taggart said. "A trip of a hundred, maybe two hundred miles would be a good way to tell if your new contraption meets all your standards, eh? Maybe just a jaunt up into the Sierras?"

Alec's eyes darkened. "Taggart . . ." he growled.

But his friend was not to be distracted. "It's perfect, don't you think, old man? Here you are with a wagon and mules, and here is Miss Trelarken in need of transport. You get to try out your wagon and she gets to Grass Valley. Very simple. What do you say, Miss Trelarken?"

Chapter Five

Startled, Rowan stole a glance at Alec. He was staring resolutely at the pale striped wallpaper that lined the hallway. "It would be a lovely gesture, but I don't think I can impose on Mr. MacKenzie any longer."

"Nonsense!" Taggart was undaunted. "This would be a venture of equal benefit to both parties. And strictly business, of course. You could bring a chaperon."

Alec shook his head. "I'm sorry, Miss Trelarken, but it would be a very uncomfortable journey for you. My wagon is hardly suitable for a lady."

"I understand."

Silence fell and grew around them. At last Taggart shrugged and gave a sigh. "Ah, well, so it must be. Seems a shame, but there you are. Good night again, Miss Trelarken. Alec, see you tomorrow?"

Alec nodded. He gave Rowan a small smile. "I hope that things go better for you tomorrow."

"Thank you." Her voice was small.

With a nod, he wheeled and headed up the hall after Taggart's retreating figure. Rowan closed the door and stood for several moments, gazing at the fire's glow. She was lost in thought when a brisk rap at the door startled her. She jumped to open it.

"Miss Trelarken." Alec stood before her, stiff and formal, with a look of stern determination on his face.

"Mr. MacKenzie?"

"I'll be leaving the day after tomorrow for Grass Valley, by way of Sacramento. It would be no trouble for you to accompany me. You may choose any chaperon you like, as you will no doubt prefer to travel in proper circumstances."

Rowan hardly knew what to say. What had changed his mind? "It's a kind offer, Alec," she said gently, hoping to put him more at ease. "But I know it's too great an inconvenience. I can find my own way."

Alec's spine grew more rigid, though that hardly seemed possible. "I doubt that you can. I'm going that way, whether you come or not."

Rowan's temper flared. "I can so find a way there! It may take me some time, but I shall earn my own fare and make my own way." She turned away and put her hand on the doorknob in a gesture of dismissal.

"Wait."

She turned to look at him. His posture had softened ever so slightly.

"I'm sorry, Rowan. I expect you can find a way to earn the fare. But I know that you're anxious to learn what's happened to your friend. I was reluctant when Taggart brought up the idea, it's true, but I see now that this trip would benefit us both." He hesitated. "I'm ready to travel, if you are."

She looked down at the carpet as she considered. "I don't know how I can ever repay you. Or Mr. Taggart."

"Taggart has oceans of money. He can wait to be repaid. And I can wait, as well. I have all the cash I need for this trip, and won't need more till I get back, which will be at least five months."

Rowan looked up. "I am worried why no one has come to meet me. But I intend to repay you both, every cent you've spent on my behalf. Are you quite sure you want to make this trip?"

"Yes. I don't make idle threats or idle offers."

She held her breath for a moment, then let it out as her decision was made. "Then we'll leave whenever you say."

"Good. Day after tomorrow, early morning. I'll come here to get you at six."

"I'll be ready. Good night, Alec. Sleep well."

"Good night."

He whirled about with almost military precision and stalked away. The stiffness of his retreating back made her wonder again if he had been as willing to make this journey as he had claimed. Had someone—namely Taggart—twisted his arm? Or did Alec have reasons of his own?

She might never know. All she knew right now was that she had decided to go with him. And then she'd simply stood there, saying inane goodbyes, all the while trying to conceal her absurd, bizarre impulse to touch him. Touch him! She had only to look up into that lean, angular face, stand near that tall, powerful body, and she not only wanted to touch him, but wanted him to touch her, as well.

She scolded herself. Nothing good could come of this. She was betrothed to Luke, she was on her way to be married, and even if she weren't spoken for, Alec MacKenzie was not in the least way interested in her.

Another knock at the door sounded. She opened it to see the bellman standing in the hall. Behind him, Molly waited with wide, frightened eyes. She had the shawl Rowan had given her neatly folded in her arms, and she shoved it forward before Rowan or the bellman could speak.

"Here's your shawl," she said quickly. "I would've brung it back, but I didn't know where you were staying, miss."

The bellman edged between Molly and Rowan. "This is the . . . person you sent for, isn't it, Miss Trelarken? I wasn't sure if I should bring her here or downstairs with the other . . . help."

Rowan stretched out her hand and pulled Molly forward. "I most assuredly want my guest to join me here. And I believe that's our supper coming now. If you would be so kind as to help the waiter set it up before the hearth?"

The bellman obeyed at once, recognizing the voice of one who was accustomed to unquestioning service. The waiter rolled the serving cart into the room, and the two men set a sumptuous table for two. They withdrew quickly, leaving Rowan and Molly standing by the door.

Molly clutched the shawl to her chest. "I—I guess your fella came for you," she said. "I'd best go before he comes home for his supper."

"Oh, no, you shan't," Rowan said. "You're my supper guest, not some fellow, and I've no intention of eating all this wonderful food alone. I couldn't if I tried, they've sent so much." She led the way to the table and began lifting the covers off dishes and sniffing with delight at the delicious aromas that wafted up to her.

It took some doing, but Rowan managed to persuade the shy, protesting Molly to come in and join her by the fire. Hesitantly Molly took a seat, smoothing the worn calico of her dress over her knees. Rowan lifted the cover off the large center dish on the table and stared in wonder. There was a whole pheasant on the platter, browned to perfection and stuffed with wild rice and savory spices. She raised her eyes to meet Molly's. Molly's eyes were wide.

"Are you as hungry as I am?" Rowan whispered.

Molly nodded. "More."

Rowan looked at the pheasant, then looked at Molly again. They both began to laugh. "Let's not stand on ceremony," Rowan said gleefully, raising a glass. "Here's to us."

The next hour passed in the kind of pleasure that only a good meal can bring to the truly hungry. Rowan hadn't eaten since the previous night, at Letty's, and she wondered what sort of diet the madam fed to her girls once they were in her employ. Judging from Molly's willowy form, she guessed it wasn't pheasant.

They ate slowly, relishing every bite, but even their hunger was no match for Taggart's generosity. There was plenty of food left by the time they arrived at the cream-covered *gâteau* that was their dessert. When they'd finished, Rowan poured more champagne in their glasses and rolled the table out of the way of the hearth. Settling back in her chair, she gave a satisfied sigh and smiled at her companion.

"That was wonderful. I'm so glad I had someone to share it with." She kicked off her carpet slippers and tucked her feet up under her. "Now, I want to know all about San Francisco."

Molly shared all she knew about the wild city on the bay, and, with Rowan's gentle coaxing, told about coming to California with her father, who had died trying to get gold out of the overpanned rivers nearby.

"That must have been difficult. I lost my father several years ago," Rowan said sympathetically.

"Was it the grippe?" Molly asked. "That's what carried off my ma and pa."

"No. He—he just left us. We don't even know where he is."

"Yeah, that's the tough one. I had a man walk out on me, but I don't ever want to know where he is."

Rowan went ahead delicately. "Your little boy's father?"

Molly's lips twisted downward. "Yep, that was him. He was no good for me, but I had to have him, you know how that is? Then he found out about Benjie and he ran like a cat that's had its tail stepped on."

"That's perfectly dreadful!" Rowan exclaimed. "How could he just leave his own child and its mother?"

"How? It was more like how fast." Molly stared at the dancing firelight before them. "It was for the best. If he'd stayed, he'd've made my life miserable, and Benjie's, too. He was one of those fellows that never grows up, you know? Had big dreams, but no grit."

"Grit?"

"You know—no backbone. Couldn't stick to any one thing or any one place long enough to make a go of it."

Rowan tried the new word on for size. "Grit. I like that. Benjie's mother has plenty of grit, I'd say. It can't be easy to raise a child up all on your own."

"Oh, he's no trouble. Benjie's just the best little fella. Hardly ever fusses. Goes to sleep and stays that way the whole night. Other women tell me I'm lucky. I agree."

"And of course you aren't the slightest bit biased, are you?"

Molly grinned. "Nope. Just telling the truth."

Rowan regarded her new friend in the rose-gold light of the hearth. Molly was thin and pale, and she looked tired inside, if not outside, if such a thing could be. Yet her smile was sweet and genuine, and her eyes, often wide with fear or anger, were soft and calm as she spoke of her child. An idea began to form in Rowan's mind—a plan.

"Could you...would you consider... Oh, blast, I don't know the right words to ask this. Perhaps I should tend to my own affairs."

Molly laughed. "I doubt that someone like you could leave off looking after folks's affairs any more than you could lift a steam locomotive. You've got that caring look." She smiled. "Why don't you tell me what's on your mind?"

Rowan sat up straight. "Well, I came to California to marry a man from my home," she said. "But it's been two days now, and there's been no sign of him. I'm beginning to worry."

"You've been here two days all on your own? That's a fix, 'specially for a lady like you. Does your fella live here?"

Rowan shook her head. "He's a miner. He lives in the Grass Valley."

"A miner?" Molly looked surprised. "I never figured you for that kind of life. What about those two friends of yours, the ones you said got you this room? Can't they get you up to Grass Valley? And it's just Grass Valley, sweetie, no 'the' about it."

"Oh," Rowan mused. "Perhaps that's why Alec laughed so when I told him I was going there." She drew a deep breath. "As it turns out, Mr. MacKenzie is going to Grass Valley, and he's willing to take me along. But I can't go alone. I need another woman for a traveling companion. Perhaps one with a baby?"

Molly looked hopeful, then amazed, then frightened. "You don't mean it."

"I do. We're leaving the day after tomorrow. It would cost you hardly anything. You'd be doing us both a great favor. And Benjie could come along, and you could see how you like Grass Valley, and we'd be able to start our new lives together." She stopped and put a hand to her mouth. "Oh, Molly, I'm sorry. I didn't mean that to sound so pompous. I don't mean that I know what's best for you or— Oh, dear."

"Maybe you do know." Molly's hands began to pluck nervously at the hem of her skirt. "What would your Mr. MacKenzie say about me? About what I do and all?"

"He needn't know, if you don't wish him to. I can tell him that you're a woman I met at the docks. We can tell him whatever you like. He's very nice, really."

Molly laughed briefly. "Yeah, I thought you might say that, from the way your face looks when you talk about him. But nice to you and nice to me are two different things. A man like him doesn't have to give me the time of day."

"Alec would," Rowan said stoutly. "He's a gentleman, and a gentleman would never question a lady about indelicate matters."

This time Molly's laugh was wholehearted. "You're a caution. You've got the nicest manners I've ever seen, and you guess the rest of the world is just as nice as you. I sure wish they were." She bit her lip. "What about Benjie? Would this Alec want a kid along? Benjie's a good baby, but he's been known to fuss with the best of them when he's hungry or wet."

"We'll both look after Benjie. Between the two of us, he shan't want for a thing. Alec will scarcely know he's around."

"You're making it sound awful good."

"It will be! Please, Molly, I need you. For my sake, won't you come?"

Rowan waited, watching her new friend struggle with her fears. She had no idea how much Molly had been through in her young life, but she sensed her longing for a chance, for hope. If she stayed with Letty Brown, another chance might never come along.

At last, Molly lifted her head. Some of the weariness was gone from her eyes. "I'll do it," she whispered, as if she feared that saying it too loudly might tip the scales of fortune against her.

Rowan's smile was radiant. "Bravo. Here's to our plan." They clinked glasses and drank, smiling at one another over the crystal rims.

Rowan slept late and spent the next day cleaning and packing up her few things and writing letters home. When she'd sealed the letters and handed them over to the concierge to be mailed, she felt relieved and satisfied that in the process some of her unruly doubts and emotions had been calmed.

Still, there were several important matters she had brushed over in her words to her family and friends, and some that she had omitted altogether. She most certainly hadn't told them that she'd been lured into a house of ill repute and had had to escape out a window. Nor had she told them much about the disturbing Alec MacKenzie. How would it sound, she asked herself, if she tried to explain that she'd thrown mud at this man, that he'd recovered her and her shoes from a brothel, that he'd bound up her wounded foot, that she'd stayed in his home, *in his bed*—albeit alone—and that now he was going to carry her and her new friend from the brothel all the way to Grass Valley in his photographic wagon? It sounded preposterous, mad, foolhardy, and improper in the extreme.

But when she went to bed that night, she had difficulty falling asleep for thinking about just these preposterous, improper turns of events. Before she could settle down in comfort in the deep luxury of her hotel bed, Rowan made three promises to herself.

First, she vowed that she would not go back to Cornwall until she had found Luke Syms. Second, she would find a way to earn money and pay her debts, whether she found Luke or not. And third, she would keep a safe distance from Alec MacKenzie.

She knew it would be difficult to keep the first two promises, but she was determined. She hadn't come all this way to fail in her mission to safeguard her family's welfare. Moreover, the memory of her father's shame and cowardice still stung her, as she knew it also stung Gil. Henry Syms had seldom let an encounter pass without referring to it in some way.

"Pity about the Thomases," he'd say mournfully to them, or to his wife, who often accompanied him on his "charitable" visits. "The whole lot of them living in that flat in London with her sister. Of course, there's no work there, no more'n there is here since Wheal Carn closed." He'd shake his head as if he could say more, but Rowan and Gil always knew what he meant to imply: So many families wouldn't be in such bad circumstances if Francis Trelarken had been looking to the needs of his workers rather than his own selfish, even criminal, interests. If Francis Trelarken hadn't taken every penny from the Wheal Carn till and payroll and run off in the night, the people of Carn Rose would be safe and content in their homes.

Rowan shook off these memories as a waste of her time. She'd been down that road far too many times. All that remained was for her to do what she could to honor her family's name and to extract them all from Henry's strangling charity.

Her third vow was a bit more problematic. She was about to embark on a journey of several days with Alec. She would be sitting by his side on the wagon seat, eating meals with him, entrusting her life and her future to him. Thank heavens for Molly and Benjie, she thought, for she was far too occupied with thoughts of Alec and what he thought and how he looked and the ways in which he moved.

With a small shiver, she recalled how it had felt to be carried in his arms, and the exquisitely gentle way he had touched her leg when she was hurt. And when she'd slid down the steps right into his lap! She knew it was shameless and silly of her, but she couldn't help imagining that he'd been reluctant to release her from his embrace. She also couldn't help wondering what might have happened had he not done so, but instead had held her there and touched her, pressed his lips to hers....

"Thank heavens for Molly!" she repeated aloud to the ceiling. It was good to have a plan, and some goals and promises to be met. It made her feel as if her life were once again within her scope of control. She'd make this trip and come out all right at journey's end, she told herself as she rolled over and prodded the pillows into a more comforting shape. Luke Syms, debts, Alec MacKenzie and all.

She slept soundly until early the next morning. Then she washed, dressed, and put the last of her things into her sack. Molly would arrive soon. While she waited, she sat down at the desk and dashed off a thank-you letter to Taggart. She'd miss him, she decided. He had a lot of Gil's mischievous qualities, and she'd never forget how he'd accepted her so completely, despite her circumstances.

When she looked up from her letter, she was surprised to see that it was almost six. Alec would be there shortly, but where was Molly?

The time slipped away. Rowan carried her travel-stained bundle to the lobby. She hadn't been waiting long when Alec's wagon pulled up before the hotel's front doors.

He entered the lobby dressed in soft corduroy pants and a worn jacket. Rowan was momentarily distracted from her thoughts of Molly as she found herself taking in every detail of his appearance, from his sturdy boots to the newly shaven cleanness of his lean face. There was something about him in his rough clothing. He looked more approachable. More inviting.

Thank heaven for Molly, Rowan repeated silently. She couldn't keep on with such thoughts about Alec. But where was she?

"Is this all you have?" Alec asked after he had greeted her.

"Yes, just the one bundle." She hesitated as he lifted the sack and started for the doors.

He stopped and looked back. "Are you ready?"

"Oh, yes. I mean no. What I mean is, I took your suggestion to heart and engaged a chaperon. I hope that's all right." She went to him.

"It's fine. Is she staying here?"

"No. She was to meet us here half an hour ago."

"Well, we can go pick her up, then." He turned to proceed.

"No!"

He stopped, frowning.

"We can't. She—she's probably on her way here right now, and we should miss her if we went to pick her up. Could we wait a few more moments? I'm sure she's coming."

"All right. I'll just put this in the wagon."

Alec departed, and Rowan hurried to the windows to peer up and down the street in front of the hotel. As she stood there, the concierge came bustling toward her. "Miss Trelarken!"

"Yes?"

"A message for you, miss."

"Oh, that reminds me, will you please deliver this to Mr. Daniel Taggart?" She handed the man the note she held in her pocket.

"Yes, miss. Right away." He bowed and left.

Rowan quickly unfolded the wrinkled scrap of brown paper. It was from Molly and said, in childish block printing, that she could not come with Rowan to "Grass Valy." Benjie's father had returned, and they were planning to make a new life for themselves, maybe even go back East. She was sure that Rowan would be all right and that she shouldn't worry. They were all going to be just fine.

Rowan was still staring at the paper when Alec returned. "What is it?" he asked quickly, seeing her face.

"It's my friend. She can't come with us."

Alec looked away, frowning. Rowan hurried on. "You'd better go on your own, Alec," she said. "You shouldn't be imposed upon any longer. I'll stay here and find another way to get to Grass Valley."

Alec straightened and rounded on her abruptly. "You're right. I won't be imposed upon any longer. Now, get your jacket on and get out to the wagon. I've laid in extra supplies and planned the route and closed my studio to take you to Grass Valley, and now you're by God going to Grass Valley!" He pointed to the doors, his face rigid with determination and anger.

Rebellion bubbled up in Rowan at his commanding tone. "Who do you think you are, ordering me about? If I'm such a burden to you, why don't you just leave me here?"

He took a step closer, looming over her. His voice was low and tight with anger. "Because if I leave you here I will only have to come get you out of a whorehouse, or rescue you from a pack of gypsies, or fish you out of the blessed bay—at midnight, in a thunderstorm, I have no doubt! No, you're going with me to Grass Valley, where I can leave you safe and sound in someone else's care once and for all!"

"I shan't be carted off and dumped like some unwanted parcel! And I won't travel without a proper chaperon."

He reached out and grasped her upper arm. He didn't hurt her, but she felt the unbreakable strength of his hold. "Don't worry about chaperons, Miss Trelarken. The way I'm feeling right now, I just may strap you to the roof and let you stay there for the whole trip. Believe me, the last thing I want on this green earth is to take liberties wi' the likes of you! Now, let's be off.''

Alec steered her toward the door, never letting go of her arm. Rowan had no choice but to go along. Still, she seethed with outrage when he almost tossed her up onto the front seat of the wagon and then climbed up right behind her. He clamped one hand on her arm again, took up the reins with the other, and gave a sharp command to the mules.

The team started up with a jolt, and Rowan was rocked sideways against Alec's shoulder. He straightened her up and held tight to her arm as he guided the mules into the street.

They'd not gone far when they heard a shout. Rowan looked up to see Taggart waving from one of the hotel balconies.

''Have a wonderful trip, Miss Trelarken!'' he called cheerfully. ''Alec, you'll know I'm right someday!''

''What does he mean by that?'' Rowan asked sharply.

Alec ignored her and shook his fist in Taggart's direction as they passed by. *''Is e so fath mo bhroin,''* he muttered.

''And what does that mean?''

His eyes glinted darkly. ''Roughly translated, it means 'You're the cause of all my problems.' ''

Rowan shrank back into the seat, frozen by the bitter ice in his tone. He remained silent all the way to the waterfront and all the way across the bay on the ferry. Rowan sat stiffly beside him for as long as she could.

But the sights and sounds of the people and animals on the ferry were too interesting, and she was soon lost in the beauty of the morning sun as it sailed up above the eastern edge of the world.

It was a long journey up San Francisco Bay and over to land. When they reached the eastern shore of the bay, they took the northern road, so the sun rode up over their heads and slid down the sky at Rowan's left side. In the hot, dry country beyond the bay, she had to drape her jacket over her head and shoulders so that she wouldn't burn in the early-summer sun. Alec made few stops, and then only for water and a bite of bread and meat, or to let the mules rest. Rowan didn't mind. At least there was more to look at on this trip than there had been on board the ship from England.

California was a revelation to her. The grassy lands that stretched before them were turning a tawny brown, but wildflowers edged the roadside in a profusion of colors and starred the grasses with vivid points of blue and yellow. Here and there, where water flowed, dark oaks clustered, their branches radiating out in all directions, their lower limbs almost touching the ground. Overhead, hawks made lazy, looping patterns in the air, then took swift, sudden dives into the grasses below. It was all fascinating, and beautiful in its wild way, yet so unlike moist, green England.

The memory of her home led her to think of Gil, and her mother. Were they well? she wondered. Gil must be settled in London by now, and studying law to his heart's content. He seldom went anywhere without a book in his pocket. Perhaps there'd be a letter waiting for her in Grass Valley. How good it would be to hear news of home.

She became lost in her thoughts, accepting Alec's silence beside her. She was startled when, as the sun began to lower, he spoke at last.

"We'll camp here," he said, and pulled the team to a halt.

Chapter Six

Camping, Rowan learned, was not unlike traveling in steerage aboard a ship. Water was provided, and fuel for a fire, but the travelers had to bring their own food, plates and utensils. They also had to cook their own food. On the trip from England, Rowan had shared her extra stores of food with her shipmate, Mary, in exchange for Mary's cooking skills and utensils. Rowan was willing to take on the challenge of learning to cook, but she didn't relish the idea of learning out in the wilds.

To her great relief, Alec had brought bread, cheese, fruit and some cooked meats for their first day out. "The rest of the supplies," he said as he handed a bundle to her out of the back of the wagon, "will keep. These have to be eaten now, or they'll to go to waste."

He didn't say much more, even after he'd built a fire for them and they'd eaten most of their meal. Rowan wondered if he was still angry with her. She'd expected him to be delighted that he wouldn't have to make this special trip for her, but she could see now that he had indeed put forth a great deal of effort in a

very short time to be ready to begin this journey today. Anyone would have been angered at a sudden
change of plans.

"I'm sorry about this morning," she ventured at
last.

Alec looked up from his meal. He gave her an assessing stare, as if judging her sincerity, then nodded.

"I appreciate all the work you must have done to get
all of these provisions and to notify your patrons," she
continued. "Thank you."

Alec looked down again. "You're welcome."

Rowan glanced up at the eastern sky and saw a large
yellow moon rising. It was almost at the full, adding its
light to that of their campfire and the kerosene lantern
that Alec had hung on one corner of the wagon. The
extra light made Rowan feel braver. "Did you camp
like this in New York?" she asked, hoping to draw him
into civil conversation.

Alec smiled at this. "Not in the city. But I used to go
on long rambles out to the country and camp there.
And I got used to traveling like this during the war."

"Did you really go out onto the battlefields to take
photographs? Now that I've seen how complicated
photography is, I can't imagine how you did it."

"I just did what I was paid to do." Alec finished his
cup of coffee, rose abruptly, and stretched. "If we're
going to make Sacramento before sundown tomorrow, we'll have to start out early. You can sleep in the
wagon, and I'll bed down out here. If you'll clean up,
I'll go get us some water to wash with."

He moved away to pick up a bucket, then lifted the
lantern and walked off toward the creek. Rowan sat

still for a moment, pondering Alec's mercurial moods. He was so methodical and orderly in all his ways, but when it came to dealing with people, it seemed, he was as unpredictable as the weather.

She gathered their plates and cups together, and the leftover cheese and bread she folded into the cloth and set aside for their morning meal. She cast the scraps out past the front of the wagon, toward the mules. Alec returned, filled a pot with water and set it on the fire to warm.

"I'll put the bucket here," he said, hanging it off the handle of the wagon's open rear door. "You can wash in this, and the water on the fire can be for the dishes." He went off into the dark again to check on the mules.

By the time she had struggled through the scrubbing, rinsing and wiping, she was wondering how anyone ever managed to have clean things in the outdoors. It was sheer luck that Alec's plates and utensils were all of unbreakable enameled steel, or they would have had only a plate and two butter knives to share at breakfast in the morning. At the end of the skirmish, she was spattered with water from head to toe, flushed from the heat of the fire, and not at all certain that the plates were fit to eat off of. Still, she bundled them all up and stored them in the wagon.

Alec returned from checking the mules and washed his face and hands in the bucket. His shirt collar was open, and his hair was damp at his forehead and temples.

"I put the dishes in the bin by the tongue of the wagon," Rowan told him.

"That's good," he said with a nod. "I left the lantern for you. I can see by the fire if need be." He reached into the wagon and lifted out a roll of blankets. "There's space to sleep inside. You'll find blankets and a pillow stored at the front of the wagon bed."

"Thank you."

He helped her climb up into the wagon and hung the lantern just inside the opening. "If it gets cold, you can pull the doors shut. I'll be sleeping by the fire, where I can keep an eye on the team. They haven't been out of the city in months, so they might be spooked."

He stood still for a moment, looking at her, the blanket roll slung over his shoulder. Rowan wanted to say something that would ease the moment. So many feelings were moving through her as he stood in the moonlight, his light shirt almost glowing against the dark background of the night. She felt gratitude and frustration, anxiety and attraction. She felt as if so many things were being left unsaid.

"I'll see you in the morning." Alec moved away from the wagon.

"Good night, Alec. Sleep well."

There was silence for a moment. Then, softer: "Good night, Rowan." She heard his footsteps moving to the front of the wagon. He lifted something down from the front seat, and then there came the quiet sounds of him settling in near the fire.

She smiled when she saw the blankets and pillow he had brought along. In contrast to his own Spartan dark wool bedroll, he had left for her the clean red-and-white quilt from his own bed, and one of the small, soft pillows. Had he been thinking of her when he packed them? There was also a pair of heavy old wool blankets, stitched together to form a mat. The floor of the wagon was spotless, and she laid out the bedding with a sigh, aware at last of how tired she was.

She had seen no other lights or fires around their campsite. They might have been the only people in the world, for all she knew. Still, she wasn't comfortable undressing before the open rear doors of the wagon; nor did she like the idea of closing the doors and sealing herself inside the dark space. She turned out the lamp and undressed quickly in the darkness that wrapped her in black velvet. Soon, her eyes grew accustomed to the dark, and the moonlight began to illuminate the space outlined by the wagon's door frame. A gentle wind moved over her as she got into her nightdress and wriggled into her makeshift bed. She sighed softly. Perhaps traveling with Alec would not be such a trial, after all.

Alec's arms ached from holding the reins all day. It had been months since he'd traveled more than a few miles at a stretch, and his body, while in good shape, protested against the new stresses and strains. He removed his shirt and sat down on a log by the fire. He pulled off his boots, laid them near his bedroll, and placed his rifle close at hand. He'd made the trip to Sacramento before, so he knew the road, but it was always smart to take precautions. The hell-raising Gold Rush days had ended before the war, but there were still dangerous men in California, and plenty of wild animals. Rowan Trelarken was trouble enough. He didn't need to invite any more.

He lay down and wrapped himself in the blankets, but found he wasn't as sleepy as he had expected. Instead of drifting off, he found himself reliving the brief argument he'd had with Taggart at the hotel.

It had been a dare, essentially. When he'd cornered Taggart in the hallway outside Rowan's door, he'd been furious and had accused Taggart of trying to railroad him into a romantic entanglement. He'd confronted Taggart about his fool notions of winning Saranne Ringlander away from Whit Carson.

Taggart had countered with his own accusations that Alec was frightened of his feelings for Rowan and was therefore acting like a damn fool about the trip to Grass Valley. When Alec had denied that, Taggart had said that a man with no such feelings would have no trouble doing a favor for a lady in distress.

Alec growled under his breath and rolled away from the fire. He'd left Taggart standing in the hall and stalked to Rowan's room, where he'd told her to be ready to travel. When he'd rejoined Taggart, he'd made it a point to say that he'd removed all doubts about his motives and feelings, meaning that he awaited Taggart's next move in the affair with Saranne.

Taggart had made his move, Alec thought, for he could only assume that the hotel balcony that Taggart had leaned from this morning belonged to the lovely Saranne. Taggart would never learn, Alec told himself. And it was no affair of his if he did or didn't; Taggart could take care of himself. As for Alec, he'd take Rowan to Grass Valley, leave her, and head south. He'd be his own man once more. That was how he liked it.

He tried again to lull himself into sleep, but his thoughts now strayed to the wagon and the woman asleep inside. He'd been so hell-bent on disproving Taggart's accusations that he hadn't given much thought to how Rowan must feel about this trip. He'd forced her to come when she'd balked at the idea of traveling without a chaperon. What feelings did she have about this trip? She was getting what she wanted. But he was sure she hadn't counted on getting it in quite this way.

He rolled onto his back and stared up at the stars. Rowan again.

What was it about this lovely red-haired marplot that reduced his famed objectivity and logic to nothing? He'd had a clear chance to back out of this trip when she'd announced that her friend could not accompany her. So what had he done? He'd grabbed her by the arm, dragged her to the wagon and driven her straight out of the city.

"Oh, no, MacKenzie," he whispered to himself. "No unchecked emotions there." Perfect objectivity? Taggart would have spilled his champagne laughing at that one.

Annoyed, he turned his thoughts to the one thing that he wanted more than anything else in this world. It was a dream that had sustained him many other times when he felt trapped by necessity.

Mathew Brady, his old employer, had made his name in the East, well before the war. Eadweard Muybridge had gained fame with his remarkable photos of Yosemite. Tim O'Sullivan, Alec's daring Irish friend from the battlefields of the war, was even now embarking on a geological expedition, photographing uncharted lands in Nevada and Utah. And he, Alec, had promised himself that he would be one of the first men ever to photograph the wilds of the Southwest. That was how he would make his name. And it was imperative to Alec that he make a name for himself, that he make his mark on the world.

He'd come to this country as an infant, the only child of a poor Scotsman who'd died before Alec was born. His mother, Rose, had taken her child and journeyed to America when she was hardly more than a girl herself, and she'd labored night and day to give her boy the best she could manage in the new home they'd found. When Alec had been apprenticed to Mathew Brady at age sixteen, he'd been the youngest man ever to work for that esteemed artist. Rose had been fiercely proud of her son, and the knowledge that Alec was on his way in the world had made the last few months of her life easier. Alec had buried Rose two days before his seventeenth birthday, and afterward had flung himself into the work at which he was already flourishing. He'd vowed he would be all his mother, with her stern ways and her sly humor, had hoped for, and more. He'd always been disciplined, determined, methodical, as Rose had taught him and as nature had made him. He'd turned those traits to good use in photography and combined with them a sensitive artist's eye and fiery soul, and he'd rapidly become a favorite in Brady's popular New York studio. Photography became his life, his sole passion.

Then the war had come, and Alec had returned from a stint in the cavalry to serve his mentor on the battlefields. But it had chafed at him when he was not given credit for photographs he risked his life to take, the photographs that wounded his heart to view. Alec and several others had left Brady's employ and formed their own loose coalition to continue documenting the true images of that terrible war. When the fighting had ended, Brady had been nearly broke, and his studio in disarray. The coalition's photographs had sold well at first, but the country had soon lost its taste for those sights. No one had wanted to be reminded of the losses of their brothers, fathers, sons. So the coalition had split up, scattering out to the frontiers to find new vistas to record.

Alec had listened to the accounts of the wonders of California and Arizona, and had formed his dream upon those images. Taggart, fresh from the service and restless as ever for new sport, had offered to come along. And so the expedition to the West had been launched.

It was a dream that had sparkled in his vision long before Rowan Trelarken had come crashing into his life, Alec thought to himself. And he still had that dream; he still had to make his name. No one could steal that from him. Nothing would turn him aside before he reached his goal.

He rolled on his side and fell asleep, content that he had conquered his demons.

Rowan lay frozen on the floor of the wagon. She'd come awake suddenly, without knowing why. Then she knew why. She heard it, alarmingly near her head.

Scritch, scritch, scritch.

Her heart surged. What was it? She could feel the vibrations of it right along her spine, as if something beneath the wagon were trying to scratch its way up inside.

She wanted to shout for Alec, but she kept still. What if this thing had already encountered Alec? What if he was unable to help her?

If she just kept quiet, it might go away. But what was it? Was it an animal? Was it some madman who lived out in the wilds, preying upon unwary travelers? What if it was red Indians?

Scritch-scritch. Scritch!

It was getting closer. She had to do something. She couldn't just let it invade the wagon and do who knew what! She had to have some kind of plan.

She sat up, moving as quietly as she could. She groped around before her and laid hands on the bundle of dishes she'd washed after supper. Slowly, with agonizing care, she unfolded the cloth and felt inside for one of the knives.

Scritch! Scritch! Scritch!

She almost screamed as the thing growled beneath the wagon. It was surely an animal, but what kind? Not a harmless squirrel or even one of the enormous white-tailed rabbits she'd seen dashing across the road that day. This was something bigger. Fiercer.

Her hand at last closed around the handle of a butter knife. It would have to do, she thought. She was shaking so badly she almost dropped it. What she wouldn't give for a stout iron skillet!

Grrr...

It had moved to the side of the wagon. Only a little farther, and it would find the open doors. She felt her breath lock in her chest.

There was another gruff sort of chirp, followed by a snorting growl. The thing was at the doors. It was time to take action. Now!

She leapt up with a piercing scream. There was a shout and a rifle blast as she tumbled out of the wagon and onto the grass below. Her arm struck something furry. She screamed again and stabbed at it with the butter knife.

"Ow!" Alec bellowed. "Damn it all, woman, have you lost your wits?"

"There's—there's a wolf!" she panted, scrambling up and struggling against his grasp. The mules began to bray, contributing to the alarm. "We have to get away!" She wrenched her arms free and began to struggle forward.

Alec grabbed her again and held her tighter, and his rifle thumped onto the grass beneath the wagon. "There's no wolf, Rowan!"

"There is! There's something, something scratching—"

"It's a raccoon! Just—" he managed to pin her flailing hands "—raccoons."

She halted, still alert and fearful. "What's a raccoon?" She could just make out his silhouette before her, looming black against the midnight-blue sky.

"It's like a..." He groped for the word as he caught his breath. "A badger, I guess. What the hell is that in your hand?"

"A knife."

"A knife?"

"Yes, a butter knife. Did you think I'd meet a wolf or even a raccoon with my bare hands?"

"I shouldn't think you'd choose to meet a wolf at all, let alone leap out at it with a kitchen utensil! But I should know you better by now. It's been almost three whole days."

"Then you must know that I don't know anything about wild American animals," she said, indignant.

"No, I don't know. After all, you invited them here."

"I did what?"

"You invited them. You left a trail of food big enough to draw every scavenging creature between here and Sacramento."

Rowan sagged a bit, dismayed. "I did?"

"Yes. And you're lucky it wasn't a wolf."

"But why didn't you call out to me? How was I to know what I'd done? I've never camped in the out-of-doors before. Why did you let them just sidle up to me?"

"I *wanted* it to 'sidle up' to us! I was going to shoot one," Alec said. "If I'd called out, I'd have frightened it away. I could have gotten us some fresh meat, or a pelt to trade, if you hadn't come out of that wagon like all the Furies on horseback. You could have been shot!"

Rowan slumped back and let the knife fall from her hands. Alec let go of her wrists and sat back as well.

"I felt fur," she said at last. "Did I stab the raccoon?"

"Och, lady, if only you had."

"What do you mean?"

"I mean that I'm your first trophy, Miss Trelarken."

"Oh, no! I didn't—"

"You did."

She covered her face with her hands, horrified and dismayed. "The Luck!" she moaned. "The unholy, misbegotten, ~~godforsaken~~ Trelarken Luck has followed me all the way around the world!"

Alec got to his feet and lighted the lantern inside the wagon. Rowan looked up and saw that he was bare-chested, and a dark stain was spreading downward from his left shoulder.

"Oh, Alec!" she cried. "Oh, I am so sorry!" She jumped to her feet and came to stand before him. "Does it hurt terribly?"

He gave her an odd look. "No. You only grazed me."

"Still, it should be attended to at once. I remember what you told me when I hurt my foot. If it goes without treatment for too long, it can become as bad as a gunshot wound."

She was already rummaging in the wagon for supplies. Alec reached in and pulled out his tin box.

"Let me," she said, taking the box from him.

She set to work cleaning the wound, and was relieved to see that the cut was neither wide nor deep. Still, there was a great deal of blood, she noted with a pang of guilt. Sheer chance had prevented her from injuring him in some more vital spot. She renewed her vow to stay away from him; she might well do something fatal next time.

She rolled a strip of cotton across his chest to hold the bandage in place, her fingers brushing through the thick, dark hair that grew there. Her cheeks grew hot to think that in her mad leap she'd mistaken him for an animal. There was no resemblance whatsoever—she could easily feel the warm, muscular flesh beneath the crisp mat of curling hair. As she stood on tiptoe to knot the ends of the bandage at his shoulder, she became more aware of the intimacy of her touch and the closeness of their bodies.

She looked up at him, her hand still resting on his shoulder. His eyes were averted, and he stood as still as marble.

"Does it hurt?" she asked softly, settling back down on her heels.

"No."

His silence seemed to accuse her. "I'm sorry that I acted so foolishly," she said. "I'll try to stay out of your way from now on."

He turned his head to face her. He seemed about to speak. Instead, he reached up and slowly lifted her hand away from his shoulder. His eyes closed as he carried her hand under his chin and carefully laid her palm against his cheek.

Now it was Rowan who could not move. She could not have been more stunned if he had hit her. The light stubble of his beard tickled her palm, and she felt a single muscle pulsing along his jaw. It was the most private, intimate gesture she had ever seen, let alone felt, far more intimate than the few times she had seen lovers kiss, or her parents share a quick embrace. There seemed to be a connection flowing from his skin to hers, a message that traveled all the way along her arm and throughout her body. The power of it rocked her and sent a quick, breath-stealing shiver down her spine.

His eyes opened, but he did not look at her. He lifted her hand from his cheek and held it gently as he lowered it to her side. Then he bent down, picked up his rifle and walked off toward the campfire.

Rowan stood staring after him as his tall form disappeared into the dark beyond the circle of lamplight. She was shaken to the very depths of her being. It was all she could do to put the tin box away, climb into the wagon, and turn out the lamp.

Huddled under the red-and-white quilt, she stared into the blackness around her and waited for her body to relax once more. She could feel Alec's presence, even through the wooden sides of the wagon, and her palm still seemed to feel his touch.

She thought she had understood what was between them, and she knew enough to know that men and women had physical desires. But this had been something so different. There was desire in it, definitely. Her body's sudden warmth and tingling had told her that much.

But there had been a new element in that simple gesture that went beyond desire. There had been a yearning in it, and a beckoning.

She shifted with frustration at the inadequacy of words. What was the word she sought? There had to be a word that encompassed all the feelings she had felt when Alec touched her, but it wasn't only desire, or wanting, or even love.

Closing her eyes, she saw Alec's face in that long moment, how his eyes had closed and how his head had bent to fit into the curve of her palm. He had not looked happy, but he had not looked angry, either. She had a feeling that if she had been able to move, to touch him in return, there would have burst forth a flood of feelings and events that neither of them could have stemmed.

That was the lesson to be learned, even if she couldn't describe the sensations she had felt. There would have been no turning back if she had met his gesture with one of her own. Though she had no clear idea where it all would have led, she knew it would have been her undoing.

She repeated her three vows once more: to find Luke as soon as she could; to earn money; and to stay away from Alec MacKenzie. If she didn't stay away from him, her whole trip to America would be for nothing. She was here to marry Luke and rescue her family from their financial woes. She was not here to ponder the merits and hazards of desire, or to puzzle over the complicated nature of American photographers.

Besides, she told herself, every time she crossed his path something disastrous happened. She had wounded him, and nearly been shot herself, in this latest fiasco. Better to stay a good distance away and hope that the trip to Grass Valley was a speedy one.

The next day brought them alongside the Sacramento River. Rowan was amazed at all the activity on the water. Steam paddle-wheel boats—some of them a hundred feet long, she guessed—chugged upstream, laden with passengers. Many people stood out on the decks and waved to Rowan and Alec as they passed. Mail packets, small and sturdy, darted in and out of the wakes of the bigger boats, while fishing boats dawdled along, trailing lines and nets.

Rowan had spent a restless night, but Alec had looked refreshed when she emerged from the wagon and joined him at the fire. He'd shown her where the raccoons had followed the scraps she'd thrown and how they'd found the leftovers she'd forgotten on the keg at the side of the wagon, but he didn't seem angry. They'd eaten breakfast and been on the road well before six. Rowan remembered her vow, and made every effort to stay away from Alec. This was difficult to do on the wagon's one seat, but she kept to one side and tried not to speak unless she was spoken to—something that was even more difficult than keeping her distance.

"We'll make Sacramento well before sundown," Alec said as they watched a barge floating heavily down the river. "But I think we should camp there for the night. I have to stop and see someone in the town."

"Will there be other people camping there, as well?" Rowan asked.

"Very likely. Sacramento's the jumping-off place for all trips north and east."

"Jumping-off place?"

He smiled. "No one goes leaping off cliffs, if that's what you're asking. But it's where everyone stops and gets supplies before they start off into the mountains. A starting point, you could say."

"Jumping-off place," she said. "It sounds like diving into cold water."

"It could be, for some. The Sierras are pretty wild, especially when you get up high and start heading over the east-west passes. The snow never melts in some spots. You can get trapped there for weeks if you don't find the right trail at just the right time."

Rowan's eyes were round with wonder. She could see the mountains of the Sierra Nevada now, off to their right. She could tell that they were still far away, but they were so tall already that she simply couldn't imagine their actual size. This was where she was going to live? "Is Grass Valley...very far up?"

Alec gave her a reassuring smile. "No. It's only a short way above the foothills. I doubt that it snows there often, if at all."

"Have you been up in those passes?"

"No. I've been to Yosemite, and you have to climb a good way before you can get down into Yosemite Valley, but from what I've heard of Donner Pass and the Truckee Pass, Yosemite's a picnic excursion."

Rowan glanced out over the river again. "I never guessed that America would look like this," she said with a sigh.

"How did you think it would look?"

"You'll only laugh."

"No, I won't. I had all kinds of ideas about what the West would be like before I came out. If I hadn't seen some photos, I wouldn't have believed it, either."

Rowan smiled. It was nice to be on friendly terms with Alec again. It was so much safer and more comfortable. Last night's events seemed far away in the sunny light of the afternoon, with all the sights and sounds of the river playing beside them.

They crossed the river aboard the ferry, and Alec took the team through town and out to the eastern limits. Under a span of oaks, near a creek, seven or eight wagons were gathered. Rowan could smell the campfires burning as they approached, and she saw one or two children darting in and out among the wagons, playing a game of tag.

She felt relieved. At least for tonight, there would be people around. They wouldn't be camping all alone in the wilds. It was almost as if they'd have a chaperon.

As Alec guided the team to an open space near the creek, her heart sank. A chaperon! They were going to be among other people; a man and a woman, unmarried, traveling alone together—with no chaperon. What would these people think of them?

"Is this where we'll camp?" she asked.

"Yes. I have to go into town and I thought you'd feel better having some people around while I'm gone."

He hopped down from the wagon and stretched, then offered his arm to help her down. Rowan looked back over her shoulder at a small group of women who were clustered about a large fire built within a ring of stones.

"Perhaps I should go with you?"

Alec shook his head. "No reason for you to do that. I'm just going to stop in at another photographer's studio, then come right back. I'm going to walk there, give the team a rest." He motioned again for her to step down.

She came down and cast another worried glance at the women. "What shall I tell them?" she blurted at last.

"Tell whom?"

"Them. Those ladies. How shall I introduce myself?"

Alec looked mystified. "What's wrong with Miss Rowan Trelarken? It's a pretty name."

"Miss! Miss Trelarken! Don't you see how it would look?"

He scowled, then nodded. "Ah, I see. Yes, this is a situation, isn't it?"

"I can't tell them I'm not married. And yet they'll know that I'm not."

"How?"

She thrust out her left hand.

"Ah," he said again. "No ring. Well, then, there's nothing for it." He fished in his pocket and pulled out his watch. He unclipped a slender gold band from the chain and slipped it onto Rowan's finger. "That should keep them quiet. We're married."

Chapter Seven

Rowan stared at the gold on her finger as he turned to unhitch the team. Seeing the glimmering band there gave her an odd feeling in her chest, a sudden tightening, a wild, sweet feeling. But it didn't solve her problem.

"Don't be ridiculous!" she said, grabbing his sleeve. "I can't tell them we're married!"

Alec straightened. "You just said you couldn't tell them we're not married. Now you say you can't tell them that we are. Can't you make up your mind?"

"It's not my mind I'm worried about. It their minds!"

"Well, that's good, but I'm starting to worry about my mind."

"Listen to me!" She stamped her foot, raising a puff of dust between them. "Listen," she continued, flapping her hand to clear the air. "If I tell them we're married, what will they think when you go to sleep outside tonight and I stay in the wagon?"

Alec shrugged and went about his task. "Tell them you're married to someone else."

"And traveling alone with another man? It's even more preposterous."

"Well, I certainly wouldn't want you to be compromised. I'll sleep in the wagon."

"You will not!"

"Rowan." His voice was stern. "I don't give a damn what a lot of strangers think of us! You do. I've made a suggestion. I've given you a ring. You can take it from there. I'll be back by sundown."

He led the team away from the wagon and went off to stake them out on their pickets. Rowan whirled about and stomped to the back of the wagon. She threw open the doors, climbed up inside, and pulled the doors shut behind her.

She promptly regretted her move. She was in utter darkness again. Damn Alec and his photographer's craze for pitch-black working conditions. She shoved one of the doors open.

"Yeow!" someone cried.

"Oh, my goodness!" she exclaimed. A man was squatting down below the bottom of the door, both arms crossed over his head. "Are you all right?"

He looked up cautiously. "Yeah. I think so." He stood and extended his hand. "'Lo, ma'am. I'm Ed Davies. My wife Melissa sent me over to tell you and your husband that you're welcome to join us at the fire."

He pointed, and one of the women waved to Rowan. "That's Lissa," he said, smiling and staring. The woman waved him off, and he came to attention again, his smile widening to a slightly embarrassed grin. "We just got married, back in Pennsylvania. We're headed for Placerville to settle near my brother's place. He's got a blacksmith shop there."

Rowan decided to go along with the man's assumption that she and Alec were married. "I'm—we're on our way to Grass Valley," she said. "Is that anywhere near Placerville?"

"No, I don't think so, Mrs.—?"

"MacKenzie." She winced inwardly at the lie.

"Pleased to meet ya. No, Placerville's east and Grass Valley's north, according to my map." He tugged at the brim of his hat and nodded toward the fire. "Just go on over when you get yourself settled in, Mrs. Mac-Kenzie. My Lissa's just so glad to see some other women that she's ready to bust."

He gave her another grin and went off, his eyes still on his wife, who kept flapping a hand at him as if to shoo him off. When he had disappeared between the wagons, she turned to Rowan and waved again.

It would be nice to have other women around, Rowan thought, giving a little wave back. And it would certainly be a way to keep a certain distance between herself and Alec.

She freshened up and looked through their supplies for their evening meal. The women at the fire were preparing food, she guessed, cooking dinner for their husbands and children. She couldn't imagine what it would take to cook on a stove in a proper house, let alone over an open fire in the out-of-doors. Even in their poverty, the Trelarkens had had a woman to cook for them, for Louisa knew as little as Rowan about such matters. Still, Rowan felt she was expected to bring along something that she could do by the fire, rather than just stand and talk. It would look odd if she, too, wasn't cooking for her "husband."

At last she settled on tea. She knew she could manage that. She filled the kettle from the keg of water that Alec carried on the wagon, found a strainer and a colorful tin of China tea and started off for the fire ring.

"Welcome." Melissa Davies came forward to greet her, wiping her hands on her apron. She was tall, like Rowan, but with a long, oval face and heavy, straight brown hair that was braided down her back and tied with a red ribbon. She had a sprinkling of soft freckles across the bridge of her nose, and that endeared her to Rowan at once. "I'm Melissa Morgan—" She blushed. "Mrs. Melissa Davies. It's kind of hard to remember that, even though Ed and I have been married almost three months now."

"I have the same problem," Rowan said, fingering the ring on her left hand. "This is all very new to me, as well. I'm Rowan Trelarken...MacKenzie. Rowan MacKenzie. It was very kind of you to invite me to join you." She lifted the kettle and strainer. "I've brought tea. Would you care for some?"

"Would I?" Melissa exclaimed. "We've been drinking mint tea, saxifrage tea, and even rosehip tea, but I haven't had the real thing in an age." She looked at Rowan cautiously. "Sure you want to share it?"

"Oh, yes. We brought quite a bit of it from San Francisco. There's plenty for everyone." Rowan's smile included the three other women, who watched them from the fireside.

"Then, if you're sure, let me provide the cups. Those I do have aplenty." She began handing teacups out of a sturdy wooden box. "Oh, but my manners! I almost forgot. This is Pru Baxter, Liza Donelly, and Jerusha Perkins. And this is Rowan MacKenzie. She and her husband just came from San Francisco, right?"

"Yes," Rowan said. "I'm pleased to meet you."

They sat down by the fire, perching on boxes or tree stumps or fallen logs that had been dragged into the circle of the wagons to serve as chairs. As the kettle boiled, the women chatted about their homes in towns Rowan had never heard of and compared notes on the joys and hardships of the trail. Rowan shared what little information about Alec and herself she could reveal without going into many confusing details.

"Well, your situation is certainly different," Melissa said. "Here you are an English girl, come over to America and married to an important photographer. What on earth, if you don't mind my asking, are you headed to Grass Valley for? Do have kin there?"

"I have friends there, yes. Have you ever been there?"

"I have," Jerusha said. "It's pretty nice."

"Land sakes, look at that sky!" Melissa exclaimed. "Sun's almost down, and here we are with no supper on except potatoes, corn cakes and hot water." She jumped up and motioned to Rowan. "Come on. We'll get our stuff out of the wagons and hustle something up quick. Those men of ours'll be coming back any minute now, hungrier'n grizzlies."

Rowan went along behind Melissa, glad to have escaped more questions about her marriage, miserable at the thought of cooking, and wondering what in the world grizzlies were. These women seemed to know everything about taking care of themselves and their men, even out-of-doors.

"I've got some fatback pork, and some beans that've been soaking all day," Melissa was saying as they came to the wagons. "That should be good with the corn bread." She saw Rowan biting her lower lip as she stared at Alec's wagon. "What's the matter? You and Alec brought provisions, didn't you?"

Rowan nodded. "It isn't that...."

Melissa's eyes closed, and she nodded. "Oh, I see," she said. She looked knowingly at Rowan. "You haven't got the hang of cooking yet, have you?"

Relieved, Rowan shook her head. "You've seen the full extent of my cooking."

Melissa slipped her arm into Rowan's. "Well, now, don't you fret. I burned bread for toast and boiled eggs till they were shoe leather when I first cooked for my Ed. I thought the poor man was going to strangle on my coffee. I think he used it to black his boots, later." She lowered her voice. "But you know what? They don't really care. Leastways, not those first few weeks. There's other things on their minds, then, if you know what I mean."

Rowan stared at her in confusion for a moment, then blushed furiously. Dear Lord, the places her lies were leading her!

"But like I said, don't worry. You just show me what you have in store, and I'll add it to what I'm cooking. Then we'll all sit down together—that's if you don't mind—and your Alec won't never need to know."

Somehow, Rowan suspected that Alec would know. There was very little that slipped past his keen brown eyes. But she'd be an idiot to refuse Melissa's offer.

"Oh, that would be ever so kind of you. You must let me help with something. I can make more tea, if you like, and I believe we have some fresh fruit to share."

"Fresh fruit? Honey, you've just made yourself some lifelong friends. All we've had in months are some sour old berries we found by the road a ways back. Lead me to it."

Suppertime was marked by the arrival of the men. There were other campfires in the area, and their smoky scent and the odor of hot food rose and mingled on the breeze. Alec appeared at the wagon, and Rowan watched as he fetched water in the bucket and rinsed off before joining the group at the fire.

"'Lo." Ed Davies jumped up and went to greet Alec. "Ed Davies. That's my wife, Melissa. Welcome."

Alec shook his hand. "Alec MacKenzie. I'm pleased to meet you both."

Rowan caught his quick glance at her left hand. She looked at him and watched his eyes begin to brighten. Was that a smile tugging at the corners of his mouth?

"Mr. MacKenzie, if you're hungry, just sit down there and we'll fill you up a plate," Melissa said quickly. "We're all kind of tossing our luck into the pot tonight."

"It smells delicious," Alec said. He crossed to Rowan's side and placed a hand on her waist. "We haven't been on the trail long, but my wife and I are glad of the company. Isn't that so, sweetheart?"

Rowan would have liked to roast him like the potatoes buried in the coals. The miserable man was teasing her—and loving it. "Yes, Alec," she murmured. "I'm especially glad to have so many others around."

"Well, I'm as hungry as a wolf, and you know how hungry they get, don't you? What have you cooked up for me tonight, love?"

Henbane, Rowan wanted to tell him. Henbane drenched in arsenic sauce. "Just take your seat near Mr. Davies, and I'll get you a plate," she purred instead. "You must be tired from your long walk into town."

"Lissa tells me you're a photographer, MacKenzie. You were in the war?" Ed Davies patted the log where he sat.

Alec gave Rowan's arm a squeeze as he moved past her to sit down next to Ed. "That's right. I've been at it since I was sixteen, and it's all I know, I'm afraid. Been on the trail long?"

"Here," Melissa said softly, handing Rowan a plate. "You just dish up some beans and pork, and I'll add the corn cakes and some of your fruit and no one'll be the wiser."

"Thank you," Rowan said. "This is so kind of you. I was afraid I wouldn't like it here, but Americans are very nice once you get to know them."

"I'll accept that compliment on behalf of these newly reunited states," Melissa said with a grin. "Out here on the trail, folks know how hard it is just to do the little things, like cooking and keeping your clothes clean. And they know how lonely it can get, even with your husband or your wife at your side. We treat one another extra good, whenever we meet." She laid two steaming corn cakes on the plate. "Besides, you never know when you're going to be the one that needs help."

Rowan smiled. "You've certainly helped me. I wish I could do something for you in return."

Melissa waved the idea away. "If it isn't you, it'll be somebody else returning the favor for you, somewhere down the road. Things tend to even out in the end. Now, go feed that man of yours."

Rowan carried the plate to Alec and handed it over in silence. She was going to move away but Alec caught her hand and gave it a tug. Reluctantly she sat down beside him, perching on the edge of the log.

Melissa came by and handed her a plate, then pulled up a crate to sit next to Ed. She winked at Rowan over the men's heads. Rowan relaxed. She was among friends, and out in public. There wasn't much trouble that she could get into with Alec while they were in camp.

Or so she thought. Some devil had taken hold of staid, calm Alec MacKenzie this evening, and he was ready to tweak her about their situation at every opportunity. He flirted shamelessly with her over his coffee mug and delivered little caresses and pats in the most astonishing places on her person, and a look of self-satisfied amusement sparkled in the depths of his eyes. She wanted to strangle him, but she knew she had to act out the part of his loving wife before all these people.

When he finished his meal, he handed her his plate with a dazzling smile. "Thank you, dear," he said, his tone warm and intimate. "Another delicious meal."

"I'll put some leftovers out for you, dear," she murmured. "In case you and the raccoons get hungry in the night."

She helped Melissa and the other women clean up, noting how they scrubbed the pots with wet sand from the riverbank and laid the clean dishes on a cloth spread out on a patch of clean grass. She thought she could manage that on her own, if she had to.

The last streaks of the sunset were fading away when they rejoined the men by the fire. Alec pulled Rowan close to his side on the log, and she couldn't find a way to object unobtrusively. She sat in tense awareness of his long thigh pressed against hers, his hip against her hip, feeling an odd, not unpleasant fluttering within her middle.

Ed Davies built a crackling, merry blaze that lighted the faces of the couples ringed around it. There was more talk of the trips people had before them, and the things they dreamed of doing when they reached their destinations. Rowan and Alec fended off inquiries about their plans as best they could. Rowan was relieved when some of the travelers brought out musical instruments and began to play. When the last note of the fiddle had trailed up and away into the night, there was a long, pleasant silence. Then Tom yawned, stretched, and dropped one arm over Liza's shoulders.

"Well, we're startin' out early, " he said to the group. He rose and helped his wife to her feet. "Guess we'll be turnin' in."

"You're right there," said Ray Perkins, jumping up. "Jerusha and I'll be home by tomorrow night if we get a good start in the morning."

Ed grinned and nodded and bade them all good-night as he stored his fiddle in its case. "Young folks need their rest," he said in a loud whisper. Melissa whacked him on the shoulder with the back of her hand, but he only grinned wider.

Alec slipped his arm around Rowan's waist. "We'd best be ready early in the morning, too. Isn't that right, angel?"

Rowan glared at him. Maybe she wouldn't just roast him. Maybe she'd cut him up in little pieces and leave a trail for the raccoons to feast on.

Alec stood up, pulling her along with him. "We'll be seeing you in the morning, Ed, Melissa."

They all said good-night to the Baxters, who were sitting hand in hand before the fire, already oblivious of all others. Rowan steeled herself against the pleasurable feeling of Alec's strong arm about her, his hand hugging her waist so that she was again held against his hip as they walked. But she was not going to allow herself to forget her vows. She went along as peacefully as she could manage, for appearances' sake, but inside, her anger at Alec's liberties was building.

Ed and Melissa left them outside the wagon and went into their own canvas-covered vehicle a few feet away. Alec helped Rowan up and lighted the lantern, turning it down low. He was about to hop up into the wagon, but he was stopped by Rowan as she thrust his bedroll into his chest. "Good night, Alec," she said sweetly. "Sleep well."

He vaulted nimbly up to her side. "Good night to you, wife. Do you prefer the left side or the right?"

"The center," she said evenly.

"Doesn't leave me much room, but I can manage. Sounds like you'll be rather uncomfortable, though."

"You're not staying in here."

"I am. What would people think?"

"I don't care what they think! Let them think what they like." She picked up the bedroll and thrust it at him again.

He refused the blankets, and they slid to the floor over their feet. "That's not what you said this afternoon." He moved closer. "I thought you wanted them to believe we're married, Rowan."

His voice had softened, taken on a deeper note. Rowan felt her breath tightening in her chest. The space between them seemed charged with a special heat and her body was tingling with the awareness that the subtlest of movements, less than a step, would bring her up against him.

"You've done quite enough to convince them," she said, finding her voice at last. "What we do—or don't do—in private is none of their affair."

He swayed toward her, and his breath stirred the delicate hairs that edged her forehead. "So, they can think what they like?" His voice was even softer, his breath a soothing touch against her flushed cheek.

She was beginning to tremble with the effort to stay straight and still before him. Her body was behaving like a traitor, warming and expanding, inward and outward, constricting here and melting there.... She couldn't think. Casting logic aside, she reached for emotions, and anger came to the fore.

"All right, I do care what they think!" she exclaimed. She lowered her voice when she realized that anyone could hear her through the open doors. "I care what they think, and so would you if you had any respect for me or for my feelings!"

His arm shot out suddenly and pulled her against him. She was caught by surprise, and her breath whooshed out of her, leaving her gasping and speechless for a moment, held tight against the hard planes of his torso.

"And just what are your feelings?" he whispered, his own anger sharpening the edges of his words. "It seems to me that you can't make up your mind about the color of the sky, let alone what you feel!"

He lifted his hand to her chin and grasped it, not roughly, but firmly, and with unswerving determination. His head came down, and his lips covered hers, angry and hard for an instant, then softening and smoothing, persuading her lips to part and swell for him, to bid him welcome, despite her inner resistance.

Rowan couldn't move. She was fitted against him so firmly, so completely, that she could feel each muscle in his chest and in his arm, which was tight and coiled to hold her for as long as he desired. She didn't think he would let her go, even if she could summon the strength to resist.

The pleasure of his kiss was far more startling than his anger, however. She hadn't known that a man's lips could be so soft and winning, and yet so insistently masculine. She hadn't known that she could be so utterly undone by such a simple thing. But she was. All her vows, all her plans, all her preconceptions were banished by that simple gesture, and in their place she found quickening desire, heady delight, and a deep-down awareness that she was being changed forever.

When he lifted his head at last, he looked down into her startled, heated face and gave a soft laugh. "And now what should they think?"

His laughter broke the spell. Her anger returned in a flash, and she shoved herself away from him with all her might, breaking his hold.

"They can think we've had a fight," she snapped. She gathered up the fallen blankets and threw them out of the wagon. "We've had a fight, and now you're going to sleep outside!"

He crossed his arms. "I'm not going anywhere."

Rowan set her jaw. "Then I shall!"

She jumped down from the wagon and hauled the blankets up from the ground. Wadding them up in her arms, she started toward the fire. She halted when she saw that the Baxters were still sitting in its light, their heads close together.

She couldn't go there, obviously. Not only was it plain that Clayton and Pru wouldn't welcome company, but it would be too ridiculous to try to explain to them why she was bedding down alone by the fire.

She rounded the end of the wagon and headed toward the creek. The moon had risen—it was at the full now, and she used its light to show her a likely spot beneath a nearby oak. She shook out the blankets and laid them down, then began to remove the pins from her hair. One of her hairpins caught on her left hand, and she saw that it was stuck in the ring Alec had given her.

Her outrage bubbled up afresh. The miserable cheek of the man! Using the situation and her scruples to make fun of her, to take base advantage of her! She turned and strode toward the wagon.

Alec stood where she had left him and tried to calm his raging spirit. He was out of his mind—that had to be the explanation. There was a full moon tonight. Perhaps that was the cause. He'd heard tales of how men and women often went raving mad under its light, behaving in ways they'd never dream of at other times.

But, God, it had felt like heaven to hold her. His body was still raging against him for the abrupt end to its pleasure. One kiss and he was toppled, all his good sense and careful reserve, his exquisite self-control— gone! If the moonlight brought madness, then she was a creature made entirely of moonlight. He had found a sweet insanity in the cool taste of her lips, and he knew that if he didn't find some way to restore his reason, he'd never stop until he possessed every maddening inch of her.

As he stood there searching his mind for an answer, something struck him hard on one shoulder, then dropped to the floor with a metallic *plink*. He heard footsteps stamping away from the wagon, and the muttered words "Insufferable American cheek!"

He knelt and grasped the object, which had rolled up against a bin. It was the ring he'd given Rowan earlier that day. He turned it to the light. Inside its circle, he read the words he'd seen so many times before: My Rose.

He clipped the ring back on his watch chain with a sigh. His father's Rose. Had his father, dead before Alec was born, ever known this madness when he'd held Rose Claymoore in his arms? Surely there must have been something for them to *ghabh an t-ainneul,* or "kindle the common fire," as his mother had called it, the fire that had begotten him. Kindled it almost two months before their wedding day, at that, leaving her to set out for America alone with their infant son. Yet he couldn't imagine anyone so confounded as he was tonight. There couldn't be anyone so completely baffling as Rowan Trelarken, or so utterly beguiling.

He undressed, turned out the lamp, and settled in under the quilt. He willed himself to relax and set his mind on the future, and his expedition. His efforts would have been rewarded with sleep if only he had been camped somewhere else. But just as he began to relax, he heard noises.

They started as a gentle creaking, now and then. There were soft murmurs that died away quickly on an indrawn breath. Then the creaking would begin again, a little louder and a little faster.

Alec groaned. Ed and Melissa, their next-wagon neighbors, were enjoying the pleasures of the marriage bed, and he would be forced to listen! He clapped his hands over his ears to keep out the lovers' moment of climax, but it was too late to halt his annoyingly active mind.

Visions of Rowan rose up before him like gathering smoke. He could see the angle of her arm as it lifted to embrace his neck, and could feel the soft giving of her breasts as he clasped her against him once more. But this time she wasn't wearing her prim black dress or her neat, braided chignon. Instead, her hair was loose and waving around her face as she embraced him, and he was sliding a gown of sheerest silk from her slender shoulders. He pulled her closer, and watched the silk flow over the inward curve of her waist and slip lower, revealing—

He shook his head, as if trying to clear the images from his brain. When he judged it was safe to listen once more, he took his hands away from his ears and sat up. Muttering curses, he crawled to the edge of the wagon and dipped a hand in the water bucket swinging from the door handle. The cold splash against his face and chest made him splutter, but it helped to clear his head. He took a drink, threw a baleful glance at the serene face of the moon above, and crawled back to his solitary bed.

Chapter Eight

Rowan woke with a start and gazed about her. It was morning, and she was alone. She frowned. Hadn't Alec been sleeping beside her? She had a clear memory of him speaking to her in the night, then a vague memory of being gently enfolded in warmth and comfort. But it must have been a dream, she thought, unable to decide whether she was relieved or disappointed.

She returned to the wagon. Alec wasn't there. She changed into clean clothes and washed up. As she stepped down from the wagon, Alec appeared, carrying feed bags for the team.

"I'd like to say goodbye to Melissa before we leave," she told him. "Is there time?"

He nodded, and she bade a hasty goodbye to her new friend.

"You and Alec be real good to one another now," Melissa said, her warm smile lighting her face. "And don't you worry about cooking till you get to Grass Valley and someone can show you what's what. Your man'll understand."

"Thanks for all your kindness," Rowan said. "I wish you and Ed all the best."

"And the same to you. If we're ever up your way, we'll come and have our pictures taken by Alec, you can be sure. Everyone back home'll be real impressed."

Rowan pondered her words as she and Alec drove out of camp and found the road north. She knew so little about him, really. Everyone seemed so admiring of his profession, yet he seemed to make light of his endeavors. Alec was indeed a man of complexities.

Alec was once again silent as he drove, keeping his thoughts, as well as his eyes, to himself. Rowan felt confused and divided by the events of the previous night. He had teased her and mocked her feelings, yet his kiss had seemed more than merely playful. She had been both entranced by his kissing and outraged at his laughing disregard for her feelings. This morning, he seemed once again cold, angry and distant, and she found she liked it no better than his mockery. She didn't know what to do to change this situation, but she felt that they could at least be civil.

"If you like," she said, breaking the silence at last, "I'll sleep out of doors from now on, and you can have the wagon. I don't mind, really."

Alec shook his head and shrugged. "I prefer to sleep outdoors, where I can keep my eye on things. You take the wagon, and I'll stay out of your way."

"Very well, if you're sure. I'm—I'm glad to have it settled." She gazed ahead at the rolling hills that were rising before them. "How much farther is it to Grass Valley?"

"I make it a hundred miles as the crow flies. Maybe longer, depending on the roads and trails."

Rowan sat silent for a while. A hundred miles was a long way, and she didn't know what concerned her more: the prospect of Alec's cool reserve toward her for a hundred miles, or the danger to them both if they dropped their guard and permitted their relations to warm. She gave a shiver that was half irritation, half pleasure.

Alec's voice cut into her reverie. "As soon as you're settled in Grass Valley, I'll have to be on my way. You'll be on your own then. Will you be all right?" His voice was oddly flat and monotonous.

"Yes. All I need is transportation to Grass Valley. If there's no one there to meet me, then I shall make other plans." Rowan congratulated herself. It was right to show him how self-sufficient she could be.

"Good. Then that's settled," he said. "I have my savings with me, and I'm planning to leave straight from Grass Valley. I won't be returning to San Francisco."

"I understand."

He scanned the horizon. "It'll be fine to be on my own again. I've been too long in the city."

"Mr. Taggart will miss you."

"Oh, I doubt that. Taggart's never without a friend or a lady. Suits him just fine."

"But it doesn't suit you?"

"Never has, never will. It's too hard to get out and see things, too hard to work, if you're always tied to somebody else and their schedules. No, this is the kind of life I like, free and clear and on my own."

Except that I'm along with you, she wanted to say, but she held the thought. It seemed that she had an answer to her wonderings. She had a lot to learn about men and their affections. Alec had been only playing last night when he'd kissed her. He wanted no entanglements, and he didn't want her. His cool demeanor would remain.

That was good, she told herself. It was a great relief. Now she knew that she could travel with him and not fear that any feelings would get in their way. She'd been hurt enough by her father's abandonment, and the parting with her family had been painful. She wasn't about to let herself in for another heartbreak when Alec disappeared, as well. She had too much to do.

They began to climb into the foothills by midday, passing the occasional farmhouse or herd of cattle grazing on the yellow grasses. They were still following the river, and where it snaked through the hills, the trees and grasses grew more lush and green.

They camped late that night, and Rowan did the washing up after Alec cooked their dinner. As she was finishing, he brought his bedroll from the wagon and laid it out by the fire. Rowan wanted to thank him for the courtesy, then thought better of it. The less said, the better, she decided.

They were quiet as they drove away at dawn the next morning. The road began to disappear as they climbed higher, toward the mountains, and they were forced to slow their pace over the rutted wagon track that replaced it.

Alec seemed more relaxed this morning, and he pointed out trees and animals to Rowan and told her their names. She was delighted to learn to recognize the small yellow-gold poppies that grew everywhere, and the coppery bark of the manzanita, as well as the great hawks overhead and the small prairie dogs that chattered at them from their roadside burrows.

Since entering the foothills, they'd been following the river, which changed as it flowed from a rippling creek to a full, rushing torrent and then back again to a quiet stream. Boulders were scattered along the river's path, some of them looking as big as cottages to Rowan. Where they were clustered in the stream, the river rushed faster, forced between their huge shoulders, causing the currents to eddy, and churning the water to a frothy white. In other places, the water slowed to a murmur, and deep, dark pools spread out to the banks. Toward the end of the day, Alec pulled up at the river's edge. The water here was neither the frantic white of the rapids nor the glassy black of the deep pools. He consulted his map, waded out a ways in the stream, then returned to the wagon.

"We're going to have to cross here, where it's shallow," he told her. "If we don't, I'm afraid we'll hit only white water or deep pools up ahead, and never get the wagon across." He held up the reins. "Can you drive? I'm going to lead the mules."

"I think I can. I've driven horses."

"Close enough." He slid closer to her and laid the reins in her hands. "All you have to do is keep the reins up and in, like this." He gave a firm, steady pull on the reins above her hands. "That way, they won't go slack. If they go slack, the mules could think they've been given their heads and pull off on their own." He looked at her, an eyebrow cocked. "Ready?"

"I think so." She pushed back the sleeves of her dress and braced herself firmly against the buckboard.

Alec jumped down, pulled off his hat and tossed it on the seat beside her. He went forward and took hold of the mules' bridles. "Go ahead," he called to Rowan.

She shook the reins and the mules started forward, into the flowing stream. Alec waded in beside them and was soon slogging along, the water up to his thighs.

Rowan bent all of her concentration on keeping the reins steady over the backs of the mules. The riverbed seemed to be all rock, and she felt her teeth jarring as the wagon lifted up, then slammed down, then lifted again. They bumped along toward the opposite shore.

Alec was holding tight to the mules' bridles, almost shouting to them over the roar of the water and the noise of the wagon. He was in water up to his waist now, his light shirt soaked through to his skin. He turned to call out something to Rowan, and in that instant he was knocked out and away from the team.

Rowan screamed as Alec was carried swiftly downstream, toward the rapids. The reins went slack in her hands. When Alec reached the white water, he was slammed from boulder to boulder, his head barely visible above the fast-moving water. The mules panicked as they felt the current cut beneath their legs as it had Alec's, and they began to thrash and struggle against their harnesses.

Rowan pulled so hard on the reins that she rose up out of her seat and was almost pulled over the buckboard into the water. The leather straps ripped into her palms, but she held on, shouting to the mules to obey. The wagon was heavy enough that she could feel the river bottom below, but she could also feel a sickening slide as the front of the wagon started to give in to the current.

"Hold!" she shrieked at the mules, the wagon, her hands. "Hold!"

Miraculously, the wheels touched bottom and rolled ahead. She shot a glance downstream. Where was Alec?

She had no more time to look. The wagon went light all of a sudden, and she felt all four wheels lift off the riverbed. She pulled hard on the reins, yanking the mules' heads above the wild water that was churning all about them. They were swimming, she thought. Thank God, they were swimming.

In the next instant, though it seemed an age to Rowan, the wagon wheels found purchase once again and began to roll. The mules scrabbled frantically and got their footing, as well.

"Pull!" she shouted, cracking the reins over their backs. "Go on, you silly beasts! *Pull!*"

At her word *pull,* the mules strained ahead and reached sand. They struggled up the bank, heaving with panic, as well as with the effort, and the wagon came to a halt at last, sunk deep in the long grasses.

Rowan vaulted down off the seat, made the reins fast to a stump, and raced to the water's edge. Stumbling over rocks and tree roots, she followed the river downstream, tucking her skirts up as she ran.

"Alec! Al-ec!" She cupped her hands to her mouth and shouted to be heard over the crashing torrent.

Where was he? There was no sign of him. Surely she would see a light shirt, the dark head—

There! He was hanging on to a twisted branch that had fallen out across the water. She clambered over more rocks until she was out as far as she could get without tumbling into the water herself.

"Rowan." His voice sounded faint.

"I'm here. Can you swim to me?" She lay down on the rock and stretched her arms out toward him.

"It's no good. Get—" His words were swallowed in the tumult.

"Get what?" she shouted.

"Rope . . . Weight it . . . Something heavy . . ."

"I'll get it! Hold on! Please, Alec, hold on!"

She raced back the way she had come, darting among the rocks and cutting around obstacles in her path. She found a rope coiled neatly and ready to hand in the back of the wagon. Bless Alec's orderly ways, she thought. But she needed a weight. What on earth could she tie to this rope?

She rummaged under the cabinet with the dishes and laid hands on a canvas sack. It hardly budged when she pushed at it, so she knew she had her weight.

"Thank heavens he's a man who likes his potatoes," she muttered.

Dragging it from its hiding place, she made the rope fast around its neck, and hefted it onto her shoulder. She thrust her arm through the coil of the rope and started out.

The trip back was agonizingly slow. She staggered along with her burdens, falling once and bruising her knee against a rock. At last she maneuvered into position and shouted to Alec from the shore.

She could see the strain in his face, even from where she stood. Still, he summoned up a nod of approval and called out his directions.

"Cast the rope to me," he shouted. "Put—" He waited for a moment of comparative quiet. "Put the weight between two rocks!"

She found two large rocks nearby and wedged the sack in firmly behind them. Climbing out onto the farthest boulder, she heaved the coil of rope with all her might. Alec reached out at the last second and caught it.

She watched with clenched hands as he circled the rope around his waist and wrestled a firm knot in the end. He let the slack float out into the river and then began to haul the line taut between his waist and the anchoring sack.

Rowan bit back a cry as he let go of the branch and was immediately swept downstream, toward a boulder that looked as big as the wagon. She sagged as he brought himself up short of it by swimming at a diagonal to the current. He then grabbed the rope and began to pull himself in toward the bank, hand over hand, his powerful arms and shoulders cutting a slow path toward his goal. She winced as she recalled the injury to his shoulder.

Rowan hopped down from the boulder and ran to the spot where she guessed he would come to shore.

She waded partway in, soaking her shoes and her skirts in the process.

At long last he was within her range, and she hauled on the rope to help him make the last drive toward safety. When he came within reach, she bent down, hooked her arms under his and dragged him to his feet. He leaned on her as he untied the rope from his waist and cast it on shore. They staggered the last few feet together and collapsed in a heap on the grassy bank, their bodies tangled together where they lay.

Several moments passed while they both recovered their breath. When his chest had stopped heaving with searing gasps, Alec grabbed Rowan and held her close.

"God, I thought you'd been lost," he said, his voice rasping with the effort to speak. "I couldn't see anything . . . the damned current changed so fast . . ."

"You thought I was lost? Alec, all I could see was your head . . . you went under— It was horrible!" Tears welled up in her eyes.

His hand came up and cupped the back of her head, and this time she met his lips as they descended to hers. Her arms came around him and held him as tight as her tired muscles would permit. All she knew was the storm of fear that was still beating at her from within, and the relief of having him safe and whole within her grasp. The kiss they shared was mindless and unreserved, and tinged with the urgent, exciting knowledge that they had just cheated death.

"It's all right," he whispered, his breath still short and coming in painful gasps. He stroked her hair; it was loose and damp from the river's spray. "It's all right now."

Rowan thought he would squeeze out of her what little breath she had left, so fierce was his embrace, but she didn't care. He kissed her again, and she rejoiced that his lips were warming against hers, and the chill of the river diminishing. She felt the soft demands he made, and felt herself answering, her body loosening and heating, her mouth moving with his.

He lifted his head to look at her, his dark brows drawn. "I shouldn't have left you alone in the wagon. I should've known there'd be an undertow. I'm sorry."

"It's—"

But his mouth was again covering hers, and this time she could feel more than the aftermath of fear in his touch. One arm held her shoulders, pressing her to his chest, while the other slipped down to her hips and drew them in, gathering her to him as if he couldn't be sure she was there unless he felt all of her. The wind blew across their damp clothes, chilling them in places, but Rowan felt nothing but welcoming, stirring warmth wherever her body touched his. Instinctively she drew closer, slipping a knee between his legs and delighting in the way he clasped that, too, the taut muscles of his thighs trapping her in his hold.

His kiss deepened. Ever so gently, he urged her mouth to open for him, and his tongue made a smooth, tantalizing search of her lips, adding more heat to their swelling, tingling warmth. Rowan had never felt anything so sensuous, hadn't known that anything could be so soothing and so exciting at the same time. She put her hand to his cheek and drew him in closer, her own tongue slipping forward to explore his lips in the same way.

The effects of her movements were gratifyingly powerful. A growl rumbled up from deep in Alec's chest. In one swift motion, he lifted her up and laid her down on her back. He slid over her, half covering her with his own hard, trembling length, one thigh resting across both of hers. Rowan found the weight of him delicious and thrilling, and she wrapped her arms about his neck, drawing him down so that she could take his kiss once more.

When it came, it was even more heated, more demanding. She felt again the tightening within her that she had felt when he first kissed her that night in the wagon. A wanting ache, it seemed, and when his hand slid upward, caressing her side from hip to breast, she felt the aching expand, causing her to press herself even more firmly against him.

Alec was lost in the surge of pleasure that followed so close upon his fear. He wanted to cover her with kisses, cover her with himself, exulting in the wild, exhilarating knowledge that they were both alive, and alone, and free under the summer sun. It was as if all of nature, all of life, were focused within him, and he longed to pour all of it into the sighing, welcoming woman in his arms. He'd never felt the blood singing within him so powerfully. He'd never wanted anyone or anything as much as he wanted her at that moment.

Yet he felt a quiet doubt as he looked at the dark fan of her damp hair spread on the grass, felt it even as his fingers smoothed across the outer curve of one breast. She would follow him into ecstasy, yes. And then what?

Then they would be on their way to Grass Valley. He would say goodbye there and disappear forever.

Very nice, MacKenzie, he groaned inwardly. Very kind. Very stupid.

He kissed her cheek, raised himself away from her, and lay back on the grass.

"Alec?" Her voice was hushed. "Is anything wrong?"

"No," he said. "Not a thing." Nothing except a resentful aching in his body, and a rushing wave of disappointment. She sat up beside him. He willed his eyes to look away from the luxuries he might be enjoying at this moment, were he not possessed of such a damnably honorable—and practical—conscience.

"Did I do something wrong?"

"No. I did." He was able to sit up now. "I just behaved very stupidly. It was just...the moment. I'm sorry, Rowan. It won't happen again."

"Oh."

That was all she said. He felt guilty again, this time for being so abrupt.

"You saved my life," he said, summoning a smile for her. "I don't know what I would've done if you hadn't managed to get that rope to me."

"I was terrified!" she said. "I had the devil's own time of it, looking for a weight. It was sheer luck that I found that sack of new potatoes."

"Potatoes?"

"Yes, that's what I tied the rope around. I found them in the bin with the dishes."

He began to laugh. Jumping to his feet, he started for the river again. "Where did you say you put it?" he called over his shoulder.

Rowan got up, pulling her clothes back into place. He was already wading back into the water. "Between two rocks, just there," she replied, pointing.

He'd caught the rope by now, and he gave it a pull so that he could follow it to the sack. To his surprise, it came loose in his hands, and the end in the water floated free, into the stream.

"Oh, no. Damn it, no!" He lunged forward, flinging the rope on shore.

Rowan stared as he reached in between the rocks and began grabbing frantically at something beneath the water. "What is it?" she called.

He made no answer, only bent farther forward to scoop his arms through the water around the rocks. He came up with something shiny, jammed it in his pocket, and resumed his frantic search.

Rowan waded out to him. "Alec, what is it?" she demanded. "What's wrong?"

"The sack," he said, his gaze never leaving the water. "Those weren't potatoes. The potatoes were just on top."

"What—what do you mean?" She felt a terrible sinking feeling within her.

"Money. Gold." He came up with a coin and thrust it at her. "My savings."

Chapter Nine

"Oh, dear God!" Rowan cried. She put the coin in her pocket and joined him in the search. "Where is the sack?"

"It opened. The damned rope came loose. Everything spilled."

"Well, it must be here nearby. Gold can't swim."

He didn't reply. She dug into the dirt of the river bottom. She soon learned that gold, even heavy gold coins, *could* swim, given the right conditions. She would feel one under her fingers, but then it would slip from her grasp and be carried tumbling downstream. Chasing it was futile—it was never where it should have been, according to her calculations, because the current was too strong and too erratic.

They searched for more than an hour, "prospecting" up and down the stretch of river where the sack had spilled its treasure. At last, Alec stood up with a salty curse and dropped his hands to his sides.

"It's no use," he declared. "It's gone."

"No," she said, stooping down to sift the sand again. "We've found some—there must be more here."

Alec waded back to her and put his hand beneath her elbow. "It's gone," he said. "Come out before you get exhausted and catch your death."

Rowan looked up at him, misery in her eyes. "Alec, this is so awful. I can't believe what I've done to you!"

He looked at her for a long moment, and then a thin smile came to his face. "You saved my life," he said, leading her out of the water. "That's compensation. And what's more, you saved the wagon, the team, and probably most of my equipment."

She frowned. "You're just being kind. I don't deserve it."

He gave her arm a shake. "I don't appreciate being called a liar. You saved my life. You're uncommonly brave."

"No, it's the Luck," she moaned. "More of the Trelarken Luck, even out in the wilderness!"

Alec gave a brief mirthless laugh and brushed a lock of her wet hair away from her face. "Come and get changed and dried off. I'll fix up a fire and we'll camp here. Then you're going to tell me all about this 'luck' you keep wailing about."

The wagon had taken on water from the crossing, but prudent Alec had placed all the perishable goods up high. Only the bedding was soaked. Rowan brought it outside after she had changed to her dry clothes and spread it out over the clean grass and on rocks in the late-afternoon sunshine. Alec had changed his clothes and was already laying a fire.

The sun was warm, but Rowan was grateful to huddle up close to the blaze. The long search in the cold water had chilled her through, and she was shaking.

Alec disappeared into the wagon and came back with his jacket and a flask.

He draped the jacket over her shoulders and unscrewed the top of the flask. "Drink," he ordered, handing it to her.

Rowan took a sip and choked. Her hand flew to her throat. "What is that?" she gasped.

Alec looked offended. "Scotch whiskey, of course. What else would a MacKenzie carry in a silver flask?"

"I'm sorry," she said, wiping her eyes and handing him the flask. "But it tastes like liquid fire."

He went and got a tin cup, filled it halfway with water and poured in a generous dollop of the Scotch. He carried it back to her. "Sip this slowly. It'll help warm you."

She obeyed, grimacing at the diluted but still-awful taste. He watched her carefully, and in a few moments was pleased to see that her shivering had stopped. He got out food for their dinner and began to prepare it while she watched from her seat on the grass.

"Now," he said as he laid baked sweet potatoes into the coals to warm. "What is 'the luck'?"

Rowan took a sip of the Scotch and shook her head. "It's hard to know where to begin. We call it the Trelarken Luck. It was first called that back in my great-great-grandfather's day, though I think we had it before that. He was Bevil Trelarken, and he was the first to make a fortune in the mines. The Trelarkens had had money before that, of course, but his luck at finding the right places to dig and to invest doubled and trebled the family holdings in his lifetime."

"But that sounds like good luck," Alec said. "Why do you keep saying it's bad?"

"The Luck can be either good or bad. Whatever the Trelarkens do, it's seldom small, but we have an uncanny knack for falling into things." She caught the mischief in his eyes. "Yes, I know, I'm the worst of the lot for falling—literally."

"Did I say anything?" he asked, all innocence.

"You didn't have to. Your eyes may be your livelihood, Alec MacKenzie, but they'll get you into trouble just as fast."

Alec laughed. "Point taken. Go on."

"The good fortune held for Bevil's son, and for my grandfather. He didn't have much to add to the holdings, but he did have one son to be his heir."

"Your father?"

"Yes." Rowan was slow to continue. She sat, turning the tin cup round and round in her hands. At last she sighed and began again.

"The Luck was with my father early on. He was healthy and strong and clever. He married well, couldn't lose at cards, or racing, or anything else he wagered on. Then, bit by bit, the Luck began to turn. We said at first that it had failed, but we soon began to believe that it had changed, instead. It was still clearly with us, only now it was all bad. The mines began to fail and close. My father lost more than he won. By the time he— In a few years, all was lost."

Alec thought about that for a time, as he poked at the fire and tended the pot he was cooking. "That was your father. Why do you say that you have the Luck?"

She shrugged. "I'm a Trelarken. The firstborn of my generation, though I am a female. And you must admit, I haven't been fortunate in anything I've done since you've known me."

Alec gave her a thoughtful glance. "That depends on how you look at it. You had the good luck today. You saved my life and my wagon. That's something."

"Maybe. But it was canceled out by my losing all your money in the river. Alec, I will pay you back for that—every penny."

"Never mind that. You saved my life. And there was over three hundred dollars in gold in that sack. It would take quite a while for you to pay that back."

Over three hundred dollars, Rowan thought. Fuzzily she tried to calculate what that amount would be in British pounds. Her arithmetic failed her. "But you wouldn't have been making this trip if it weren't for me," she told him. "You wouldn't have had to cross that river and been swept downstream. You wouldn't have lost all the money you worked so hard to save." She waved her cup at him. "I owe you a debt, and I honor my debts."

"We'll discuss it another time."

By now, she was feeling very relaxed and warm. There seemed to be a smile on her face, though she was smiling at nothing in particular. She beamed at Alec as he dished up their meal.

He chuckled. He needn't worry about her being cold now, he thought. She was evidently feeling the effects of the Scotch, and enjoying it mightily.

"These are wonderful," she murmured, tasting the sweet potatoes. "It's ambrosial. Voluptuous, really."

Alec's mirth was barely contained. "Thanks," he said wryly. "Glad you like it. The Trelarkens must be quite a clan. What are they doing while you're in America?"

Rowan's smile faded. She was on guard, despite the giddy effects of the Scotch. "They're in England," she said, hoping she sounded nonchalant. "Gil is in London. Reading law."

"That must make you proud. What about your parents?"

She waved her arm in an easterly direction. "Over there. I can't wait to hear from Gil, though. He left for London just as I was leaving for America. Have you ever been to London?"

"No. But I'd like to go someday. There's a grand exhibition of photographic works there every year. I'd like to submit some of my pictures of the Southwest when they're done."

"That would be wonderful. You are so looking forward to traveling there, aren't you?" Her eyes widened. "Oh, no! You haven't the money to go, have you?"

"Let's not get off on that subject again," he said. He rose and stretched. "I've got to feed the mules. They've had a tough day, the miserable wretches. Can you manage the washing-up?"

"I can."

"Good. I won't be long."

She watched him go whistling off in the dark with the lantern, his broad shoulders displaying their usual powerful grace. Her thoughts flew back to that afternoon, when he had lain with her on the riverbank. She could feel again the breath-stealing delight of his kisses, and her body, giddy and relaxed from the effects of the whiskey, responded as strongly to the memory as it had to the reality of his hands and his lips and his long, hard form pressing against her.

She'd wanted it to go on and on. Nothing in her experience had prepared her for the way she wanted Alec MacKenzie. Wanted him with her whole body, and wanted him with her mind and heart, as well. The closeness between them in that moment had been magical, and she wished she could find a way to bring it about once again. But did Alec share that wish?

The ascent into the Sierras began the next day. Rowan could see the changes in the landscape as they moved from the scrub brush and oak of the foothills into the evergreens and bracken of the mountains. The trees were enormous, extending far higher than any trees she'd ever seen, and their ruddy bark had turned the earth around them redder than her hair.

Alec pulled to a halt early in the day and hopped down to stretch his legs. Rowan climbed down and had a drink of water while he went for a quick look around. He came hurrying back with a light in his eyes.

"I'd like to stop here for the day," he said, heading for the back of the wagon. "There's a view just over that ridge that will take your breath away. If I can get a good picture of it, I can put it into a Sierra collection. Be some quick money for me."

"By all means, let's stop, then!" Rowan said. "An extra half day won't matter."

The extra half day stretched into two days. The beauties of the mountains were myriad, and Alec found he couldn't resist just one more shot at dawn or at sunset or under the full light of midday. Rowan added fuel to his creative fires by showing him how this wild, overwhelming place looked to a foreigner's eyes.

The weather was perfect, as well. Rowan thought she could live here forever, drinking the pure, icy creek water, wandering through the trees and meadows by day and sitting spellbound at night as the brilliant stars appeared, so close they seemed to hang down just out of reach.

Alec was utterly absorbed in his work. Even when he was waiting for the wind to die down, or the light to be exactly right, he seemed to be in his element. He quit at night with obvious reluctance and rose each morning before the light had even filtered through the trees to their camp. They didn't talk much. Rowan could see that when Alec worked he was transported into another world. Yet she was never bored or lonely. She accompanied him to the spots where he would set up his camera, and spent her time roaming the area all around him. In the afternoon, they moved a couple of miles ahead.

One day, he brought along his sketchpad, and she amused herself by drawing the delicate wildflowers and ferns she found. When he could tear his eyes from his work, Alec helped her label them, and soon they grew into a long, richly illustrated letter to Gil. At other times, she simply sat and stared out at the far-reaching landscape below their mountain perch, never growing tired of the view.

Rowan felt the intense wanting within her growing as she watched Alec's shining-eyed absorption in the natural wonders around them and enjoyed the quiet, almost intimate conversations they shared by the firelight in the evenings. From time to time she would see his eyes turn her way as she moved about the camp, and she thought she caught a glimpse of the heated interest she'd seen in them when he embraced her on the riverbank.

At last they began to descend from the higher ground, and Rowan knew without consulting Alec's map that their route was sloping toward a valley. It could only be Grass Valley.

"We can make it down today," Alec said that morning at breakfast. "But I'd like to have one more shot of the ridge in the mists, if I can get it. Do you mind?"

"No. Of course not."

They climbed up the short path to the ridge, Alec's equipment loaded onto one of the mules. The early-morning mists hung in shreds around the tops of the trees, and filled the valley beyond like a great bowl of clouds. Alec developed his negatives in the little portable darkroom he carried with him, and then they sat down to lunch, there on the rim of the world.

"I've been up here before," Alec said as they ate. "But never in summer. I had no idea it would be so..."

"So magnificent."

"Yes."

"I shall never forget it." She went to a rock at the very brink of the ledge and perched on it, her knees drawn up beneath her skirt. "I had no idea that anyone could ever get this high up in the air and not be a bird or in one of those enormous balloons."

Alec got up from his place in the grass and went to his camera. He swung it around to face her and began to focus.

"What are you doing?" she asked.

"Hold very still, please, Miss Trelarken."

"Alec, you're not serious."

"I am. Hold, please." He looked up over the camera with a grin. "Call it a way to repay me."

Rowan took him at his word. When he had taken the picture and developed the negative, he came away from his darkroom-box with that odd, utterly absorbed look once more on his face.

"There," he said quietly, pointing to a patch of wild roses and blue lupine.

Rowan got up, hesitantly, and went to sit amid the fragrant blooms. "Like this?" she asked, spreading her skirts around her.

"Yes."

He didn't move to his camera right away. He stood looking at her, the expression on his face unreadable. Then, to her surprise, he stooped down quickly and kissed her. His kiss was lingering, and soft, and she felt herself melting and kindling at the same time. The scent of the flowers rose to tangle with her other senses, making her feel as if Alec's touch were a part of the wild, lush scene around her.

He stood up abruptly and walked to the camera, still holding her gaze.

She was speechless, so thoroughly aroused that she had no time to change expressions or react in any way. Alec took the picture before she could move a muscle.

"You scheming wretch!" she cried, half angry, half amused. "How dare you use me that way?"

Alec paid her no heed, but she could see that he was smiling at his negative as he transferred it quickly to the darkroom box. She waited while he worked, picking some of the flowers and weaving them into a wreath.

He came striding toward her again, that look of absolute authority and concentration on his face again. He dropped to his knees beside her and began pulling the hairpins from the knot at the back of her neck.

"What are you doing now?" she demanded, but she knew it was useless to try to dissuade him. "Here, let me," she said at last. Her precious hairpins were flying about at an alarming rate, and she couldn't afford to lose a one.

When she was finished and her pins safely tucked into her pocket, she shook her hair down over her shoulders and looked up at him, laughter twitching at her lips. "Is that what you want?"

"Yes." He lifted his hands to her throat and slid his fingers up behind her ears, combing her hair out and letting it drift down in soft waves wherever it willed. She closed her eyes and leaned into the gentle, massaging touch of his fingers against her scalp. She felt him lean over her shoulder, and felt something settled on her head. Lifting a hand to her temple, she felt the flower wreath.

He made two pictures of her wearing the wreath, moving the camera to different spots, so that in one view she was backed by the far hills, and in the other she was looking over her shoulder at him.

When he returned to her side, she was prepared for anything. This time, he led her to the boulder where she first had posed. He helped her up and turned her body so that she was standing in a three-quarter pose, facing out across the far valley. The wind lifted her hair, teasing some of the heavy curls that lay on her breast and fluttering her skirts. Alec muttered an oath as he ducked down behind the camera. They waited a long time for the wind to die down. Finally, everything was still.

"What is it you see out there?" he said.

Rowan's eyes widened as she looked out over the panorama before her, a hundred thousand thoughts and emotions racing through her. Alec took the picture.

"May I see?" she asked, crossing to where he was storing the day's negatives in a box.

"Not yet. Not until I print them."

"That doesn't seem fair," she said. "After all, I'm the one who had to sit still for all that time."

"It's still no." He looked up and gave her a smile. "Thank you for posing."

"Hmph." She began to pin up her hair.

"Don't." His hand reached out and stopped her. "I like to see it."

She looked at him quizzically, then nodded. A small shiver of pleasure and pride raced up her spine. She was flattered that he liked her hair—the symbol of her flame-quick temper!—and that he had wanted to photograph her. Alec saying that he liked seeing her was better than any compliment he could pay her, for she knew now how much he used his photographer's eyesight to discern the truth or beauty around him.

They packed up Alec's equipment, but stayed on the ledge for the sunset. Rowan felt Alec watching her as they sat side by side on the grass, listening to the wind and watching the sunlight break into high golden shafts that rose from the far-off hills. He was in such an odd mood. She felt that at any moment he would speak....

"Rowan."

She looked at him. Her heart caught when she saw the banked heat in his dark eyes. Did he feel the same anticipation that she felt?

"We should go now," he said. "We don't want to have to find our way back in the dark."

Disappointed, Rowan nodded, and they started back to camp. She felt his eyes on her many times that evening, but when she looked up, he was always looking elsewhere. The tension in her rose each time they played this game. Were they indeed thinking the same thoughts?

He went to the wagon and got his bedroll and laid it out by the fire. Rowan wasn't ready to retire to the wagon, but Alec's actions were tantamount to a dismissal. She was about to say good-night and go to bed when he finally spoke. "We'll be in Grass Valley tomorrow."

"I know," she said gravely, stopping at the edge of the campfire.

"I just want you to know that I'm glad I made the trip."

Her eyebrows went up as she stepped closer. "Knife wounds, lost money and all?"

He shook his head and smiled. "Well, perhaps some of it I could have done without, but in general, I've enjoyed the journey."

"I've especially enjoyed these last few days," she said with a sigh and a glance around their campsite. "I think I can honestly say that I've seen the most beautiful place on earth." She reached out and laid a hand on his arm. "I know I've said this before, but I thank you so much for all your help. And your kindness."

He lifted her hand and kissed it. "We've had quite a time, haven't we?" he murmured.

Her answer was to step up and kiss his cheek. "That we have."

She stood there before him, her eyes searching his for a sign that he was feeling what she had felt all day. His chest rose and fell, so close to her own, but he made no move. She felt the tension, the anticipation in her, tighten another notch. She wanted more than goodbye for them. She wanted more.

But he didn't move.

She stepped back. "Good night."

"Good night." It was a whisper.

She turned away. Before she could take a step, he whirled her around and enveloped her in a crushing embrace.

Relief flooded through her. He did share her feelings, after all. She was free now to express the joy, the excitement, the yearning, and the hundred other confusing, swirling impulses and emotions that were woven around this man. She raised her face to kiss him, and was rewarded with a kiss so heated, so hungry, that she moaned beneath the onslaught and was left gasping in its aftermath, her cheek resting upon his shoulder.

Alec felt again the blissful feeling of freedom that he had known that day on the riverbank. Rowan in his arms seemed the most natural thing in the world. The awareness of how alone they were, here among the trees and the peace of the wilderness, worked magic on him, and he forgot all care and time and practicalities, living only to hold Rowan and make her sigh for his touch. "What do you want?" he whispered. "What can I give you?"

"I don't know what to ask for," she replied. "Hold me. Touch me. Stay with me."

Cupping her face in his hands, he kissed her tenderly on the forehead, eyes, temples, cheeks, lips. He gathered a handful of her rich, heavy hair, and swept it back to kiss her neck in the soft, vulnerable spot just beneath her ear. He went carefully—his methodical, thorough ways were not limited to his possessions or his work. He wanted her to know every comfort, every nuance of touch and tease and give and take. He wanted to give her everything, and if it wasn't enough, he'd dream up still more ways to bring her joy.

Rowan held still, letting her long-held anticipation run free as he meticulously undid the top buttons of her dress. She wanted him to touch her now, but she sensed that there was a ritual he was teaching her—a dance, almost, a dance of give and take and touch. The anticipation was no longer a torment, but a beautiful part of the whole, magical dance.

She felt deliciously drugged with sensations as he eased her down until they were kneeling on the blankets by the fire. Everywhere he touched her brought satisfaction for an instant, and then the wanting returned, more powerful than before. His hands caressed, his lips soothed and tantalized, his arms warmed and bound her. A small hum of pleasure emanated from within her as his lips formed kisses to match the delicacy of her collarbone, then danced still lower, just touching the swell of her breast. Rowan held her breath and waited for what was to come, rejoicing in how completely her wanting of Alec was being fulfilled.

When he returned to claim her mouth with light, teasing light kisses, she reached up and pulled him to her, demanding that he give her all. He responded with a gratifying heat, parting her lips and thrusting his tongue inside, showing her that he did indeed have more pleasures to share.

She was like no other woman he'd ever been with, Alec thought. For one thing, she was innocence itself. She brought no guile, no polite pretensions or feigned enjoyments, to the moment, and what she felt showed clearly in her face and in her actions. She smelled of roses and lupine and the faint musk of the fire; she had become a part of the beauty of the world around them. And she was so soft and vital and strong in his arms. She felt like life. She felt real.

He slipped a hand inside the soft wool of her dress and smoothly cupped the perfect curve of her breast. She sighed and buried her face in his shoulder, arching against his hand, begging the soothing, exciting motions to continue and build. He caressed the fullness of her, then brushed the delicate tip and heard her smothered gasp. He waited, fearing he'd shocked her.

"Please," she whispered against his cheek. "Oh, Alec, more, please."

He wanted to laugh aloud for the sheer joy of her. He granted her request willingly, the pad of his thumb circling and smoothing over the taut crest.

Rowan was mesmerized by his touch, her world now reduced to her body and his body and nothing else. Heat was spiraling downward inside her; she could feel it settle in her very core, a pleasant, swelling ache that begged for some fulfillment she couldn't have named. "I've never— I never knew anything could be this wonderful."

"Then hold fast to me, angel. There's wonders yet to come."

His loving became the center of her universe, his touch the one thing her existence demanded. As he carefully undressed her and worked loving, heated ministrations over every available inch of her, she felt as if she were walking the golden rim of the world again, becoming a part of the fiery sunset they'd shared that afternoon. And as he covered her body with his own, and gathered close for the ultimate act of joining, she almost sang aloud for the sheer joy of her wanting fulfilled.

Unreasoning, she disregarded his murmured warnings and pulled him to her. She felt the pain of her maidenhead's loss, but she was too far gone to care. She took the lead now, arching and clasping him with a desperate, joyous greed, reveling in the sensations she found as his mouth and hands and arms showed her the way to completion. There couldn't be anything more than this, she thought, but in a moment she learned there could be, as a wild, shaking sweetness engulfed her, and she fell over the rim of the world into the fiery paradise below.

Alec heard her musical cries, felt the fevered tension in her as she climaxed. With a shout of equal joy, he followed her into ultimate pleasure, until they both collapsed and fell, tangled and gasping, to the cooling earth. And there they lay, their bodies lulled and sated, their eyes closed to the shining stars above.

Rowan stirred presently and nestled herself more closely into Alec's side. He reached out for his bedroll and shook out a blanket to cover them. She was asleep within moments, her breath soft against his shoulder.

Alec blinked at the stars overhead. Lying here, with Rowan in his arms, her lustrous hair tangled about them, her sweet scent covering his body, seemed the most normal, natural thing in the world. He couldn't remember when he had last felt so at home in his skin, so much a part of the world. Certainly not since the war, when the shocks of death and dying had been all around him and he had spent his days staring into the faces of young men lost to the ravages of war. The experience had made him feel somehow tainted and alien, for there were few who had seen what he'd seen, and fewer still whose job it had been to record it for all time.

He'd kept his distance from everyone after that, with the exception of Taggart, his loyal, longtime friend. But in the past few days, Rowan Trelarken had been closer than anyone had been to him in years. And in the past hour or so, she'd been closer than anyone in his life. He couldn't fathom how it was that this woman had managed to launch an assault on all his defenses, but she had done it, and the payback had been lovemaking of such potent bliss that all his past liaisons paled beside it.

He shook his head. This couldn't be happening. God help him, he wanted her again, right now. He wanted to pull her soft, sleeping form beneath him and love her into waking. He needed to rouse those musical, singing sighs from her once again. He needed to know she was his.

His. He closed his eyes tightly. What the hell was he thinking? She wasn't his. And he wasn't hers. He had made other plans. He'd made promises to himself, to the memory of Rose MacKenzie. He couldn't take another person into his life! It was too dangerous, too energy-consuming.

And what did he have to offer her, even if he did ask her to be with him? He had no money. He was essentially an itinerant photographer, with no home, no fixed address. He was nobody in the world of his profession, only one of the Brady men, and now that meant little or nothing. He was a man whose dreams were incomplete, and the fulfillment of those dreams rested with him alone.

God, he'd been a fool. He'd taken her innocence, and he had nothing to offer her in return. He couldn't marry her. He couldn't take her with him—even if he were so inclined—for she'd never fit in on the rough journey he had ahead of him.

He was different. He wasn't a man who could take on the likes of an innocent Cornish lass. Whatever the cost, he had to break away.

He went still in the dark, holding Rowan in his arms, willing his arousal to die away, slowly and reluctantly. After a short while, she raised her head from his shoulder and blinked at him. "Is there something wrong?" she whispered.

"I'm going to go check on the team," he said, abruptly letting go of her. "Here's my jacket. You should get to bed, where you'll be warm."

"Oh, but I am warm." She raised her arms and stretched, giving a throaty laugh. "Deliciously warm."

"That won't last if you stay out here," he said brusquely, getting to his feet. "Go to the wagon."

He stalked away, leaving her blinking in surprise at his back. What on earth had she done wrong? She'd never seen him so cold.

She was shaken by his sudden displeasure, following so close upon the heels of his embrace. She went to the wagon and washed up. The scent of him was still upon her, and the memory of pleasure was still tangible in her body and on her skin. Was she wrong to feel so good? Didn't he enjoy what they had just shared?

Rowan frowned as she got into the wagon and began to make up her bed. She pondered what she could have done—or not done—that had made him turn from her with such cool displeasure. It must have been something about her, or the way she had responded to him. But what could that be? She cursed her ignorance of men and women and all that should pass between them. It wasn't fair to be thrust into such a heady, delightful and overwhelming endeavor without any sort of training whatsoever. There was so much she didn't understand.

She was exhausted, but she couldn't sleep. She heard Alec moving restlessly about the camp long after she had gone to the wagon. He seemed to be as wakeful and tense as she. It felt wrong that their idyllic stay in the Sierras should end this way. Tomorrow they would reach Grass Valley, and their association would be at an end. He would drive away, and she would be left to marry Luke Syms.

This last thought settled into place in her mind at last. Marry. She'd been worrying about "relations" with Alec, forgetting all the while that she was promised to Luke. She'd just experienced the full measure of lovemaking with Alec, and yet she had vowed to preserve that gift for Luke alone.

She pressed her face to the pillow, wanting to weep in frustration and shame. Alec had awakened so many new feelings in her, feelings that she felt she could only express in his arms. But she had almost abandoned her family—all for a starlit night with Alec. It was as if the very wilderness itself had canceled out all she knew of propriety and courtship and the way a well-bred young woman should behave. She had felt as if she and Alec were the only two people in the world, as if the only rules that applied to them were the dictates of their own desires.

It was a sobering discovery. She had never before known the power of human passions. Was she at all ready to accept that power?

Perhaps it was sheer chance that had caused her to forget all she had planned for her life and her loved ones. But from now on she would be on her guard, lest her family suffer by dint of her foolish heart and her wayward body. She would keep her promises.

Chapter Ten

They heard Grass Valley long before they saw it. Over the rumble of the wagon and the clop of the mules' hooves, they heard a deep, rhythmic pounding that shook the earth and echoed around the ring of hills that rose over the little town.

"It's the stamp mills," Rowan said, catching Alec's curious frown. "Great weights that crush the ore after it's brought up from the mine. You get used to the sound."

He shook his head. "Sounds like the gods themselves are mining."

Rowan smiled, glad that he didn't seem as cold and stiff as he had earlier that morning. "No, just ordinary men. When you live near a mill for a long time, you grow so accustomed to the sound that you'd be awakened by the quiet, not by the noise. That's the loudest I've ever heard them, though."

She looked down from the hillside into the town below. Grass Valley was plainly not San Francisco, or even Sacramento, with their bustling waterfronts. But it was a prospering town, that was clear. She could spot shops and lumberyards, stables and homes, from their vantage point, and on nearly every hill, in every ravine, along every creek, stood a mine of some kind.

She felt a chill as she realized that one of those mines was Luke's workplace, that this was his town. She might very well spend the rest of her life here. And she would never see Alec MacKenzie again.

The long trip was over. It was time to face the true purpose of her journey.

"I think we should go straight to the Kingsfield Mine," she said to Alec. "They'll know what's happened."

Alec shot her a curious glance, but didn't say anything. He spoke to the mules, and they started their descent into the valley.

They located the mine on one of the tallest hills. They wound their way up the well-used road until they came to a cluster of buildings and the high, slanting tower of the headframe, where ore and men were hauled up and down the main shaft.

Rowan and Alec stopped before the building marked Manager. The door was open, so Rowan knocked at the frame. Someone barked, "Come!" and they went through a large room with several clerks' desks into a smaller, well-furnished office. A stout, red-faced man with a bristling mustache glared at them from behind a massive oak desk.

"Yes?" he demanded, giving them both an appraising stare.

"I'm looking for a miner," Rowan began.

"Well, you've come to the right place for it," he barked. "Any particular one you got in mind?"

"Yes," Rowan said, her tone cooling to something more like the one her mother employed in her regal moments. "I'm seeking Mr. Luke Syms."

"Syms, eh?" The man creaked back in his leather-covered chair. "Cornish, are you?"

"Yes."

"Lindsey!" the man bellowed. Rowan jumped, but Alec caught her elbow and held her steady.

A small man bustled through the door, pen in hand and an exasperated frown on his lips. "Yes, Mr. Dewey?" he asked, tapping his foot.

"We got a fellow name of Syms? What was the name?"

"Luke Syms," Rowan supplied quickly.

"We got one of those? A Cousin Jack."

"Luke Syms is in San Francisco," Lindsey said with an irritated little smile. "Went to meet his wife there yesterday. I told you that. He's the one that wanted the leave several days ago, to meet his wife's ship from Cornwall." He turned to Rowan. "That would be you."

She wasn't sure if he was asking her or telling her. The manager spoke again before she could reply.

"Well, when's he due back? The man can't just leave his wife standing here in my office."

"Oh, but I'm—"

"It takes five days, by stage, there and back. This is Thursday. He'll be back on Monday, first shift." Lindsey was edging toward the door, more important matters clearly drawing him back to wherever he'd been hiding. "Nice to meet you, Mrs. Syms."

He trotted away, and Dewey slapped his meaty palms on the desktop. "Well, there it is, ma'am. Come Monday, your husband'll be back in town. Whyn't you go on down into town and find a place to stay and wait. Nice to meet you, Mrs. Syms." He threw open a huge ledger and set to tracking the columns with a stubby finger while he groped in his ashtray for his still-burning cigar. The meeting was plainly at an end.

Alec turned and stalked out to the wagon. Rowan bade the manager a polite goodbye, which was answered by a grunt, and hurried after Alec.

He had the mules moving almost before she was on the seat of the wagon. She sat down with a thump and held on tight as he swung the mules out in a circle and started them back down the hill at a rattling pace.

Rowan stared at him. The look on his face was thunderous. "What's the matter?" she asked, but she knew the answer before the words were out of her mouth.

Alec drew up hard beneath a stand of pines and let the wagon rattle into silence. He stared straight ahead, his jaw clenched, his hands gripping the reins. "Why didn't you tell me?" he asked at last.

She sat silent. There seemed no words suitable for explaining.

"What kind of game were you playing? Or maybe this was all an act to you. Which parts were real? The poor waif left all alone in the new world, helpless and forlorn? The honorable lady swearing she'd repay all her debts? The innocent begging me to hold her?"

This last stung Rowan the worst. "It was all true! I told you the truth about everything!"

"Everything, Mrs. Syms?"

"I'm not Mrs. Syms! I'm who I told you I was. I'm Rowan Trelarken."

"Not according to those men back there at the mine. Your husband's bosses."

"Those men are mistaken. I am not Luke's wife."

Alec stared at her, his eyes still dark with suspicion. She went on, trying to fill with words the gap that was opening wider between them with every second.

"I am not Luke's wife," she repeated, emotions rising. "I am his *intended* bride. I didn't tell you about our betrothal, because I can scarcely believe it myself, and because it is a matter born out of painful circumstances, being carried out over long distances." She knew she wasn't making much sense, so she hurried on. "I've told you about the Trelarken Luck, and how my father saw it turn against him until everything he had was lost, except his family. Evidently his family were not enough to comfort him, for he... he stole some money and fled and left my mother, my brother and me, to carry on by ourselves, penniless and without a soul to care for us. The mine failed soon after. Everyone blamed my father, and all the Trelarkens. One benefactor came to our rescue—Henry Syms, Luke's older brother. He offered us a cottage and other necessities, and allowed my mother to live on his credit until we were far beyond any hope of repaying him. And he knew this. Henry is the sort of man who takes pleasure in holding that sort of power over other people. He even treats his own kin as if they were in his debt. He's always refused Luke the opportunity to help out in his business, insisting he first 'prove' himself in the mines.''

She paused and stole a glance at Alec. His eyes were still as dark as the deepest lakes, and his expression was still as hard as stone. She gathered her courage again and continued.

''At last, there came a way to end our bondage to Henry Syms. His brother, Luke, wanted a wife. He'd known me as a child and offered to marry me if I came to California. Henry said he would cancel our debts to him if I married Luke. That's why I've come here. That's why I must find Luke. I made a promise to marry Luke Syms, and I keep my promises.'' She reached out and touched his arm. ''But I had no idea how difficult that might be.''

He straightened at her touch, and she quickly removed her hand. ''Difficult?'' he said with a rueful laugh. ''Yes, I guess it has been difficult for you to lie at every turn and play upon my sympathies, and Taggart's, as well. It must be difficult to have had your whole plan revealed before you played the last trump. I didn't get out of town soon enough, did I?''

''Alec, you're being ridiculous—''

''You're so right. That's exactly how I feel—ridiculous. I don't know how much of your story is fact, and how much fiction, but this ride is at an end. I'll take you into town, and then I'll be well out of your way.''

He snapped the reins, and the mules started off. Rowan attempted to speak, but he refused to notice her. Fury was evident in the corded muscles of his arms as he drove, and in the rigid square of his shoulders. He was beyond the reach of her words. She retreated to her side of the wagon seat and waited out the short, miserable ride down the hill and onto Mill Street. Alec pulled up before a sign that swung out over the board sidewalk. Rowan read the words: "Osborn Hotel—Reasonable."

Alec hopped down from the wagon and went around to the back. He yanked open the doors and reached inside to pull out Rowan's canvas sack. He swung it down at her feet just as she came around the corner. She had to stop short to keep from falling over it.

"Here's three dollars," Alec said, stuffing three gold coins in her pocket. "That'll get you through until your fiancé gets back, or until your next fool comes along."

He brushed past her like an icy wind and climbed up to his seat, calling out to the mules as he went. The wagon was moving away before Rowan could run after him.

"Alec!"

He ignored her. The people in the street and on the sidewalks stared as she raced after the wagon, but it soon gained speed and was on its way out of town.

Rowan stopped in the street, letting the dust of the wagon wheels settle around her. He was gone.

She glanced up at last to see the eyes that were all directed toward her. She was too hurt and bewildered to care. She trudged back to where her sack lay by the sidewalk, hefted it, and headed into the Osborn Hotel—reasonable or not.

If there were many amenities that Grass Valley lacked in comparison with San Francisco, speed of communication was not among them. Rowan's arrival in Grass Valley was common knowledge by Friday noon. The town's formidable gossip mill had it that she'd arrived with an outlaw and been thrown off the back of his wagon while it was still moving. It was said that she had walked into town with a burlap sack over her shoulder and had begged gold from a passing tinsmith. It was said that her sack contained nothing but silk petticoats and satin slippers, while she went about in dusty rags and black high-buttoned boots.

Lowella Tolbathy, the most recent arrival from Carn Rose—Rowan excepted—took center stage with great relish as she told the rest of the Cornish community in Grass Valley just how low the Trelarkens had sunk, and how the outlandish daughter was here "expectin' to fit in, like as if she were one of us 'erself." The others listened with awe or recounted tales of the Trelarken fortunes and of the eccentricities of the family.

And the old story of Francis Trelarken's ignominious flight from Carn Rose was given a thorough airing out. Everyone knew of the theft, everyone knew of the gambling, and many other twists and turns and embellishments were added to fill in the gaps where truth or ignorance left the storytellers dissatisfied. The Trelarken name was on every tongue.

Everywhere Rowan went, there were curious stares and abruptly ended conversations and whispers as she passed. The feeling of being under surveillance made her uncomfortable but she persevered, beginning her search for employment first thing Friday morning. She wasn't going to give in to the pain of seeing Alec depart in anger. She intended to keep her vows and stick to her plan, beginning with paying back the money she owed to Alec and Taggart.

After her bitter parting with Alec, Rowan had spent considerable time listing her skills and trying to imagine what job she would be qualified to do. Her list wasn't any too long, to her chagrin, and the list of possible jobs was even shorter. She decided that she had enough education to perhaps act as a schoolteacher or a governess. Failing that, she thought she might manage as a clerk in a hotel, if it didn't require much arithmetic or writing. Or be a shop girl, if she could just remember what all the American coins were worth.

Beyond that, she didn't see much hope. She wasn't a seamstress, or a cook, or a baker, or a housekeeper. She didn't know how to do laundry or press clothes. She knew a bit about horses, but she knew no one would give a woman a job in a stable. She would have to try her luck at the schools, or the shops, or in private homes. She decided that work in a shop would pay the soonest, so she started there.

But nothing prepared her for the resistance she met as she went up and down Mill Street, and then up and down Main Street, searching for employment. It was as if someone were going before her into each of the shops, warning the proprietors that she was coming.

"I wish I had something to offer you, miss, but I don't hire single girls."

"You fit the bill, miss, but I was lookin' for someone who's used to good hard work. One day of hauling dry goods over the counters and you'd be done in."

"Oh, heavens, Lady Trelarken, I couldn't possibly give you orders! No, you go on and don't give working another thought. You'll have a husband to look after, soon enough."

"What's 'e want to work here for, then? 'E had more'n your share over 'ome, but when 'e comes 'ere to America, 'e must take what 'e's husband provides for 'e."

By the end of the day on Friday, shoulders sagging, feet sore, Rowan had been in almost every shop and mercantile business in town. No one would give her a job, though they all had comments and advice about her upcoming nuptials. Most of the refusals seemed to fall into two groups—those who thought a woman of her background couldn't work, and those who thought a woman of her background shouldn't work. One merchant had even implied that, as a Trelarken, she might be tempted to steal if she were hired. She had stalked out before her temper could explode and ruin all her hopes and plans. Saturday was no more of a success, and it was a dispirited, exhausted Rowan who returned to her room that afternoon.

She spent the evening lying on her bed and composing a letter to Gil. Her mood improved as she thought of ways to minimize the difficulties and hurts of her first days in her new home. She didn't want Gil to think that she wasn't capable of coping with a new life; nor did she want to bring him bad news. So she concentrated on telling him about the town and the huge stamp mills that ran twenty-four hours a day and all the best tidbits of local color until at last she fell asleep. But before she slept, she laid out her clothes for church the following morning. That was one place where she was fairly sure she'd be accepted in this strange new town.

John Wesley Methodist Church was one of the finest structures in Grass Valley, simple and white, but with Gothic touches at the windows and eaves to emphasize the reverence of its purpose. On this Sunday morning, the air was still cool and fine, the sun shone brightly off the high white belfry overhead, and it seemed a shame to come inside and shut out the beautiful day—though no one would have said as much out loud.

Rowan didn't wait outside on the walkway with the others. There was no one she knew to speak to, so she went inside the church and found a seat near the front.

The bells halted their tolling, and there was a rustle of noise as stragglers hurried inside to find seats as the minister strode to the pulpit. The choir filed in from one side to take their places. The minister nodded to someone at the back of the church, and Rowan saw the sunlight diminish as the doors were drawn shut.

But they didn't close all the way. A whisper rippled through the sanctuary as someone came through the doors at the last instant. Rowan didn't turn her head and look, though she was sorely tempted. She watched the minister's face for some sign that the latecomer was settled. The minister continued to stare until his gaze came to rest on her row, and finally on Rowan herself. She looked up, startled, to see a man with a soft dark brown mustache standing beside her, dressed in a neat, well-cut black suit and hat. He was looking at her with mild blue eyes, and she had the vague notion that he was trying to tell her something. Taking his hint at last, she blushed and slid to the left to make room for him. He sat down slowly and removed his hat, placing it on his right knee. The minister nodded. The man nodded. The choir began to sing the Doxology, and the congregation joined in.

Rowan wanted to laugh at the solemn exchange between the minister and the man beside her. It was as if a whole conversation had passed between them, without a single word being spoken. Idly she wondered who her pewmate was. Probably a warden of the church, she guessed.

During the service, Rowan stole a glance or two more at her seatmate. He was an inch or two taller than she, with a long oval face, prominent chin and narrow, long nose that stamped him as a Cornishman. The battered hands that gripped the brim of his hat, nails blackened and forever bruised, told the world that he worked hard for his living, while the pallor of his skin made it clear that he labored underground. A miner, she thought. Plenty of those in the congregation.

She was in better spirits when the service, with the glorious hymn singing that was a hallmark of Cornish tradition, came to a close. The man on her right stood up and backed toward the altar to allow her to go ahead of him. She nodded her thanks and proceeded toward the door.

The minister was waiting on the walk outside, along with just about every member of the congregation. All eyes were fixed on Rowan as she stepped out onto the sunlit steps.

The minister looked past her with a wide smile. "Well, Luke, I see you've found her, safe and sound at last."

Rowan felt as if the minister had thrown a bucket of cold water over her. She gaped at him in stunned silence as he shook the hand of the man behind her.

"We were surprised that she arrived in town without you, Luke. I hope this isn't a sign of things to come!"

"Happen it won't be, Mr. Chapham, sir," came the quiet reply.

Rowan turned and looked at the man who had sat beside her all morning. Luke Syms! No wonder there had been such a stir at his arrival. Thank God they'd been in church when they met, for she certainly wouldn't have recognized him. He bore no resemblance to the tall, beefy Henry, or to the boy she remembered from years ago.

"Miss Trelarken, welcome to Grass Valley."

She managed to gather her wits in time to respond. "Thank you, Mr. Chapham. I'm glad I found your church this morning."

"I know our ladies are waiting to make your acquaintance, Miss Trelarken. There's nothing like a wedding to be planned to stir things up among the wives of our parish."

Rowan nodded and took a nervous peek at the "ladies," who were waiting on the walk and on the lawn. They were openly scrutinizing her, and it was clear that it wasn't a wedding they were planning.

"Another time," Luke said, leading the way down the steps. "Good sermon."

Rowan trailed behind him, half annoyed at the way he'd spoken for her, and half relieved that she had an excuse to escape the women who were plainly waiting to interrogate her. Luke waited at the gate for her to catch up and then proceeded toward Mill Street in silence.

Rowan was tongue-tied. Here was the man she was to marry, and she could think of nothing to say to him. She was still shocked that she had sat next to him in church and not known who he was. Stealing a sidelong glance at him, she tried to guess his mood. She could gather no clues from his face, only that he looked tired. Finally the silence wore on her, and she had to speak.

"I hope you aren't angry that I left San Francisco," she ventured. "Did you get my telegram?"

"Aye. Foolish expense. I'd have come for 'e."

"But I had no idea when you would come. I knew no one. And I had no place to stay in San Francisco."

"Maybe. Maybe not."

"What do you mean?"

He looked at her, no rancor in his face. "'E found your way here, didn't 'e?"

She flushed quickly. "Yes. Mr. MacKenzie was kind enough to bring me."

There was silence as they crossed the street to Osborn's. "Well," he said at last. "'E's here now."

"Yes, I am." Rowan hesitated at the door. "Won't you come in? There's a lot we have to say to one another."

"Aye."

They took seats in a corner of the room that served as the lobby and dining room of the Osborn Hotel. Mrs. Osborn hung over the desk and watched with open curiosity as the pair settled in and looked at each other expectantly.

"Your brother and his wife were well when I left Carn Rose," Rowan offered, hoping he'd be glad of news from home. "His business is doing quite well, especially now that the American war is over."

"'Tes well." Luke sat still before her, hat on his knee.

Rowan didn't know what to say. The man was clearly not one for small talk. She elected to seize the moment and plunge into the topic that had been on her mind for so many months.

"Shall you tell the Reverend Mr. Chapham that we'll be married soon?"

"No."

She stared in surprise. "No?"

"I can't marry 'e."

Chapter Eleven

Rowan could only gape at him. Her worst fear, that Henry had played a monstrous trick on her, and her fondest wish, that she would not have to marry this stranger, seemed to be coming true in the same instant.

"I've no house for 'e," he continued, after a long moment of silence. "Can't have a bride and no home to take her to. Wedding'll have to wait till I can build." He looked away, as if embarrassed at this long speech.

Rowan felt her heart sink. She hadn't imagined that this could happen. She might be dreading marriage to a stranger, but if it must happen, she would prefer that it happen quickly. That way, the matter would be settled, once and for all, and she wouldn't have to think of other things, things she might have missed. More importantly, the sooner they were married, the sooner Henry would destroy the credit note against her family.

"I don't need a house," she said. "I can live anywhere, really. Here. Or a boardinghouse."

"I'll not take a wife into a boardinghouse. 'Tisn't proper. I'll build."

Luke's chin rose a notch. Rowan saw that this was a matter of pride to him. Her heart sank, but she respected his feelings. A man who couldn't provide a roof over his wife's head would of course feel shame.

"How—how long might it take?" she asked. "To build, I mean."

"Month. Maybe two, working the odd hour here and there."

Two months! What would she do with herself in this place for two months?

"'E can stay with Mrs. Grey. She takes ladies. I can pay the keep."

She smiled. "I can't expect you to pay my way when we aren't even married. I'll get a job. Perhaps I can teach at one of the local schools."

Luke frowned and shook his head. "No. 'E's not workin'. I'll pay."

"But—"

"'Tes my fault I didn't get the house built. There was a contract to finish down the mine. Mrs. Grey's is cheap enough."

She saw from the rock-jawed look on his face that it was his final word on the subject. For all his quiet manners, Luke Syms appeared to have a rock-solid will. There was no doubting that he had the Syms tenacity, if nothing else. If there was a way around him, it was beyond her skills to find it just now.

"All right," she said. "We'll wait." She paused. "Is there anything that I can do in the meantime? I don't want to sit idle."

He gave her a frankly curious look. "'E never did naught before."

"What do you mean?"

"Over 'ome. 'E were a lady. Ladies don't do naught."

She bristled. "I've done plenty! I can ride, and draw, and read and write. I can hunt and I can play the pianoforte. I can even wash dishes!" she declared proudly.

He was plainly unimpressed. "'E'd best find some needlework or some such to do," he said, getting to his feet. "'Twon't be long before the house is done."

She sighed and rose to accompany him to the door. "When shall I see you again?"

"I'll move 'e to Mrs. Grey's tonight. Six o'clock." He put on his hat and stuck out his hand. "Afternoon."

"Good afternoon, Luke."

They shook hands, and then he was gone, quietly and slowly, up the sidewalk, past the other churchgoers heading home to their Sunday dinners. They greeted him warmly and strained to get a peek through the mosquito netting that screened the front door to Osborn's.

Rowan went to her room and sat down on the bed. Nothing to do for two whole months except sit and dread her wedding day! She would have to do something—anything. She had debts to pay. She had to keep from going insane from boredom and worry. She had to keep from thinking about Alec MacKenzie. She had to make a plan.

*   *   *

Luke saw her settled into Mrs. Grey's neat, comfortable rooming house on Sunday evening, then left with a shy nod and a tip of his hat. The following morning, Rowan got up, brushed her best black dress to immaculate cleanliness, took extra care with her hair, and set out once more to seek a job. She had decided that, even if it angered Luke at first to have her working, she would prove to him that she could indeed do something worthwhile and earn her own way.

But by midafternoon Rowan's sense of worth was sinking lower. She'd never imagined that getting a job could be so difficult. She was told she was underqualified, overqualified, about to be married and therefore bound to quit, too refined, too soon, too late, even too pretty. How did other people manage to gain employment here? Was it like this everywhere in America?

Mill Street was as busy as ever at five in the afternoon. Her steps slowed further as she passed the dry goods store. A new sign, the paint still glistening wet, hung out over the sidewalk just ahead: MacKenzie Photographic Studio—Portraits and Scenic Views. The sign had not been there on Sunday, when she had passed by here with Luke.

Alec was here! The miserable man was going to stay for a good long while, too, judging from the sign. What had brought him back? And why would he want to stay here?

She decided to find out. She followed the arrow on the sign and climbed the stairs that rose alongside the dry goods store. There was a door at the top, with more fresh paint spelling out MacKenzie Studio. She knocked twice and opened the door. "Alec? Are you here?"

"I am."

Her heart gave a jump as he stepped out from behind a curtain at the back of the long, echoing room. It had been only a few days since she'd last seen him, but she'd almost forgotten how strongly his physical appearance affected her. Just looking at him in his shirtsleeves caused her to recall the strong and tender magic he could work on her in just one moment, with just one touch.

"Are you really staying here in Grass Valley?" she managed at last.

"So it would appear."

"Why?"

"Why not?"

"You're being deliberately infuriating!" she said, her temper flashing up to drive away her confusion.

He looked her up and down, a bitter twist on his lips. "Haven't you a wedding to plan?"

"The wedding! Everyone in this town is an authority on my wedding!" She moved across the room with a twitch of her skirts. "Why can't they mind their own affairs?"

"Why can't you?"

She came about with a glare. "I think I have some right to know why you insist on staying here. You can go anywhere you like. I can't. How do you think it will make me feel to see you every day?"

He crossed his arms. "I don't know. How would it feel?"

She realized her mistake and tried to escape his trap. "You were so angry with me, I thought that you'd never want to see me again. Are you staying just to punish me for not telling you the truth about Luke?"

His eyes were veiled. "So, you admit that you lied."

"Yes, I lied!" she exclaimed. "If by lying you mean that I didn't tell you everything that was true."

"That pretty well covers it. But I still don't understand why you're here today. And where is Mr. Syms, by the way?"

"He'll be here soon, so I shan't waste any more time talking with you. Do as you like. I don't care." She stalked toward the door. Why was everything so complicated with Alec? "Stay or go," she said in frustration. "It doesn't matter to me."

"Liar."

She whirled on him, temper flying. "I admitted it was wrong not to tell you about Luke, but you don't have to keep repeating it!"

"I'm not talking about Luke."

"Then I can't think what you mean."

He approached her, slowly, his gaze holding hers in a steady, heated line. "I mean, you're a liar if you say you don't care what I do."

"That's nonsense." Her voice was smaller now, and he was coming still closer.

"Is it? I don't think so." He was a step away now. "Remember I told you never to play poker? Your face gives you away every time."

He reached out and ran a fingertip over the curve of her cheekbone. Her cheeks flamed beneath his touch.

"You're blushing. You have something to hide, as usual."

"I have nothing to hide."

His hand slipped beneath her chin and lifted it. He was so near that she could feel his whole warmth. Frantically she tried to distract herself from the temptation of his lips, so close to hers, but to no avail.

"You've already said that you care if I stay in Grass Valley. That's why you came in here, isn't it?" His thumb gently massaged the delicate bone of her jaw.

She wanted to touch him. She ached to have him touch her. She could barely catch her breath. "No. I— I don't care," she managed to say. "Go or stay."

"And if I stay, what will you do?" His head was bent to hers. She couldn't think. She didn't answer. "Liar," he murmured, just before his lips came down to cover hers.

Rowan felt an ocean wave sweep beneath her feet and cast her adrift. She was helpless to fight the tide of emotion and desire that he unleashed with just his kiss. She reached up and clung to him, desperate for his embrace. How could he do this to her, so quickly and so thoroughly?

When he raised his head at last, he smiled mockingly into her eyes. "Well, it seems your lips tell the truth sometimes, at least."

She pulled back her arm and slapped him, hard, across the cheek. He stepped back, rage kindling in his eyes.

"If I'm such a poor liar," she whispered, "how is it that you never guessed about Luke in first place?"

She didn't wait for his reply. Yanking open the door, she took the steps two at a time to the street.

Alec sat in his new digs and stared out the window over the tops of the houses that spread down the hill behind the store. He'd been sitting there ever since Rowan had left, and he still felt some of the sting of her hand, as well as the sweet taste of her lips.

He wished she'd struck him harder. He deserved it, for acting the fool. What an idiot he was when it came to her! He'd been torn by his emotions, and he had succumbed to them all—she'd had only to show her face. He'd wanted to hurt her and drive her away as much as he had wanted to kiss her and bind her close to his side forever. So he'd tried both. Neither was satisfying in the event.

If only he could have stayed in Nevada City. But Nevada City already had a photography studio, and one was the limit that such a small market could bear. He wasn't going to cut the business out from under a fellow photographer. It had been the same story in Marysville. Grass Valley was thriving and growing, and there hadn't been a photographer in residence here for over two years. He could earn the cash he needed in short order.

He'd tried to convince himself that seeing Rowan wouldn't matter. After all, he reasoned, he wasn't in love and she wasn't free, and he had no interest in the sort of games she had played with his feelings. He was well rid of her.

He shoved away from the window seat and stalked about the room, trying to pick up the threads of what he'd been doing before she came in. He couldn't seem to concentrate. He kept recalling her last words. Why *hadn't* he guessed about her ties to Luke?

Why? Because he was a born fool. Because she'd seemed so utterly guileless and true. Because he'd never asked. Because he hadn't wanted to know. Damn it! He'd been sidetracked by a mere woman, he thought, lulled into believing for a time that he could be like other men, like other people, and laugh and fall in love and worry over a woman's simple lies. But he'd been wrong, of course. He was a loner. He always had been, and he always would be.

He set briskly back to work setting up his studio. He needed to earn his money and set out on his journey as soon as possible. Rowan again, he thought. She'd managed to sink his fortunes to the bottom of the river, even though she'd saved his life in the process. He needed to be extra careful, but he would do it. He would concentrate on the task at hand, earn back his savings, and be on his way to fulfilling his dream. Rowan Trelarken, with her famed "Luck" and her distracting charms, would soon be a fading memory.

Rowan moved at a clip down the street, going over in her mind the confrontation she'd had the day before with Alec. Why was it that she was so flustered by him? She was always coming away from dealings with him wishing everything she'd done and said could be erased and rewritten, as on a slate in a schoolroom.

As she approached the boardinghouse, she looked up from her reverie, stopped, and stared in disbelief at the small figure that rose from the rocker on Mrs. Grey's front porch. Then she began to run.

"Molly!" she cried in joy.

Molly's face was wreathed in smiles. She carried Benjie on one hip, and Rowan caught them both up in a hug. "I can't believe it! How did you get here? Have you been waiting long? How are you? Oh, it's so good to see you! Do you have a place to stay?"

Molly laughed. "We got in not twenty minutes ago on the stage. I asked where you were and came straight here. Nobody's home, I guess, so I sat down to wait."

"And Benjie's father? Is he with you?"

Molly's gaze dropped. She shook her head. "I never saw him."

"You didn't?"

"Uh-uh. He never was there."

"I don't understand—"

"Would you have gone if you knew he wasn't?"

"No, of course not."

"I kind of figured. I made it up so you'd go off without me."

Rowan stared at her friend for a moment. "What changed your mind?"

Molly lifted her eyes to meet Rowan's. "After you'd gone, I got to thinking about what all you said that night in your hotel. About how this might be the only chance you get to change things for your mama and your brother. Well, I thought this might be my only chance, too. I mean, who would've thought that you and I'd ever meet and get to be friends?" She hoisted Benjie farther up on her hip. "This here's all I've got, but I'm willing to gamble on something better for him.

Maybe I'll be scrubbing floors, but at least I'd be taking the money home to my own house, not Letty's, every night.''

Rowan hugged her again. ''Well, you're the best thing that's happened to me since I arrived. Come talk to me and tell me everything that's been happening.''

She led Molly into the boardinghouse and up to her room, talking the whole time. Molly listened and laughed and sympathized, and it wasn't until they heard Mrs. Grey downstairs preparing dinner that they stopped talking and thought about the future.

It took some persuasion, but Mrs. Grey agreed to allow Molly and Benjie to stay in Rowan's room for a little extra rent. When Molly saw that their landlady was struggling with several pots, she quietly and efficiently tied a large dishcloth at her waist and set to work in the kitchen beside her. Mrs. Grey was wary at first, knowing already that Rowan's lack of domestic skills was extensive. But when she saw that Molly knew her way around a kitchen as a fish knew the ocean, she was soon beaming upon her new boarder and making clucking noises at Benjie.

Rowan fed Benjie a crumbled biscuit while the others worked. She felt herself relaxing for the first time since she had come to Grass Valley. With Molly to share her room, she no longer felt so absolutely alone. Later that night, she told Molly more about what had passed between her and Alec, and about her plans and vows for the future and how she had encountered failure and resistance at every turn. Molly listened with solemn gray eyes.

"Been feeling kind of sorry for yourself, haven't you?" she asked. Her voice was kindly.

Rowan looked shamefaced. After all that Molly had been through, what did she have to complain about? "Oh. Yes, I guess I have."

"It's all right, long's you don't make a habit of it." Molly patted Rowan's knee. "It kind of looks like you've been doing all the wrong things for all the right reasons, you know what I mean?"

"I think so," Rowan said slowly.

Molly leaned forward. "What do you want most of all?"

Rowan didn't hesitate. "To help my family! I want to be free of this debt to Henry Syms, and to repay everyone I owe and be done with it! I hate my father for running out on his debts, and I will not do the same! I want everyone to know that Trelarken is still an honorable name."

"Good girl. Then you need to do all you can to get those debts paid. Everything. Don't wait. I waited around, thinking something would just come along, but you showed me that if I don't act, I just stay stuck. I was stuck at Letty's, but I made the move here. I aim to see that I don't miss out on a single opportunity to help me and my boy from now on."

Rowan looked at Molly's shining, determined face with admiration. She was right, of course, and she knew what she was talking about. This was no time to give up and wait for things to right themselves.

"But where can I get some money, if not from Luke?" Rowan asked, drooping a bit at the memory of her fruitless job search.

"I know somebody right here in town that'd give you a job. Be a good one, too, just right for you."

"Tell me! Who?"

"Alec." Molly laughed. "Now, don't look at me as if I just said you oughta fly to the moon. You told me he was looking to get out of town as fast as he could make up the money he lost, right? Well, he'd get there a whole lot faster if he had some help, and who better to help him than you?"

"But he despises me! And besides, I've only watched him make photographs, I can't do it myself."

"You could learn. I say give it a whirl. What have you got to lose? Tell him it's strictly business, you can read and write and draw and all that stuff, and you know how he works. You'll be his right-hand man—er, woman."

"Strictly business," Rowan mused. "I suppose the worst he can do is tell me no, just like every other businessman in this town."

"And that hasn't killed you yet," Molly said with a grin.

"I'll do it," Rowan said firmly. "If you can come all this way just on the word of a crazy girl from Cornwall who's always in a scrape, then I can ask Alec MacKenzie for a job!"

Chapter Twelve

"God save me, they've taken a penknife to my floorboards looking for hidden treasure, and used iodine to paint a beard on Mrs. Pengelly's aunt. Now I've lost one of them, and I think he may have gone out the window and gotten stuck inside the rainspout!"

These were Alec's first words to Rowan when she rapped on the door of his studio. His hair was nearly standing on end, and his voice was choked with panic and fury. His usually impeccable collar had rotated to one side, as if he should be wearing his tie under his left ear. A smudge of blackberry jam decorated his forehead, and his eyes had a dazed, hunted look.

Rowan was too astonished at the aspect of Alec MacKenzie minus his composure to say a word. She peered around him to see inside the studio. Two small boys were wrangling on the floor, their brown velvet suits collecting the remains of the bread and jam that seemed to be everywhere around them.

"The Meecham triplets," Alec intoned, as if naming the chief tormentors of hell.

"Triplets? I see only two."

"That's what I mean. One of them's escaped. Down the rainspout. Perhaps in the ceiling." He took a few hesitant steps in their direction. "Boys. Fellows? Come now, let's be a little quieter, shall we?" Bedlam continued to reign. He turned to Rowan with a desperate grimace. "They've been like that ever since their mother left to finish her shopping."

"I see." Rowan set aside her pocketbook and hat and pushed up her sleeves. She strode across the room to the center of the squabble. Reaching down, she seized an ear of one boy and a lock of hair of the other. With a gentle but steady pull, she brought them scrambling to their feet, heads down in an effort to escape her grasp.

"Find your brother and bring him here," she ordered in clear, ringing tones. "Now."

She released them, and they scampered to a trunk at the back of the room. It took them a moment or two to get the key fitted into the lock, but they soon had it open, and a third, identical Meecham erupted, redfaced and squalling, clawing his way out from among Alec's shirts.

"Come over here." Rowan's tone was like steel.

They obeyed, though not without taking several swipes at one another along the way. At last they stood before her, hardly contrite, but certainly quieter.

"Now, I want the lot of you to march to the kitchen basin, fetch a wet cloth and begin cleaning up the mess you've made here. But first, I'll have that knife." She looked meaningfully at the left-hand Meecham and held out her hand.

"It's mine. Pa give it to me for our birthday!"

"You'll spend your next birthday standing up, laddie, unless you hand me that knife right quick."

The boy squinted at her, then apparently decided that she just might make good on her promise and handed over his weapon.

"March to the kitchen. No dawdling, and no fighting!"

"You talk funny," the center Meecham said as they shuffled toward the sink.

"You'll be talking funny, too, if Mr. MacKenzie loses his temper," she said briskly, hurrying them along. "Now, no more of your sauce. Do as I tell you."

Alec almost gaped in amazement as the terrible trio turned wary eyes his way. He caught himself just in time to register something closer to a frown. They didn't seem convinced, but when their eyes turned to Rowan, it was plain that they believed her, at least.

Order was restored, and by the time Mrs. Meecham called to collect her charges, Alec had taken several poses, most of them guaranteed to make the viewer believe that a small band of cherubim had gathered for the camera. He watched Rowan escort the family to the door and waited as blessed silence fell over his studio.

"Thank you," he breathed when the last clattering footstep was heard on the stairs. "All I could think was that next they'd discover the stove and decide to set fire to the place."

She smiled. "You just have to know how to speak to them in a way that they understand." Her eyes twinkled. "You were trying to be rational and reasonable with them, weren't you?"

"Well, yes, but they'd been so good and polite when their mother was here."

She nodded. "Of course. The little terrors know they can't get away with a thing when she's about."

He crossed his arms. "How did you get so wise?"

"Mmm, perhaps I shouldn't say." She smiled. "Let's say that I learned the technique from my nanny."

Alec laughed. "Well, it was a—"

But Rowan held up her hand. "Shh! I believe someone is coming up the steps."

She crossed to the door and opened it before the visitors had a chance to knock. "Hello. Won't you come in? Mr. MacKenzie will be with you in a moment." She waved a hand behind her back, shooing Alec toward the darkroom. In his state of utter bewilderment, he went, leaving the door open just a crack to hear the conversation in the studio.

"I am Miss Trelarken. May I bring you a cup of tea while you wait?" Rowan's tones were warm and beguiling. "There are a number of photograph albums there on the table. Perhaps you'd like to glance through them to see the poses for which Mr. MacKenzie is so famous?"

Alec turned, running a hand through his hair. He caught a glimpse of himself in the mirror by the door and saw why Rowan had waved him away. He was still in a state of dishevelment from the Meecham fiasco. He quickly put himself to rights and faced the new arrivals.

His new clients were Mrs. Winthorp and her daughter, Corliss. Mr. Winthorp ran the town bank and the family fancied themselves the arbiters of culture and grace in the community. Languid Corliss Winthorp had come equipped with yards of white muslin, clumps of purplish-red oleander and a stuffed parakeet, asking that she be posed as the muse of music.

Alec opened his mouth to protest. He knew that he'd just end up wasting his time and his equipment on such nonsense. Rowan intervened before he had the chance to speak.

"If I might make a suggestion, Mr. MacKenzie?"

He glared at her. She continued with an engaging smile. "Don't you think that Miss Winthorp, standing just as she is, is the very likeness of the portrait of the princess that Gainsborough painted? I recall that you said you'd seen it when you were at the palace."

Alec's mouth moved, but no words came out. Corliss Winthorp perked up noticeably. "What portrait?" she demanded. "Which palace?"

Alec stared at Rowan for an instant and then nodded. "Ah! The royal portrait at . . . at . . ."

"Balmoral," Rowan put in, prompting him.

"Balmoral! Yes, Miss Winthorp would show herself to great advantage in such a . . . a dignified, regal pose."

"Yes, quite," said Rowan, making her accent as crisply British as she could manage. "If you would step this way, Miss Winthorp, I would be pleased to show you just how the princess was standing. . . ."

The session flew by. Rowan managed the Winthorps with as much grace as she had shown authority in the face of the Meecham triplets. The Winthorps left the studio twittering with delight and promising to send all the very best folk of Grass Valley to the MacKenzie Studios.

Rowan closed the door behind them and leaned against it, shaking with laughter. "I thought I'd burst when she held up that pathetic old bird!"

"You thought you'd burst! You were diplomacy itself. I was ready to tell her I'd rather be the photographer at the funeral parlor than shoot a ludicrous tableau like that. Where did you learn to handle people so well?"

Rowan shook her head. "I have no idea. I just try to imagine what I would want if I were in their shoes." She glanced down at her worn boots. "Though Miss Winthorp's 'Grecian sandals' are hardly the thing I'd choose."

Alec joined in her laughter. "Well, no matter how you came by the skill, you saved my sanity. I wish I had you around every day."

They both paused. His words hung in the silence between them.

"Do you mean that?" Rowan asked at last.

"Well, yes. That is—"

"Good. Then it's settled," she said quickly. "Here's my plan. I'll work here every weekday and a half day on Saturday. You can show me what to do, and what not to do and I shall follow your instructions implicitly. You needn't pay me, but with my help, you should be able to take on more patrons, and thus you should be able to earn the money I lost for you in half the time it would have taken you to do it alone. Shall we shake hands upon it?"

Alec's head whirled. He wasn't sure what was happening. He hadn't intended to make her a job offer. But what had he meant?

"Rowan, I think—"

But Rowan held up her hand. "Shh... I believe someone is coming up the steps."

She crossed to the door and opened it. "Hello. Won't you come in? Mr. MacKenzie will be with you in a moment. I am Miss Trelarken, Mr. MacKenzie's assistant. May I bring you a cup of tea while you wait? There are a number of photograph albums there on the table. Perhaps you'd like to glance through them to see the poses for which Mr. MacKenzie is so famous?"

"What has she done to me?" Alec whispered as he strode to the darkroom to prepare fresh plates.

How did she always manage to duck under his best defenses and place herself right in the middle of his life? A short time ago, he'd vowed that he never wanted to see her again, that he couldn't have another person in his life. Yet here he was, taking her on as his assistant!

Rational and reasonable, she'd called him. He caught himself gazing at her slender form as she moved about his studio, imagining the pleasure of seeing her whole, glorious body clad only in summer sunlight....

Rational and reasonable, he thought to himself. Well, rationality and reason didn't stand a chance against Rowan Trelarken.

Luke was irritated when he learned that Rowan was working, but she was in too buoyant a mood to let him discourage her. Instead, she talked fast and made sure that he knew that it was a respectable job and that she was doing it not for cash but for the sake of repaying a debt. By the time she was finished, either he was too confused to protest or he'd just resigned himself that his fiancée was too daft to argue with. Also, Molly appeared, and Rowan swept them both up into a flurry of introductions and plans for the three of them.

Alec bore three days of working with Rowan—three days of making sure that he maintained a safe distance, of reminding himself of her deceit about Luke and her pretenses in San Francisco. Only the dream of his expedition, and the reminder that she could cause more trouble in his life than the Meecham triplets combined, kept him from reaching for her and carrying her off to his bed—and finally even those safeguards began to falter. On the fourth day, he sent word to Mrs. Grey's that he was taking a day off and that Rowan needn't come to work. He closed the studio, took his camera and one of the mules, and headed up into the hills and ravines, looking for places to photograph.

His wanderings took him up to the Kingsfield mine, where he saw Cornish miners heading home at the end of their shift, and heard them lift their voices in perfect harmony, despite their weariness. His curiosity roused, he went to find the mine manager and obtained permission to visit the mines. He arrived at the headframe early the next morning, a small pack of food and drawing supplies slung over his shoulder.

Dewey escorted Alec to the main shaft and showed him the skip cars, which were long, open metal boxes on wheels, pulled up and down the shaft on two tracks. One man stood by the skip, greeting the men as they clambered single file into the steeply inclined cars and sat, their knees around the fellow in front of them. Dewey led Alec to the man who stood on the platform.

"Luke Syms, Alec MacKenzie," the mine manager grunted. "Syms is captain on this shift."

Alec was startled to come face-to-face with the man who would soon be Rowan's husband, but he managed to maintain an affable expression as he offered his hand. As they shook hands, he wondered just how much Luke knew about him. He knew precious little about Syms, beyond what Rowan had told him of her family and their debt to his brother.

Dewey explained Alec's presence. "MacKenzie here is a photographer. He's gonna take some pictures of the buildings and the men after the shift comes up. In exchange, he wants to go down with you and take a look around, see what we do around here."

"I'll stay out of your way, you can count on that," Alec said to Luke.

Luke took a long, appraising look at him. No emotion was betrayed in his face. At last he nodded and turned back to the skip. Dewey motioned for Alec to follow Luke. "There'll be an engineer going down around noon," he said. "You can come back up with him."

Alec thanked him and went after Luke, who stood waiting by the skip.

"'E can sit there," Luke said, pointing to the second seat from the bottom on the skip. "Keep hands in."

Alec stepped over the edge of the car and took his seat. The car was so narrow and the seating so cramped, his knees felt as if they were folded up about his ears. The man behind him gave him a poke in the shoulder. "Look sharp, son," he said cheerfully. "'E'll 'ave to duck come first level. That or go on bowed. Mine's not th' place for 'e's lank."

Alec gathered that he was being warned not to bump his head. A quick glance behind him showed he was roughly a foot taller than most of the men in the skip, and that all of them wore some sort of soft, padded headgear. "Thanks," he said over his shoulder. "I'll keep an eye out."

Luke climbed in before him and handed back a candle. "'E'll need this at th' end."

Alec accepted the candle with thanks. The car jerked into motion, throwing Alec's head back and then snapping it forward as it lurched ahead. The skip slid away on the tracks, traveled along a gentle slope for a few yards, and then headed into the maw of the main tunnel, which slanted sharply downward into the dark.

As the men talked and exchanged jests over the echoing rattle of the car, Alec considered the irony of going below in the care of Luke Syms. He'd known that he would meet up with Luke eventually; the town was too small to avoid it. But he certainly wouldn't have dreamed of this encounter.

This was the man that Rowan would marry, he thought. The man who would take her to his bed and share her life, whose children she might bear. The idea sent a bolt of hot resentment through him. She'd be Luke's for the price of a cottage and food for her brother and mother. Damn her useless cur of a father, anyway. She would give herself to a stranger in payment of a debt. His hand tensed on Luke's shoulder. Some deep, undeniable source within him roiled up in jealousy and anger and cried aloud for him to challenge this man for the right to possess a woman—even though he had originally come to the mine just to avoid that woman.

By the time they climbed out of the skip at the five-hundred-foot level, his temper had cooled and he was ready to be a more impartial observer. The men lighted their candles and a few lamps, and Luke led the way to where their tools lay waiting for them to resume work. Alec followed, remembering just in time that he'd have to stoop to avoid crashing into the heavy timbers that bore the weight of the ceiling.

The air was heavy and moist, and surprisingly warm in this man-made cavern. Here and there, water dripped along the walls and fell in echoing drops into puddles below. The men set their lunch buckets down on one side and began to doff their jackets. Moving to various positions in the cavern, they hung their candles off any protruding surface, or lacking that, jabbed the pointed ends of their candlesticks into a stretch of timber.

He watched as the men began their labor in the passage, working in teams of two or three to drill, pick and hammer at the rock walls. The skip returned to their passage, with high-sided cars this time. Two men set to work "mucking out," which consisted of shoveling up the mined rock and loading it into the skip.

Alec took out his sketchpad and a pencil, sat down, and began to draw. He sketched rapidly, his skilled hand working to capture the movements of the men as they swung their heavy tools, and the looming shadows they cast on the walls by the dim light of their candles.

Presently one of the men working at widening the main tunnel motioned to him. "Eh, lad, can 'e manage hammer and nail? We're short a fella."

"I've banged a few boards," Alec replied.

"Then set to that 'un there." The man pointed to a massive log that lay nearby. "I'll hold 'er steady and 'e can set 'er in proper."

Alec laid down his sketchpad and went to where the man pointed. He wondered if this was a test to see if he was a man to respect, or a prank to prove that he was not only an outsider, but a fool, as well. Glancing to his left, he saw Luke watching him with mild interest. Alec rolled his shoulders and bent to the task.

The log was heavy and rough-hewn, but years of lugging his heaviest cameras and equipment up and down hills had suited Alec to the task. He squatted, got both hands under the timber and hefted it up. He transferred the weight to one shoulder, wrapped his arm up around it and swiveled to face the man. "Where do you want it?" he asked blandly.

The miner gaped at him. "Damn, but the Scots're just as mad as th' Irish."

There was laughter all around, and the men returned to work, seeing that there wasn't going to be any display of ineptitude on Alec's part. They'd finished their lunch, or "croust," as they called it, of Cornish meat pasties and tea, and had returned to their work, when a rattling sound was heard in the passage and then a screeching like a rusty door dragged shut. A man in a neat, clean jumper stepped out of the dark passage, a notebook in his hand.

One by one, the men on the shift slowed and finally stopped their work. They leaned casually on the handles of their picks or shovels, or slouched against the walls, watching the man with studied disinterest. Luke went to greet him, and together they walked the length of the open passage, checking the work and taking ore samples here and there.

At last they came to Alec, who'd been helping to pick out a section of wall and pile it behind them to be mucked out. Alec wiped his forehead on his sleeve and nodded to the newcomer.

"You must be MacKenzie, the photographer fellow. I'm Ted Sinclair, the engineer and inspector on this shift. Didn't expect you to be working with the Cousins." Sinclair laughed nervously and offered his hand.

Alec took the man's measure coolly. Sinclair wasn't a bad sort, he judged, but he had the stamp of the company man all the same. His independent, rebellious nature recognized their fundamental opposition. He kept his hand on the pick.

"Just trying it on for size," he said nonchalantly. "Luke and his men were willing to take me on for a day."

"I see." Slightly flustered, the inspector raised his offered hand and pushed his spectacles up on his nose.

"Well, you can ride back up in the cage with me." He started toward the passage.

"I think I'll wait and go to grass with the others at the end of the shift. If it's all right with you, Luke?"

Luke shrugged. "We're short a fella. 'E's no Cousin, but 'e'll do for now."

"But—" the inspector sputtered. "Aren't you supposed to—"

"Man's his own boss," Luke said quietly.

Alec shot him a glance, and saw a faint flicker of approval in Luke's blue eyes. He felt a strange twist as two conflicting emotions met inside him. He still harbored jealous resentment of the man who would take Rowan as his wife, but he now felt admiration and appreciation of him, as well. "Tell Dewey I'll stop by his office before I leave," Alec said.

Sinclair left, looking dubious. Luke looked at Alec and shrugged again. "School of Mines fella," he explained briefly.

"Ah. An expert," Alec said with a grin.

Luke's mustache twitched. "That's it."

The shift was a long one, Alec realized. Every muscle in his back, neck, arms and shoulders told him that. The men still took little notice of him, but he could sense that their nonchalance was the acceptance of him as a friend, rather than the cool resistance they'd shown Sinclair.

He was treated to an impromptu concert when they broke for water and a stretch in the afternoon. Their voices were rich in the passage, the songs rolling out to the rock walls and then echoing back, magnified. Alec sat immersed in sound, feeling that he'd crossed the border into some strange new land.

Luke came to sit beside him in the quiet aftermath. As they sat sipping water and letting their bodies cool, an idea came to Alec. He quickly ran over the obstacles and the advantages in his mind and then broached the subject to Luke.

"I'd like to come back and take some photographs," Alec said to him. "Of you and the men at work. People should know about what you do down here, especially the people back east. I can show them with my photographs."

Luke shrugged. "'Tes no matter, except for Dewey. 'E'll have to ask him." He slanted a keen glance at Alec as he sipped the last of his tea. "I seen a fella taking some of them photo pictures. Needed a window and lamps, beside. That was above. In daytime."

Alec nodded. "I will need extra lighting. That's where things get sticky." He turned slightly so that he could meet Luke's eyes. "In order to get enough light down here, I'll have to use flash powder to make the exposures. I have magnesium flares that will work. But it'll be chancy, all the same. Your men might not want to take the risk."

Luke considered this for a moment. "John Samuel," he called out. "Scotsman 'ere says he'll need to bring powder below to make photograph pictures. Says it could be chancy."

The big man raised his chin. "Black powder or giant powder?"

Alec nodded in understanding. There had been talk of the dangerous dynamite, or "giant powder," being used in other mines. Most miners wanted no part of its massive explosions or noxious fumes. Besides, it was a laborsaving device brought in by the mine owners, which meant that if it was used, some miners might soon be out of their jobs. "Strictly black," he said. "Dynamite'd wreak hell on my camera."

"Then what's 'e waitin' for?" John Samuel grinned and resumed his task, humming.

"Dewey's the one to ask," Luke repeated. "The man can show his mettle some days. On others, he's naught but an old woman. Be his to say."

Alec couldn't resist the next question. "Is every man here named John, except you?"

Luke almost smiled. "'E's hit on it, just about. Mr. John Wesley come through the duchy a ways back. Converted all of Cornwall to th' Methodism. Folks been namin' sons upon him ever since." He tossed away the cold dregs of his tea. "'E's heard us called Cousin Jacks. That's because every time the shifter needed another man, one of the lads from over home'd say, 'Eh, I got just the fella. Me cousin Jack from the old country.' The Cousins are the finest there is below, so they'd take him on."

"Of course," Alec said, with a grin, recalling Rowan's proud words about her countrymen.

"Mine comp'ny men come in once. Wanted us to take numbers 'stead of names." Luke shook his head slowly, in disbelief.

"What happened?"

"Well, it was a daft idea, wasn't it? Fancy a man shoutin' 'Look sharp, Thirteen!' With names, all a fella has to do is shout 'Mind yer arse, John,' and every man below and half up at grass'll be gettin' out the way. We kept with names.''

When Alec entered Dewey's office at sundown that day, the mine manager nearly dropped his cigar at the sight of Alec's mud-encrusted pants and shirt. "MacKenzie! What the hell happened to you?"

"Nothing much. Just an honest day's work."

"Hmph. Hope you aren't expecting to be paid for it."

"No, but you might consider giving a bit more to Luke's crew. They're top-notch, if I'm any judge."

"Fortunately, you're not," Dewey replied dryly. "When are you going to take your pictures?"

"Tomorrow, I hope. I'm going down with Luke's shift again and take pictures there."

Dewey drew back his chin in a gesture of disbelief and disapproval. "It's impossible. You won't have enough light."

Alec paused for a second. Then: "I'll use magnesium flares."

"I won't permit it."

"Why not? I've handled the flares before, and the men have handled black powder. It'll be done by experts."

"There are gases down in those tunnels. They're volatile. One good spark and the whole place could blow."

"I know what I'm doing, and the men working on the shift know how to play it safe."

"You'll disrupt my workers."

"Luke Syms doesn't think so, and he's the man responsible for the whole shift."

"It's nonsense, MacKenzie. Nobody wants to see pictures of a bunch of dirty Limeys."

Alec bit back an insult for the degrading way he spoke about these men who worked so hard for him. Instead, he placed both hands on Dewey's desk and leaned toward him. "You'd be surprised how many people will want to see these pictures. I have contacts in Washington, D.C. The government is looking for every opportunity to exploit the resources of the new western states. Photos of real men working in real gold mines in California? They'll eat it up for breakfast. You couldn't ask for better publicity. Not to mention making friends in Washington."

"I won't have you disrupting my men at work."

"Do it of a Saturday night."

Dewey and Alec turned to see Luke standing in the doorway, a lighted pipe between his teeth.

"That's right," Alec said, with a cautious nod to Luke. "We can work it this way. I'll go down with Luke and a couple of his men on Saturday night, last shift. You can come along—"

"Oh, no," said Dewey, red-faced. "Not me."

"Fine. Then send your man Sinclair to keep an eye on things. If things look bad to him, we'll pack up and clear out."

"Damn." Dewey gnawed at his cigar. "All right, I'll talk it over with the big boss in San Francisco this week. But if there's any funny business, the pair of you will hang for it, you understand?"

Luke nodded, impassive. Alec adopted his cool stance and said, "I'll be back here next week, early."

Chapter Thirteen

Rowan's face went ashen when Luke told her of Alec's plan. She groped behind her to find the front porch rocker and sat down abruptly. "You can't be serious."

Luke pulled his pipe from the pocket of his waistcoat and tapped it against one of the pillars supporting the porch at Mrs. Grey's. "Don't believe the man were makin' jest. I'll be goin' below with him."

Rowan felt a wave of sickness pass over her. She wanted to say something, but a high-pitched whine of fear was wailing in her head. Alec going down underground? In one of those dank, narrow tunnels? It was horrible.

She'd lived among miners for most of her life, but she'd been in a mine only once. She never wanted to repeat the experience. The trip into Wheal Carn had been nightmarishly dark, full of echoing chambers and the tapping of hammers beyond the walls. They'd gone too far for her to find her way back; the passage had grown narrower, and she'd felt as if the breath were being squeezed out of her. Panic had dogged her every step, until she was sobbing and begging her father to find a way out, quickly.

They'd come to the end of the passage, and her father and Gil had comforted her, but the terror she'd felt had never left her. It had become her greatest fear to be confined in a small space, with life-giving air slowly vanishing. She never would have survived the ocean voyage from England if she hadn't been able to steal out of the coffinlike stacks of berths in steerage and climb on deck, where the air was bountiful.

And now Alec wanted to go down in the mines! She'd always closed her mind to the idea of Luke's occupation, and she also harbored the feeling that miners were somehow special, or protected from the dangers of the mines. Perhaps because her ties to Luke seemed so vague and unreal, the danger didn't seem to touch her. But Alec—Alec was very close, and very real.

"You mustn't do this," she whispered. Then, finding her voice: "Luke, don't let him do this. Tell him he can't. He doesn't belong down there."

Luke looked at her as he lighted his pipe. "Didn't seem to bother 'im much yesterday."

"Yesterday? He went down with you yesterday?" She shivered involuntarily.

"Come up beggin' to go again." Luke pondered a moment. "Man's either plain mad or there's some of the duchy running in his veins."

Before Rowan could reply, Molly came out on the porch. "Oh, I'm sorry," she said hastily, seeing Luke. "I didn't know you had company." She gave Luke a shy smile, then turned to look at Rowan. "What's the matter?'' she asked, seeing Rowan's pale face. ''Sickening for something, are you?''

''No. No, I just—'' Rowan shook her head. ''Luke says that he and Al—Mr. MacKenzie—are going down into the mine to take photographs. I say it's too dangerous.''

Molly laid her hand on her shoulder and squeezed comfortingly. Rowan had told her of her special fear. She looked at Luke. ''Is it dangerous?'' she asked.

Luke shuffled a bit, and looked away from Molly's questioning gaze. ''Might be. Not the goin' down, but the powder could be a bother.''

Molly's eyes narrowed. ''How much of a bother?''

Luke lifted his head and looked at her squarely. ''Flash powder and flame are always a risk, below. We'll be carryin' both.''

Rowan drew a strangled breath. Molly patted her shoulder, looking thoughtful. ''It's brave of you to go down with Mr. MacKenzie,'' she said to Luke. ''Not many men'd put their lives on the line for a plumb stranger.''

Luke shrugged away her praise. ''Not much more risk for myself. Scotsman could be a little mad, but he's no coward.''

Rowan bounced up from the chair, suddenly furious. She ran down the steps of the porch and out to the street. ''A little mad!'' she exclaimed as she went. ''The man's fair bird-witted!''

Luke and Molly stared after her as she marched away.

''Scotsman'd better look sharp,'' Luke observed, puffing on his pipe.

Molly threw him a curious glance. "You don't mind?" She flushed quickly, realizing what she had said.

Luke seemed unperturbed by her question. "Not much."

Molly peered at him, was about to say something, then changed her mind. Benjie began to cry indoors.

"That's my little boy. I better go see to him," she said.

"A lad needs his mam."

They stood silent for a moment. Finally, Benjie's crying grew insistent. "Goodbye, Mr. Syms," she said, sidling toward the door.

"'Evening," Luke said with a nod.

He stood on the porch for a few minutes after she'd gone inside. Then he turned, went down the steps, and headed up the street. Two of his fellow miners hailed him as he passed, but their shift boss seemed to have his mind turned to other things.

Rowan burst into Alec's studio without knocking. She found him at his worktable, mounting some portraits on pasteboard. She crossed the room with determined strides.

"Are you mad?" she asked him.

"Am I what?" He wanted to laugh, but he could see from her expression that she was genuinely disturbed about something.

"Luke says that you and he are going down into the mine and take photographs! With flare powder and flash—flash things!"

"Luke's right. We are." Alec removed the excess glue and laid the print under a flat, heavy weight to dry.

Rowan caught his arm as he turned toward her. "You can't do it! You mustn't!"

Alec's mild expression faded. He pulled his arm away. "What do you mean?"

"It's far too dangerous. You could be hurt. You could be killed."

He shrugged. "And I could step out of my door and be struck down by a runaway horse and wagon."

Rowan followed him as he went to the kitchen area to clean his brushes. "That's foolishness. There's a difference between an accident and a deliberate deed. One can't be avoided. The other most certainly can."

Alec's face grew darker. "Luke goes down there every day. He's your *intended,* isn't he? Why aren't you after him to quit working in the mines?"

"Because Luke knows what he's doing. He was born to it. I don't like that he has to go down into some horrible dark hole in the ground, but it's what he does. You're different."

Alec noted the high color in her cheeks, and the way her breath was coming quickly. She was truly worried. But he wasn't in a mood to placate her. Her protests and warnings only made him more resolute.

"Luke was born to it?" he asked. "You make it sound as if the man were some kind of dog, bred to hunt or retrieve."

"Now you're being insulting."

"No more insulting than you've been, coming in here and telling me what I should or shouldn't do." He moved away from the kitchen and began putting away his mounting materials. "We have a business arrangement, Miss Trelarken. That's all. I'm your employer. You're my employee. You do as I say, not the other way around."

Rowan caught the last edge of her temper before it went sailing off. She had to make him see that she was in earnest.

"If you care about Luke, as you obviously do," she said, approaching him as calmly as she could manage, "then won't you please see that what you want to do isn't the same as what he and the other men do every day? They don't go down and stand frozen in place, waiting for someone to make a photograph. They don't use explosives every day, and when they do, they put them in with a long fuse, so that they have time to get far away from the blast." She stepped closer and laid her hand lightly on his forearm. "They can't escape your flash powder when it goes off— I've seen you work with it, it has to be right in front of them. Please, Alec. Their jobs are dangerous enough, without adding more to their lot."

Alec glared at the tools he was putting away. Damn her, he thought. She was forever catching him off his guard. She'd come in ranting incoherently, and just when he'd thought he'd won out over the emotional fit she was throwing, she'd gone and turned rational on him. He'd never learn.

To complicate matters further, he was only too aware of how close she was, and how beautiful, with her high color and brilliant eyes. He wanted to take the hand on his arm, press its palm to his chest and slide it up and around his neck. He simply, elementally, wanted to pull her into his arms, and raise sighing whispers and panting cries from those lovely, curving lips.

Her eyes were searching his for some sign of his capitulation. He wanted her. But he wasn't about to back down. "If Luke thinks the chances are good, I'm not going to argue with him. As you say, he knows more about the risks down there than I do."

"Will you at least consider it?"

He stood for a moment in silence. "I'll think about it."

Her smile was radiant. "Oh, I'm so glad—"

"I said I'd think about it. I make no promises."

Rowan nodded. "That's all right. This will do for now. Take as long as you like to think about it."

She stood still for a moment, smiling at him. Then she glanced around her, as if trying to remember how she came to be here. "Oh. Well, that's all that I came to say," she said, fluttering a hand in Alec's direction. "I shall be off—that is, unless you want me to stay?"

He blinked. Did he want her to stay? Had she read his thoughts? He looked at her and realized she was talking as he had ordered her to—as an employee to her employer.

"No, I can manage on my own this evening. I have some work in the darkroom." He felt a rushing mix of disappointment and relief at his words. The tension of his wanting was fed by his refusals of her. He was tormented by her absence as well as her presence. But to be safe, it was best that she leave.

He watched her disappear out the door, leaving him alone in the studio. Still, he seemed to see her everywhere. He turned toward the darkroom with a growl.

"She's right. I must be mad."

* * *

The congregation at the church had plenty of grist for their formidable gossip mill when Luke Syms arrived at Sunday services flanked by two young women. Speculation about the slim, petite Molly Jenkins began at once, and when it was learned that she was a friend of Luke's fiancée and a single woman with a child besides, their curiosity increased. Lowella Tolbathy took it upon herself to investigate, saying that it was high time she took tea with Mary Ellen Grey.

Rowan caught bits of the gossip that traveled so quickly through the community and realized that it would soon reach back to Carn Rose—the mail went overland now, by horse across Panama and then out on fast merchant clippers to England, Luke had told her.

A letter had already arrived from Gil, no doubt written soon after they had parted. It was full of fond wishes and clever descriptions of his new life, but Rowan could tell that he, too, was feeling a bit alone in the world away from Carn Rose.

The rest of his letter disturbed Rowan even more. "I've been making inquiries," he wrote. "And though I know you won't approve, I've located Father in London. Sister of mine, there is so much more to say than I can tell you in this letter, but please understand that I had to find him, just as you had to carry out your famed plan to marry Luke. Father is not well and was not happy to see me, but I made him tell me a little of what happened in Carn Rose. He was in his cups, but from what I can make out, he says he stole nothing from the mines. He left in utter financial disgrace, true, and for that he is sorry, but he vows he'd never have stolen from Wheal Carn or anyone in Carn Rose. I want to believe him, Row, so I'm going back home to look into matters there.''

Rowan hardly knew what to think or feel. She'd long ago set aside all thoughts that Francis Trelarken would return or be found. The rumors in Carn Rose had all indicated that he'd sailed for France. But Gil had found him, and was trying to clear his name. She shook her head as she set the letter aside. She prayed he wouldn't be too disappointed. She couldn't imagine that her father would have left his beloved Nanstowe, Louisa, his family, for any reason less than terrible shame. Why else would he have stayed away so long?

Rowan wrote back to Gil warning him not to get his hopes up too high. The letter and the gossip in Grass Valley made her more wary; she knew that her actions were being closely watched by the Cornish townspeople, who must in turn be writing home to Carn Rose and other, nearby villages with all the latest news about Luke Syms and the Trelarken heiress. It reminded her that she must do her part to protect her family, and keep her agreement to marry Luke Syms. Whether Gil managed to clear their name or not, there was still a debt to be paid.

Luke came to visit almost every evening, occasionally bringing with him news of his progress on the house. Molly took a keen interest in the details of the building, and the times spent on Mrs. Grey's front porch were pleasant.

Rowan continued to work for Alec, still troubled by the confused state of her emotions. He'd been turned down by the mine company in his bid to photograph underground, and he seemed to be taking out his frustration by doubling his workload. As Rowan helped with the poses, corralled children and served tea, she wondered if he was also taking the extra work so that he could leave Grass Valley even sooner.

Whatever his motives, their hectic schedule left them no chance to be alone together. This was a relief to Rowan at first, but after a day or two she found that she was still keenly aware of his presence, and the shuttered heat behind his eyes. A simple gesture could make her recall all the tempting, intoxicating ways he had touched her. A stolen glance at him could bring to her mind the hundred ways she wanted to touch him. She wondered at the desire that was so easily awakened when she was around him, and struggled in vain to find the same spark when she looked at Luke.

One Saturday, Luke sent word to Mrs. Grey's that Rowan should walk out to see the new house, so that she could tell him what she wanted in the kitchen and the pantry. Rowan had no idea what to ask for, so Molly and Benjie joined her.

Luke had chosen a small, isolated lot at the western end of town. The land had been cleared, but an oak tree grew beside one corner of the house. The little house was just framed in, and Molly told Rowan that the structure was much sturdier and better crafted than the wooden shacks that many of the miners had tacked up to provide shelter for their families. "Looks like he's planning to stay a while," she said.

Luke was nowhere in sight when they arrived, so they went in and looked around. A plank floor had been laid, and the whole place smelled of fresh-cut pine boards. Molly's eyes lighted up when she saw that the house was divided into five separate rooms.

"There's a kitchen, a parlor, two bedrooms..." she said. "And space for a real pantry just off the kitchen, too."

"Is that good?"

"Yes, it is. And this last room must be a bathroom, Rowan! Just like in the best houses in the city."

"Really? Now, what am I supposed to do about the kitchen?"

Molly shook her head. "You are a one. He wants to know where to put the bins and shelves in the pantry and where you want the drainboard. I brought a measuring tape so we can fit for curtains in here. You can get good muslin real cheap at Youngman's general store."

"Mm-hmm," Rowan said, gazing out the window. "Oh, look—there are wild irises growing over by the creek! I'd love to have some for our room, wouldn't you?"

Before Molly could answer, she had darted out the back door and was hurrying across the meadow toward the winding creek. Molly shook her head at the mercurial nature of her good friend and set to work measuring the windows.

"Mornin', missus."

Molly turned, startled, to see Luke standing in the doorway to the parlor. "Oh, good morning, Mr.

Syms," she said. "I was helping Rowan plan for her
kitchen. Hope you don't mind."

"How does 'e like she?"

Molly looked mystified. "Pardon?"

"The house. Does 'e fancy it?"

Her face brightened. "It's a wonderful house. So
many rooms! And I can— Rowan can do so much in a
kitchen like this."

Luke's mustache twitched. "What 'e does in a
kitchen and what 'er does is two different things besides."

"But she's doing much better," Molly said
staunchly. "I've shown her how to make biscuits already."

He nodded. "'Er's lucky to have 'e along. Tell me
what bins and boxes ye needs, missus, and I'll put 'em
in next week."

Rowan was returning to the house several minutes
later, her hands full of delicate purple blooms, when
her heart gave a jump at the sight of Alec's wagon tied
at the side of the house. She came in through the
kitchen and crossed to the doorway to see Molly, Luke,
Alec and Benjie all gathered in the parlor. Her eyes
quickly widened at the sight of Molly expounding on
the joys of a good potbellied stove while Luke listened
with rapt attention. Benjie was fussing in his basket,
and he suddenly let out a squalling cry. To cap Rowan's astonishment, Luke bent down, picked up the
boy and laid him casually over one shoulder, his eyes
never leaving Molly's face. He was patting the baby's
behind with a big, rough hand when Molly spotted
Rowan.

"You're back!" she called out. "Come and see. Luke was going to put in a fireplace, but I think he should put in a stove, instead, don't you?"

"Absolutely, I do," Rowan said absently. She caught Alec's gaze above Molly's head and found it icier than ever.

"Luke," he said, "I need to talk to you about taking some of the pictures of the mining operations aboveground. I trust you more than Dewey to tell me what's what."

Molly headed toward the kitchen door. "Come in here and tell me if you like where I've put the shelves and bins, Rowan. There's not a lot of room in the pantry, but Luke's got ways to fit it all in nice and snug."

Rowan followed, but not without stealing a look at Luke's face. What she saw there pleased her greatly. It also filled her with doubt.

Luke was taken with Molly. She couldn't think of a better match. Alec had seen their feelings, too—it was as clear as day in their faces. And he heartily disapproved of what she, Rowan, was doing.

But she had to marry Luke or lose all.

Chapter Fourteen

Molly never spoke a word about her feelings for Luke, but Rowan could sense that they were growing and strengthening with each passing day. The evenings on Mrs. Grey's front porch were filled with unspoken wants among the three of them. Rowan gathered up her courage at last and walked out to the new house one Saturday afternoon.

As she approached, she saw that Luke had whitewashed the exterior walls and installed clear, sparkling glass panes in the windows. From its crisp gray shingles to its broad front porch, it looked snug and cozy and welcoming.

Rowan hated it already.

She went inside, hoping to see that some of the walls weren't finished or that there was some other big job left to be done. She was disappointed. She went from room to room, noting the neat, simple beauty of the house and seeing Molly's deft hand in the details. Everything was in place except the furniture. She was in the pantry, wondering what all the bins and drawers could possibly be for, when she heard footsteps echoing in the parlor.

"Luke?" she called out. "Molly?"

"Wrong on both counts."

She stepped out of the pantry and saw Alec standing in the doorway to the kitchen. He was bareheaded, and dressed in the corduroy pants and soft muslin shirt he'd worn so often on their trip from San Francisco. The breeze outside had tousled his hair, and she was reminded of that last day on the road, when they'd sat on the edge of the cliff and watched the sun go down. She caught his eyes assessing her, as well, and felt a quick pulse of excitement at the way he seemed to gather in every detail, as if he could see not only her body, but what she was feeling inside, as well.

Unconsciously she took a step toward him. "Are you looking for Luke? I haven't seen him."

"He's gone to pick up a kitchen stove in Nevada City." He gave her another long, measuring glance. "I was looking for you."

She felt another quick pulse. "Why?"

He left the doorway and crossed to the counter. "I want you to answer a question for me."

"I will if I can."

He turned and faced her, challenge in his eyes and in his stance. "What are you intending to do about this marriage of yours to Luke?"

"What do you mean?"

"You know what I mean. Molly's in love with Luke. He feels the same for her. Isn't it time you bowed out?"

Rowan felt the color rush to her cheeks. She avoided his eyes. "I can't," she said at last.

"Can't? Or won't?"

She bristled at his contemptuous tone. "Can't. And won't," she said, meeting his gaze.

He regarded her coolly. "You're quite a piece of work, aren't you? You talk a good game about caring for Molly, but when it comes down to you having to change your precious plans, that's where you draw the line, isn't it?"

"I'm not going to listen to this." She headed for the parlor door.

He caught her and held her before him, his eyes smoldering. "Yes, you are going to listen to this. The way I see it, you have a choice. Either you marry Luke and break two hearts with one blow, or you can call this wedding off and save everyone the grief."

"It's not that simple." She held herself stiffly in his grasp, struggling to maintain her composure under his merciless gaze.

"Really?" He pulled her closer and held her still before him. "And why is that? Don't tell me you've fallen in love with Luke?"

Her eyes flashed defiantly. "Yes, perhaps I have! What business is it of yours?"

He laughed. "You're no good at lying, angel, remember? I've seen you lie before, and I know that you're lying now."

"I don't think so. Luke's a good man. I do love him."

The angry light in his eyes flickered and brightened. He pulled her still closer, his hands clenched about her upper arms. "I say you're lying, and I can prove it."

His voice was lower now, but somehow more powerful, like a lion's roar in the distance.

"I don't believe you." Deep within, she felt a trembling response to his words, and to the tantalizing nearness of his body. "You can't prove anything."

He pulled her into his arms, his voice a dark velvet whisper. "Then I'll just . . . have . . . to show you. . . ."

It was only a kiss. A kiss that started sweetly, achingly, on her lips, and then quickly kindled into something so lush, wild, and searingly hot that it threatened to engulf her whole being. She twisted in his arms, seeking escape, not out of fear or anger, but out of her need to resist the overwhelming desire that rushed in to blot out all other feelings, all other thoughts. Stripped at last of all pretenses and doubts, she clung to him, breathless and shaking, aching to have him love her as he had that magic night in the Sierras.

"You can never lie to me, angel," he whispered against her hair. "You'll never feel this with Luke. He'll never find a way to raise those fires within you." He pulled back and met her eyes. "You're not in love with Luke."

"Perhaps . . ."

"Not perhaps," he said roughly. "Absolutely. Because if you were in love with Luke, you wouldn't feel like this—" he kissed her breathless "—or like this." His hand stroked upward to caress the soft swell of her breast, and she swayed in his arms at the pleasure. "Or this." He lifted her up into his arms, raising her off the floor so that she was fitted completely against him. His kiss was almost savage in its intensity, rousing a fierce, answering need deep within her.

When he finally released her from his embrace, it required the very last ounce of her will to back away from him. She felt bereft inside, but she forced herself to back away and stand upright before him.

Alec glowered at her. "You're determined to do this, aren't you?"

"How can I explain it to you? Things are more complicated than you know." Rowan felt her frustration rising.

"Yes, yes, I've heard the pathetic story before. You're trying to pay back a debt. Well, let's do this then, shall we?" He reached in his pocket and pulled out several gold pieces. "How much do you owe old Henry Syms? A hundred? Two hundred? I'll pay it, and you can call off this nasty little masquerade."

Rowan shook her head. "It won't change anything. In the first place, the amount is far more than you could pay, in a year or more. In the second place, I've signed a contract, and so has Luke. It is binding, believe me. Luke has chosen me for a wife." She lifted her eyes to his. "It's for my family, don't you understand?"

Alec's fist closed around the money. "You'd do anything, and use anyone, to get your own way in this, wouldn't you? You and your family and the holy Trelarken name come before honesty, fairness and friendship."

"Yes!" Rowan cried. "And not you nor anyone else can sway me from my course! I will keep my promise to my family. The name of Trelarken is an honorable one. We pay our debts and keep our word."

She went to the back door and yanked it open, then turned to face him. "Perhaps if you didn't spend all your time hiding behind a camera, life wouldn't seem as simple as you appear to believe. Perhaps then you'd know what it feels like to want to do something for others, for people you love, and to want it so much that it pushes out everything else. But I doubt if that's possible for you. You don't live life, you just take pictures of it! You'd never allow anyone to come close enough for you to care!"

She fled through the door and raced across the meadow. Alec stared at the open doorway for a long moment after she had gone. Then he turned with a curse, walked to the front door, and put his fist straight through it.

That evening, he came to Luke's boardinghouse and handed him several coins. Luke looked at him quizzically.

"You need a new front door," Alec said, and left as quickly as he had come. Before daybreak the next day, he was on his way to San Francisco, hoping that a few days spent in Taggart's congenial company would take his mind off Rowan, and the soul-stealing enchantment of her kisses.

Rowan lay long awake that night, thinking over all that she and Alec had said. Her feelings seesawed between outrage and hurt, ecstasy and irritation. She had said that she wouldn't be swayed, but in truth, she had been. She knew that Luke and Molly were in love, and that her marriage to Luke would destroy both their love and her friendship with Molly. Not to mention black-

ening Alec's regard for her. There was also no denying
the proof of his kisses, and the way her body had
clamored for more of his touch. The night they'd
shared in the mountains had never faded in her memory.

In the wee small hours she concocted a plan, and by
the time the sun had risen she was on her way back out
to the new house. This time, it was Luke in the sunny
little kitchen.

"Luke, I have something that I want to talk to you
about."

He looked up from the chair he was building and
regarded her warily. "Has 'e?"

"Yes, and I'll be Joan-blunt about it, as we say over
home. You love Molly, don't you? And she feels the
same for you?"

He nodded, still wary.

"Then my next question is, why haven't you broken
our engagement and asked her to marry you?"

Luke's eyes widened. "'E's askin' why I haven't
jilted 'e?"

"Yes."

"Well, I—"

"Wait, you don't have to answer. Let's just go on
from here—you love Molly, and not me—"

"And 'e doesn't love me. Truth to tell." His face
held no rancor.

Rowan colored up, but she nodded. "Truth to tell.
But why do you still act as if our marriage is an inevi-
table event?"

Luke put down his rag. He looked like an unprepared schoolboy called on to recite. "Was a time when I wanted nothing but," he said, eyes downcast.

Rowan was startled, but kept silent.

"Over 'ome, when 'e was a girl, 'e was the finest thing I'd ever seen. And good 'e was to me, too, when I come to do errands for 'e's dad, mine errands. I never dreamt of marryin' till I caught word about 'e's dad and all. I wrote Henry and said would he ask for 'e."

"But?" Rowan knew there must be more.

"That were a time or two ago. I wasn't countin' on being made captain at th' Kingsfield and folks lookin' up t'me. I wasn't countin' on waitin' all this time for 'e. I wasn't countin' on 'er."

Rowan's eyes narrowed. "How long ago did you ask Henry to propose?"

"Three, maybe four year now."

Rowan stared at him, stunned. "Three or four years! Luke, Henry only asked me last winter."

Luke blinked. He considered her words for a moment, then nodded slowly. "Henry and 'e's dad."

"What about them?"

"Him and Mister Francis was never friends. Truth to tell, Henry hated him. Fell out over an old wager when they was boys. Always called him His Majesty Trelarken."

"But why would he wait— Oh, my." It was Rowan's turn to fall silent.

"He said 'e was refusin' me on account of 'e was a Trelarken, even though 'e was in hard straits." Luke wrung the rag in his powerful hands. "Henry likes havin' power over folks. Used to say there was only two things worth havin' in this world, money and the power 'e could buy with it. I never could do things his way. Guess I had my pride. This time he's gone a step too far.''

"Oh, Luke, I am so sorry." Rowan's eyes went from sorrowful to snapping in an instant. "He's played us all for fools. And he shan't get away with it."

"But the contract—that's all legal-like. Be hard to break, knowin' Henry."

She paced around the room a few times, as Luke sat and rested his chin in his hands. She came to a halt before him at last, her blue eyes gleaming with purpose. He looked at her as if he were facing a skittish horse. And with good reason.

"Luke Syms," she asked brightly, "how would you like to elope with me tonight?"

Chapter Fifteen

Lowella Tolbathy flapped out a length of calico and yanked on it, testing it for strength. The shopkeeper winced at the sight, but kept silent, as Lowella had the most delicious news she'd heard in an age.

"And you say they went to Sacramento all alone together, and was married by the judge there?"

"That's what they did. They never bothered with church nor chapel, just went and had one of them civil weddings—all in a day. But they wasn't all alone." Lowella wadded the fabric in her hands, checking for wrinkling.

"That photographer fella? The one who brought her here?"

"No, not he. He's been away in San Francisco, I heard tell. 'Twas that friend of hers, the skinny little thing with the baby."

The shopkeeper's eyes widened. "Not the one our Luke's so taken with?"

"The very one. Matron of honor, I heard tell, not that that sort of thing counts for much in a judge's office." Lowella abandoned the stretch of calico and reached for a bolt of muslin. "And they all come home together, smiling."

"If that doesn't beat everything. So, the high-and-mighty Trelarkens get their way again. Couldn't even stand the thought of losing a miner to a little widow woman with a baby."

"Seems like it. But don't it seem queer they went about it so powerful fast? I was sayin' to— Well, if it isn't one of 'em, now," Lowella said, nudging the shopkeeper.

Alec and Daniel Taggart had caused quite a stir as they strolled up the sidewalk together on this sunny afternoon. Whispered discussions followed behind them, along with not a few sighs and admiring stares from the females of Grass Valley. Dark Alec and blond Taggart, two handsome and "foreign" males, were apt to draw attention. And the Syms-Trelarken wedding, and the speculation over Rowan's relationship with her employer, added considerable spice to the whole affair.

"Good afternoon, Mr. MacKenzie," the shopkeeper said, popping to attention behind the counter. "Is there something I can show you today?"

"My friend here is looking for a razor, and some other items." Alec motioned to Taggart, who stepped forward with his most disarming smile and proceeded to charm the shopkeeper into a rosy blush as he made his purchases.

"Good day to 'e, Mr. MacKenzie," Lowella said. "And how was the visit to the big city?"

"Fine, thank you," Alec said with a polite nod.

"Happen 'e'll be the next to tie the knot, I reckon," Lowella said, fingering a length of ribbon. "Perhaps there's a young lady in San Francisco?"

"No, I'm afraid not." Alec started to move away.

"Well, 'e's sure to be drinkin' the health of Mr. and Mrs. Syms, though 'e'll no doubt be sorry to see her leavin' 'e's photograph shop for a housewife. I see the two lovey-birds all over town of late, lookin' like they discovered the secret of life, if 'e take my meanin'. Newlyweds—you know how they are."

Alec froze for a moment, then turned and looked at Lowella with a thin smile. "I'll most certainly drink a toast to them both."

He stood by Taggart while the shopkeeper wrapped up Taggart's purchases. As soon as Taggart was ready, Alec strode out of the store and was gone up the sidewalk toward his studio, with Taggart hurrying along in his wake.

"Do you think he knew?" the shopkeeper asked, chewing her lip.

"I'd say not," Lowella replied. "But it's better he knows right away. Not good to keep bad news away from folks, just on account of they've been away. One shock and it's all over, and that's kindest." She plopped the spool of ribbon down on the counter. "Just a yard of this today, Mariah."

"Alec, old man, you're not making sense."

Taggart followed Alec into the storeroom at the back of the studio and watched as he grabbed boxes and equipment down off the shelves. His face was pinched with rage, and his dark eyes held enough fire within them to set off an explosion in the little room.

"What the hell happened back there? I knew you were in some kind of a foul mood when you showed up at my place last week, but I fancied you were in better spirits this morning. Now what did that old cow say to you?"

"Nothing. I'm just going to do something I should have done a long time ago."

"What's that?"

"I'm going to be the first photographer to go down into a gold mine and take photographs."

"That old bat told you to go take pictures underground?" Taggart crossed his arms and leaned against the doorway as Alec sorted bottles and boxes into a big crate.

"No," Alec said, hefting the box and carrying it into the studio. "But I want it to be the last thing I do before I leave Grass Valley for good. And that," he said, as he went to dismantle his camera and tripod, "is what I'm going to do first thing tomorrow."

That morning, Rowan and Molly had met on the porch of the new house in the faint glow of first light. They'd hugged in silence, exchanging radiant, mirthful smiles, and then Molly had picked up Benjie and hurried off toward town. Every night since the three of them had returned from Sacramento, Rowan and Molly had changed places, coming and going under cover of darkness, so that the real newlyweds could have some time together.

Rowan knocked as she came in the front door. "Luke?" she called softly. "It's Rowan."

"In the kitchen."

She wanted to laugh as she came into the kitchen and saw Luke seated at the table, a lopsided smile lighting his face. Before him was a plate of hotcakes, crowned with melted butter and maple syrup, a steaming mug of tea, and a small plate heaped with crisp bacon. Molly had made him breakfast before she left, knowing that Rowan's culinary powers had yet to reach the point where they could be tried out on others.

"Go ahead and eat," Rowan said, returning his smile. "I'll start the dishes."

When Luke had finished his repast and was looking like a man whose fortune was made, Rowan brought up the subject of their secret.

"So," she said, "we're married, 'officially,' and the town believes we've consummated the marriage. Let's hope that the gossip starts to spread back to Carn Rose as soon as possible."

"Happen the word's flyin' over home this minute. We been makin' plain fools of ourselves before every Jack and Ginny in this place."

Rowan smiled. "I know. You've been so good about this, Luke. I won't forget what you've done for me."

"Oh, no," he said, holding up his hand. "Don't 'e start in with me. I won't be havin' 'e owin' me a debt. Can't afford it. Molly's all to me, and that's enough."

Rowan sighed. "I suppose you're right. I mean well, I truly do, but my plans always seem to come out other side to. But I have faith in this one. Anything that brings you and Molly together, frees my family from debt and saves us both a loveless marriage can't be wrong.''

"What about th' Scotsman?"

"Alec? What about him?"

Luke shook his head. "A pair, the two of 'e. 'E always talkin' and 'im never talkin' and the two of 'e goin' off like a pair of cartwheels every time one of 'e looks the wrong way. Isn't 'e goin' to tell him, then?"

Rowan's shoulders slumped. "I will. But I'm afraid to. I'm afraid he won't—"

"He will."

She looked at him, eyes wide. He nodded. "He will," he said again.

It was late afternoon when Rowan returned to town. As she walked toward Mrs. Grey's house, where she was to meet Molly, she passed the dry goods store. She recalled that Molly had said she needed something called a churn-dasher for the kitchen of the new house, so she went in. The shopkeeper was all smiles and chatter, saying Mrs. Syms this and Mrs. Syms that.

"Making your own butter, are you? I imagine you'll be staying home now and cooking for Luke all the time, instead of working down here in the town," she said, laying out three or four types of dashers for the bewildered Rowan. "When your boss was in here today, it looked like maybe he had him a new assistant."

"He was here today? With a new assistant?" Rowan frowned.

"Oh, yes, just an hour or two ago. Tall and fine-looking fellow, the other one was. Fair hair. And not tight with the purse strings, either, I might add. Maybe he's not an assistant after all, 'cause it sure didn't look like he needed any cash to hand.''

"Perhaps not," Rowan murmured, trying to remain aloof. "I think I'll take that one there," she said, pointing to one dasher at random.

"Very good. I'll wrap it up." The shopkeeper began to bundle up Rowan's purchase. "Yes, your Mr. MacKenzie and his friend could cut quite a wide swath in this little town, if you know what I mean. Especially now that he knows you're taken for good."

Rowan paid and left the store in a daze of delight and apprehension. Alec was back, with Taggart. She could tell him the whole story about her and Luke and Molly's trip, and the wedding charade. But then what? What would he say? Would he care at all that she was free, or be pleased that she had found a plan that would solve so many problems at once?

She hurried up the street to his studio. It was nearing five o'clock, and she knew he always closed the studio at five sharp on Saturdays. She took the steps in a rush. She was baffled when there was no answer to her knock.

She knocked several more times, then gave up. He was probably out somewhere with Taggart, showing him around Grass Valley.

When she returned to the house, Molly greeted her at the door with Benjie in her arms. "How's my fella?" she asked softly as they went upstairs.

"Luke was fine when he went off to work," Rowan said warmly, handing over the churn-dasher. "Full of your good cooking, and smiling like a king."

"I'll be glad when this business is over with and me and Luke and Benjie can be a real family. How long do you think it'll be before they catch on that you and Luke got married?"

"Luke sent telegrams to Henry and to an old friend who isn't at all shy about chattering on at the pub. It was expensive, but I'd guess that half of Carn Rose knows by now, and if I know the way gossip goes there, my marriage to Luke will be a matter of fact within the week. I just hope that Gil can pressure Henry into tearing up the note he holds on my family without having to produce a marriage certificate."

"Won't he be mad when he learns that you and Luke lied?"

"Hopping mad," Rowan said with a laugh. "And more power to him. Once he's torn up the note, there's nothing he can do. Luke and I will announce that we're having our marriage annulled, and that will be the end of it."

Molly shook her head as she dressed Benjie for sleep. "It seems pretty crazy to me, but then, everything always is kinda crazy with you, and you seem to come out all right."

"I hope you're right. I just found out that Alec is back from San Francisco. I'm going to tell him as soon as I can."

Molly gave her a hug. "I know he'll be just as glad as glad can be, sweetie. He can't see the sun for lookin' at you, you know."

Rowan shrugged. "I know that I love him. It's all I can think of. But I'm so afraid that he...that I... Oh, I don't know."

"Love's pretty hard on you both," Molly said with a laugh. "I'll walk over there with you. I got to leave Benjie off with Mrs. Grey's niece so's I can work the dinner shift at Osborn's."

"All right."

They made it a leisurely stroll, as Molly had time before she had to get to work and Rowan was still nervous at the idea of telling Alec about her latest scheme. They left Benjie in good hands and went ahead to the studio in the growing twilight. Rowan turned to Molly and gave her an anxious smile.

"It's gonna be fine," Molly said soothingly. "Just tell him the whole story, and how Luke and me are in on it, and it'll be all right."

Rowan squared her shoulders and marched up the steps to the studio door. She looked down, and Molly gave her a warm wave and a smile from the street below. She knocked and waited. There was no answer. She tried the door. It opened to a silent, darkened room.

"Alec?" she called out. "Taggart? It's Rowan. Are you here?"

No one spoke. Could the shopkeeper have been wrong? Were Alec and Taggart still in San Francisco? But that couldn't be. No one had ever seen Taggart in Grass Valley before, and the woman had described him to a T.

"Alec? Anyone home?" A small needle of worry began to prick at her. She strode forward and lighted the gas lamp over the kitchen area. No one was around. Two cups stood by the sideboard, and a fine-quality leather valise stood by the counter. Taggart's case, she thought. So they both had been here. But where were they now?

You're just being silly, she told herself. Two grown men can certainly go out by themselves. There was no evidence that they were in any kind of trouble.

She lighted a small lamp and carried it into the back. The door to the darkroom was open, and several boxes stood out on the long counter where Alec developed his photographs. She frowned. Two cups out of place, and now developing supplies were sitting out of place. That was most certainly unlike the Alec MacKenzie she knew.

She hurried to the storeroom. Small boxes and some jars stood out on the floor. A canister of some kind of powder had been knocked over. She lifted an empty box and read the label: Magnesium Wire Ribbon.

"Magnesium wire!" she exclaimed. It was used for only one purpose that she knew of. Alec ignited it and used its intense flaring light to illuminate pictures when the available light was at its weakest.

"Oh, dear God," she gasped, and raced for the door.

Down the street she ran, stopping only to dash in, gasp out her suspicions to Molly and fling herself out into the street once more, headed for the Kingsfield Mine. Molly was right behind her, but she veered off and headed for the new house, shouting that she would get Luke to come help.

Rowan arrived at the headframe winded and sidesore from her headlong rush to the site. No one stopped her as she entered the dim, dusty room that echoed with her footsteps.

Rowan prowled around the platform, but there was no sign of anyone about. The silence was more disturbing than any sound. She was about to turn and call out when something by the skip operator's station caught her eye.

"Oh, no!"

"That's Luke's pipe," Molly said, running up beside her, breathless. "He says he always leaves it here when he goes below."

"That's what I thought." Rowan bit her lip. "Luke's down there. And Alec's with him. Molly, what on earth—"

"Hello there, ladies." Taggart came strolling in from the outside, tucking a silver cigar case into the front of his jacket. "Lovely evening, eh?"

Rowan pounced on him. "How could you let him go down there? Do you have any idea how dangerous it is? Do you know what he's going to do? Taggart, why? Why did he do it?"

Taggart raised his hands reassuringly. "It's all right. That miner fellow, Luke Syms, is down there with him. I admit I was worried at first, especially after he heard about you and your recent nuptials, but he seemed to calm down when he got here and your Luke showed up."

"He heard about the wedding and then he decided to go down there?" Rowan covered her face with her hands and turned to Molly. "Oh, no, I can't believe it. It's the Luck again. I try to do something right, and it all goes wrong. Molly, I'm so sorry."

"Hush, now," Molly said. "Luke's down there with him, and Luke knows rock, as all you Cornish say around here. He'll tell Alec the truth, and he'll take care of them both.''

"Do you think so?"

"The truth?" asked Taggart.

"Luke and Rowan didn't get married. Luke and me did. But we made it look like they did so's they can get Luke's brother to let Rowan out of her debt back home in England," Molly explained hastily.

"Somewhere in there is something that makes sense, but I can't quite put my finger on it," Taggart mused. "But you're right, Mrs. Syms—Alec is safe down there with your husband. I can sense these things. Though Alec didn't look exactly pleased to see him when he showed up."

"Why did Luke let him go down? They don't have permission, do they?" Rowan glanced at the dark mouth of the tunnel and shuddered.

"Oh, yes," Taggart said. "He talked to some of the bigwigs down in the city, and they gave him the go-ahead. I didn't expect him to go at it right away, but I guess he had the urge all of a sudden."

Rowan paced to the edge of the platform, straining to see into the blackness beyond, trying to take it all in. Alec was down there. He was angry, and he was with Luke. Would he take his anger out on Luke? Would he even listen to Luke's story, and if he did, would he believe it? Would he care?

She closed her eyes and willed her shivering body to calm itself. There was nothing to do but wait and make sure that he heard all the truth from all three of them when he came up. They'd make him see that her plan was for the best—

The earth began to quiver beneath her feet. She heard Molly cry out, and turned to look behind her. The vibrations increased, and dust began to shake down around them. Then it came: a huge, rumbling tremor that jolted the platform, and the very beams that held it. A few seconds later, a great wind blew up and out of the tunnel, a storm of black dust and debris that looked like the belching of hellfire to the frightened Rowan. The noise arrived with the cloud of dirt, a deep and mighty roaring far below.

The planks of the platform were dancing beneath her feet, but Rowan had no thought for that now. On the echoes of Molly's shriek of terror, she rushed for the great bell rope that hung down from the tower of the headframe. She gave a pull on it that might have yanked it from its moorings had it not been securely anchored. She pulled and pulled and pulled on the rope, ringing hand over hand, mindlessly sounding the alarm that rang out over the valley and signaled disaster at the Kingsfield.

And still more dust was blowing up from the shaft, and the awful rumbling went on and on.

Chapter Sixteen

Rowan felt the minutes crawl by, each one lasting at least an hour, as the whole of Grass Valley labored to clear away the rock and dust and timbers that filled the tunnel. Miners from all over the valley had answered the ringing of the bell, and they spelled each other at the digging. The men from Luke's shift were always at the front of the line. Slowly they cleared the rubble that had shaken loose along the level entry of the main tunnel.

"John Samuel," she said, catching his sleeve as he went to take a dipperful of water. "How bad is it? Can you get through to them?"

"I'm not sure, missus. Looks like the main's just dusted, no real damage. But what's below—that's anybody's guess." He wiped the sweat off his brow with a red kerchief. "But don't 'e fret about it. Our Luke knows rock, and he's got as many lives as a cat. The Tommyknockers'll be lookin' after he."

"Can you get a skip down?" Molly asked.

"Happen we might. Not all the way, likely, and we'll have to see what timbers could be rotten from the blast. But we'll be doin' all we can, I promise."

"I know you will." Rowan touched his arm. "Thank you, John."

"Anything for a Cousin," he said, flashing her a bright grin from out of his sooty face. "And anything for Luke. The fella's stone brave, I tell 'e and every one of us owes him."

The men in the lead had disappeared down the passage at last, the clanging of their shovels and the thudding of their pickaxes growing fainter as they progressed below. Molly put her arm around Rowan's waist.

"I can't bear it," she murmured to Molly. "It's too dark and lonely down there."

"Hush," Molly said. "They have each other. They're not alone."

"I hope so."

Rowan grew more restless as the work dragged on. She paced away from the group and then back, away, then back. The waiting wore on her nerves like a rasp, making her jumpy and anxious. She could concentrate only on one thought, and that was that Alec was trapped deep in the silent, cold ground. It wound through her head in an endless circle, always bringing her back to one fearful image of his still, pale face.

She had to do something. She didn't care what.

Her opportunity came an hour later. One of the men from Luke's shift had gathered a group of boys around him, and Rowan paused at the edge of their circle to hear what he was saying.

"The passage ends at six hundred. That's as far as skip'll take 'e. When 'e gets there, 'e'll need light, a shovel, and a pick. Anything starts to slide, 'e scut out'n there right smart. Understand?"

There were nods all around. "Now then. Which of 'e is it going t'be? Must be one of th' smaller lads, as it gets tight besides, down there."

Several hands went up. Rowan bit her lip. They were sending children down into that dreadful hole? She shuddered at the thought.

"Good then, John Wesley, 'e can be lead man. Tom Polvethy, 'e can go behind. Just two—that's all we can spare of 'e just now." There was some grumbling but the boys seemed to accept the decision without question. "Good lads. Now, Tom and John, 'e's been below grass for a year or two now. 'E knows what to expect. No larkin' about, eh? Wait back there, out th' way, till I give the signal."

The crowd of boys scattered as the man left to confer with the others on the front line. Rowan moved quietly out of her hiding spot and slipped in behind young Tom, intent upon following her new plan.

Alec raised his head and spat dust. He blinked and nearly panicked, for he was surrounded by a darkness so profound it seemed to be tangible, something that pressed against his eyes as he strained to see into it. He passed a hand before his face. A piece of the darkness went even darker, if that was possible. Then he knew: he wasn't blind, he was in the Number 7 mine at the Kingsfield. And he was alive.

Where was Luke? The meaning of the darkness and the ringing in his ears came to him in a rush. Luke had been talking to him, telling him about Rowan's mad marriage scheme. There had been a rumbling, an explosion, and then—the blackness. But Luke had been at his side when everything blew. He should be here, too.

"Luke?" he croaked, dust still choking in his throat. "Luke, are you there?"

Silence.

"Damn!" Alec whispered. He pulled himself up into a sitting position. He managed to get an extra candle out of his pocket, and when he lighted it a blessed ring of light opened up around him, pushing the solid dark away. The air was still full of falling dust, so thick the place looked smoky. His eye was drawn to the area on his left. There was a more irregular pile there, and he felt a prickling at the back of his neck as he guessed at what could be beneath it.

He crawled to the pile and brushed away some of the rocks. A boot appeared.

"God help me," he said, teeth clenched. He moved to the other end and scrabbled away at the debris. Luke's face, gray with dust, appeared at once. Alec felt for a pulse at his throat, and found one, faint and slow. He doubled his efforts, and soon had Luke's torso dug out from under the pile.

Alec listened for a breath, then slapped him lightly on each cheek. He got behind him and began to lift his shoulders. Breath hissed through Luke's teeth, and he stiffened in Alec's grasp.

"Luke!" Alec cried, shaking him. "Talk to me, man."

Luke stiffened again. "L-l-leg . . ." he gasped out.

"Hold still." Alec lowered his shoulders as gently as possible and went around to dig out the lower half of Luke's body. He swore under his breath when he saw the awkward angle at which the left leg lay.

"It's a break," he told Luke. "Not a pretty one, but not a bloody one, either. Can you feel anything else? Anything else hurt?"

"Pride."

Alec grinned briefly. "I know what you mean. But we're not licked yet." He glanced around the "cave," then back at Luke. "I did some medic work in the war. I'm going to try and splint your leg, to keep it still until we can get out of here."

"Got to start diggin'. Only hope." Luke tried to struggle up, shuddered, and fell back.

"Don't move. First things first. You'll only hurt that leg more if you try to shift on it. Let me get the splint on it, then I'll start digging."

"Scotsman, 'e's got to dig now."

"Not until—"

"Dig, man!" Luke's voice was strained with the effort to speak over his pain. "Air won't last."

Alec paused. He hadn't thought of that, but of course there were no outlets or inlets to this little chamber of theirs. In time, they would use up all the available air. Even the precious light of the candle was eating up their supply. But Luke would be in greater agony, and in danger of losing his leg to a doctor's saw, if it wasn't held firmly in place to avoid new injuries.

"I'm almost ready," he told Luke. "I'll slap these boards on you, and then I'll start digging."

"'E's stubborn as she."

Alec moved to Luke's leg. "This is going to hurt like hell. Howl all you want—any man would. I'll be as quick as I can." He cleared away more of the rubble around the injured leg. "Stubborn as who?"

"Rowan— Ah, damn!" Luke sucked in his breath as Alec touched the leg.

"Don't try to talk—just yell if you need to."

Working as quickly and carefully as he could, Alec got the leg splinted and bound with his own torn shirt-sleeves. He knotted the bindings tight and sat back to look at Luke. "You all right?" he asked. Livid white patches showed through the dirt on Luke's face.

"Dig."

Alec moved to the pile that he guessed blocked the passage to the skip car rails. He raised the candle and saw that the pile of rocks, timbers and other debris reached up to what was left of the ceiling. He jammed two stout pieces of wood under his belt to use as shovels and tucked the drill bit into his shirt pocket. He stuck the toe of his boot into the foot of the pile, wedged it in firmly, then proceeded up the slope. He climbed for a yard or so, until his head was up near the ceiling.

"Can 'e hear aught?" Luke asked, his voice tight against his pain.

"Nothing. But I think I should start digging here. That way, the whole pile is less likely to come down on top of us."

"Eh, Scotsman, 'e's beginnin'... to know rock."

"I'm going to blow out the candle," he called to Luke. "I want to save the light."

"Aye."

Alec carefully studied the pattern of the rocks before him, and then, taking a deep breath, he blew out the light. He blessed his photographer's visual memory, which allowed him to recall the finest details of a scene. Working with the image in his mind, he began to dig.

Rowan crawled along the rock pile behind John Wesley, pausing only to push back her hat so that the candle would stand upright. They traveled that way for several yards, and then John halted.

"It's dropped off here," he called back to her. "We'll have to climb down."

"Is it a long drop?" she asked.

John whirled around as fast as he could on his hands and knees. "What the—? Where's Tom?"

"He's back at the platform. My name is Rowan, and I'm going with you."

"Oh, no, lady, 'e mustn't do it! It's bad luck! This be too dangerous a place for wimmin."

Rowan darted out and stopped him before he could head past her toward the main shaft. "I'm as hale and strong as you, and if you go back now, you'll only be robbing those men down there of precious time. We've come too far to turn back now." She stared at him intently. "I'm Cornwall born. My family owned Wheal Carn. Rock's in my blood, too."

"But I—"

"I'll take all the responsibility," she said firmly. "Now let's get down there and find those men. Their very lives depend on us."

The boy looked torn. This was clearly not something he had counted on when he had taken the job of going down.

"Eh, lad," Rowan chided him softly. "You know what they say over home. *Nyel jy dha gregy*—they can't hang us. Doesn't 'e want to do somethin' rare?" She flashed him a beguiling grin.

He looked worried, but then a bit of a grin began to play at the corners of his mouth. "'E's right—they can't hang us."

"Then let's move."

They clambered over the rocks and dropped to the floor of the original passage. They could feel some sort of worn path beneath their feet in places, and could almost stand upright. Rowan felt some relief in this more open stretch, but it wasn't long before they came to another pile blocking their way. They wetted their handkerchiefs with the water in John Wesley's flask and tied them over their mouths, to keep out the dust. Then they set to work digging out with their small shovels.

It felt good to work, Rowan thought. It made the dark less fearsome, and the nearness of the walls less oppressive. She kept her mind trained on Alec, and followed John's lead. Soon they were crawling and digging their way through the pile, wondering if the mass would ever end.

* * *

Taggart stretched upward and scanned the crowd.

"Do you see her?" Molly asked, tugging at his elbow.

"I'm afraid not." Taggart's brow was furrowed as he met Molly's gaze. "Where might she have gone?"

Molly shook her head, not wanting to say what she suspected. What she suspected was impossible, insane. And yet, when had she ever known Rowan to take the safe or sane route in any matter?

"Maybe she went to see Dewey, the manager," she said, moving toward the back of the room. "She must have felt she had to do something."

Taggart shook his head and guided her toward the alcove by the bells. "I don't think she'd leave the site, knowing that Alec's down— What is it?" he asked when Molly gave a faint shriek.

Molly bent down and came up with a handful of glossy deep red hair. Taggart stared at it in shock.

"Good God, who would have done a thing like that to her?" he sputtered. "This isn't some Indian camp out on the plains!"

"Nobody did it to her." Molly's voice was flat.

"You think she did it to herself? But why—? Oh, no. No, you don't mean you think that Rowan is—?"

"I know she is," she said slowly, pointing to a huddled figure trying to scrunch deeper into the shadows. "Come here, boy."

"Can't," a muffled voice said.

"Why not?"

There was a long pause. "Don't have no clothes on."

"You don't know how sorry I am to hear that," Molly said. She looked up at Taggart, her eyes wide and dark with new fear. "She's down there, Mr. Taggart. They're all down there now."

Rowan and John Wesley had come to a fork in their road. At seven hundred feet, the tunnel plainly branched off in two directions, but it was anyone's guess as to which direction Alec and Luke had chosen.

"Let's not waste time," Rowan said. "You go left and I'll go right. We'll go just until we're out of earshot. If we haven't found anything by then, I'll come to you and we'll work that way until we break through. All right?" He nodded. She took a deep breath as she stood before him, hands on her hips. "Ready?"

"As ready as ready," he replied. "Let's go."

They paced away in opposite directions. Every few yards, one of them would turn and shout down the passage, wait for the echoes to die away, and then listen for an answering shout.

Rowan trudged on, sending her mind out toward Alec, wherever he was at this moment. He couldn't be dead, she thought. She would know if he was dead, and she could still feel his presence, somehow, could still conjure up his voice and his image in her mind.

She longed to be in his arms right now, and to shut out the world of dangers and heartbreaks and compromises. She wanted to feel that perfect, elemental sensation of his skin on hers, that feeling that made all others seem small and unimportant. It had been such a short time, really, since he had found her in San Francisco, and yet it seemed a lifetime. They'd traveled together, fought, struggled, laughed, talked, and made fiery, soul-touching love.

"Oy!"

John's faint shout woke her from her reverie. She turned and shouted back down the tunnel. "Here!"

She resumed her trek. The debris was piling higher now, rising as she proceeded. John's voice floated to her, and she shouted back with all her lungpower. She knew she should start back, but something was nagging at her. There was still more of this passage ahead, and she found it an irresistible lure.

Soon she was climbing on piles of rock mounded almost to the tunnel's ceiling. She reached the end of the space, gave a long shout behind her, and waited to hear John's reply.

Nothing but silence filled the tunnel. It pressed around her ears as she strained to hear a far-off voice. Suddenly, into the silence, there came a tapping sound.

She froze. It was like a distant hammer, she decided, working on rock somewhere beyond—or inside—these walls. It was not coming from the rockpile in front of her. It was beside her.

The skin at the nape of her neck tingled. It was an eerie sound, like no other she'd ever heard. Rhythmical, ringing, steady, it made her think of granite caverns and fine metal hammers wielded by wizened hands.

"John?" she shouted, wincing at the sudden force of her own voice in that darkened space. "Is that you?"

There was no reply. The tapping went on.

"Alec? Luke?"

Silence was her answer. Then she gasped. "Tommy-knockers!"

John Samuel's words came rushing back. Tommy-knockers were said to live in the depths of every mine, and their tappings could lead men to treasures, or to folly and death. Every good Cornish miner respected their powers.

Well, she'd respect them, too. But would they lead her to treasure or folly?

Alec punched through the top of the pile and wriggled out, his broad shoulders scraping against the rough timber above him. He slid down the other side and struck a light to see what lay before him.

More rocks.

He sat down for a moment and rested his head against the outer wall. His mouth felt as if it were lined with wool, and his eyes burned with the soot and grime that flew everywhere when he dug. He was sweating from his efforts, his bare chest and back were scratched and bruised, and his hands and nails were torn from the jagged edges of the rocks he'd had to move.

He had no way of telling how far he'd come. But he knew he had far to go.

He rose and found his next target, pinched out his candle, and started to dig once more. The thought of Luke lying in the dust behind him, and of Molly, who waited above, spurred him on. He hoped Taggart was with her. And Rowan.

Powerful feelings suddenly rushed in to fill his chest. God, he needed her. He wanted her. But after all the harsh things he'd said to her, and the way he'd pushed her away so many times, did she want him?

He tried to imagine her waiting at the platform above. If she was, she wouldn't be able to keep still, he knew. She'd be pacing up and down, pestering the men....

Pestering the men to let her go down below. The idea entered his head like a bolt of lightning. Rowan wouldn't wait. Not his Rowan, not the woman who'd attacked a "wolf" with a butter knife, and driven his wagon across a flooded stream, and taken it upon herself to sail halfway around the world for the sake of the people she loved. His Rowan would have concocted one of her famous plans. His Rowan would be down here, in the mine, searching for him and Luke.

The idea of her lost beneath the earth made him go a little mad. He began to tear at the rocks around him, burrowing ahead with his powerful arms and shoulders. He had to get to her. He had to have her safe within his arms.

Rowan was tunneling ahead with the single-mindedness of a badger trying to escape a bear. She'd forgotten about the signals to John Wesley—had forgotten John Wesley, truth to tell. Every so often she would pause, lift her head, and listen for the tappings. And always they were just ahead, as if someone were leading her on from a vantage point on the other side of the wall.

Then there came a thud.

She stopped so quickly that she lost her balance and tipped over onto one shoulder. She rolled up and listened again.

Another thud, and a scrabbling sound. Not from the side walls, this time. From straight ahead.

She dived into the rocks, too frantic to stop for her shovel. Rocks flew out behind her, and she was panting with the fever of her efforts.

The sounds came closer. Tears welled in her eyes, and she rubbed them off hurriedly on her shoulders. She wriggled forward on her stomach, clearing a narrower hole in order to push ahead faster.

There was a shout—faint, far off, and muffled, but human!

"Alec!" she croaked, her mouth and throat choked with dust. She pulled down her mask, swallowed convulsively and tried again. "Alec!"

The sounds of rocks moving on the other side was becoming clearer. She redoubled her efforts, almost tearing the tips from the fingers of her gloves with the fury of her digging. She reached out again and again, until at last she grasped at a rock and it fell through to the other side.

"Alec," she gasped. "Alec!"

Sobbing, she thrust her hand through the opening. Strong fingers grasped hers and held them as if this were the last human touch they would ever feel.

Chapter Seventeen

Their first kiss was like the first sip of water after an agelong thirst. Alec vaulted through the opening they'd made and caught her to him in a crushing embrace.

"God, angel, I can't believe it's you," Alec groaned against her lips. "I thought I was losing my mind when I heard your voice."

"I had to come," she gasped. "Had to get to you. Your signals led me here. Where's Luke?"

"You should have waited with the others," he said, raining more kisses on her dusty face. "We have to go back and get Luke. What signals?"

"The tappings," she managed, when she could draw a breath. "I heard you tapping on the walls all the way along here. I knew it was you."

"I don't recall— Angel! What's happened to your hair?"

His hands had come up to her head and knocked off the cap she wore. He frantically traced the soft, curling locks that ended so abruptly in blunt, jagged ends.

"I knew they wouldn't let me go down. I had to disguise myself as a boy. Tom Polvethy traded places with me. There was too much of it to fit, so I cut it off with Tom's penknife.'' Rowan wrapped her arms about his neck once more and began to kiss him.

Alec pulled her arms down to her sides. "You did what?"

"I traded places with Tom Polvethy so that I could come down and look for you. I had to cut my hair off, because it wouldn't fit under his cap.'' She reached for him again.

"God in heaven, woman, you are the most exasperating, foolhardy, single-minded—'' Words failed him and he grabbed her to him and kissed her again, hard, and though she tried to protest and to defend her behavior, he wouldn't let her speak until he had poured out all the anguish and fear and love he felt filling his chest.

When he could think again, he loosened his embrace and sagged back on his heels. Rowan, her head spinning with the intensity of his kisses, leaned forward to rest her head against his bare shoulder.

"I love you," she whispered. "I had to come."

His hand caressed the line of her neck. "I know, angel. I love you, too."

"Luke!" she exclaimed, coming to attention. "Is he all right?"

"Yes. At least I think so. He broke his leg in the cave-in. I splinted it up, but he was unconscious when I left him to get help. How far is it up to the entrance?"

"Hmm... about six hundred feet," she said.

"Six hundred—?" Alec shook his head in shock.

"It's not far back to where I left John Wesley—John Wesley!" she gasped. Her hand flew to her cheek. "I was supposed to stay within calling distance. But I heard the tappings, and I just had to go on.... Alec, did Luke tell you the truth about the marriage?"

"Let's get going," Alec said, blowing out his candle. "We'll talk about it later." He took Rowan's candle from where she'd stuck it in a pocket of clay in the side wall. "Ready?"

"Yes," she said slowly, reaching for the candle.

"Do you have any more of these?"

"One, I think." She put her hand on it, but Alec held it firmly.

"I think it'll be better if we save them," he said. "There weren't any cave-ins behind you as you dug through, were there?"

"Not—not that I heard." She swallowed hard, her eyes trained on the candle.

"Then it should be a straight shot to where you left young John, right?" He didn't wait for her reply. "We can find our way back without this."

Rowan flinched as the light vanished. Alec reached for her and gathered her into his embrace. For a moment, the tight little lump of fear in her stomach loosened and quieted.

"I love you, angel," he said fiercely. "I never want to lose you." He kissed her with swift efficiency, and then began to move past her. "I'll lead off. Call out if you want me to stop."

The relief of finding Alec had freed her mind of concern for him and, somewhat, for Luke. Now she could recall another, older fear that was just as daunting. She was underground, in utter darkness, shut off from air and light and hope.

Get hold of yourself, she thought, going to her hands and knees once more. Alec was here with her, and they were on their way out. John Wesley would be waiting with more candles at the end of this passage. She could make it that far, surely. Think of Luke, she told herself. Think of Molly—and how frantic she, Rowan, would be, if she were the one waiting back at the platform.

"I'm going to have to widen the passage," Alec said over his shoulder. She hung on the sound of his voice, feeling it was her only link to calm and sanity. "It's a tight fit for me, and we'll need more room to get Luke out," he continued. "Might as well start now. I'm going to light the candle again."

Rowan felt her own spirit come alight again with the wavering flame. It shamed her to be so fearful, but she found the feeling was impossible to shake. She wondered at how she'd managed to come so far in this place, candle or no candle.

They worked quickly and presently began to hear a change in the sounds ahead of them. They soon tumbled out into the open space, calling excitedly.

"John!" Rowan shouted down the opposite passage. "John, I've found them!"

Alec called down the main passage. "John Wesley! Shout if you can hear us!"

There was no answer, only the mocking echoes of their own voices. Rowan looked to Alec in alarm.

"He was to go down the other passage," she said. "I went down the other. We were supposed to stay within earshot. But when I heard you tapping, I just went on. I didn't even stop to think— Oh, Alec, you don't think something's happened to him? He's just a boy...."

"No," Alec said decisively. "No, I don't think anything's happened to him. Look here."

He strode to the opening of the opposite passage, bent, and picked up something. He held out his hands to Rowan.

"Two candles!" she exclaimed. "He left his extra candles. But what makes you think—?"

"They were arranged in a neat line, right where you'd see them when you came out again. Which makes me think that he came out, couldn't raise you, and decided to go back for help. He left the candles for you to find, just in case you returned."

Rowan raised dark, worried eyes to his. "Do you really think so?" she asked, her voice tight with feeling. "If anything happened to him, it's my fault. I should have—"

"Should have left Luke and me trapped down here?" Alec put down the candles and took her into his arms. "Angel, I wasn't even sure that I was headed in the right direction until I heard you. John is a good lad, I've seen him working with Luke and John Samuel. The first thing they teach these boys is to use good sense—otherwise, they couldn't depend on each other down here."

"Good sense," Rowan moaned. "Where was mine?"

He gave her a gentle shake, and then he grinned. "You're Rowan Trelarken. You don't need good sense, remember? You've got the Trelarken Luck."

She raised her face to his, shocked at his levity in this awful place. He shook his head. "You're a wonder," he mused. "You risk your neck to crawl down here in this bloody hole, and, miracle of miracles, you find me—and all you can do is blame yourself for not looking out for yet another soul you've taken under your wing." He kissed her eyelids solemnly. "I've never seen your like for loving, angel. And while your methods could be a wee tad less dangerous, I hope you never change."

Rowan drank in his words and felt them soothe her heart like a balm. He had never said such things to her before. He'd always raved about her impetuosity and her insistence on carrying out her plans, regardless of the cost. She liked what she saw in his eyes now. She raised up on tiptoe to place a kiss on his lips, a kiss that spoke of love, and gratitude, and renewed faith.

"We'd better get on with it," he said at last, pulling away gently.

"If John Wesley went back to the mine entrance," Rowan said, brightening suddenly, "then more of the men could be on their way back here right now! Alec, do you think Luke can hold on until we get there?"

"I don't know," Alec replied. "But he's not going to disappoint Molly, not if he can help it."

They went on for some time, going slower now that Rowan was only working with one hand. The candle was burning low and she felt the sick feeling in her stomach return.

"Hand me another candle," she called forward, pleased that she sounded less shaky this time.

Alec paused and wrangled into his pocket. He searched the other one. Rowan felt a shiver course down her back, anticipating what he would say next. "I don't have one. That's it."

"But you must," she said quickly. "You have to. John Wesley left us two more! That's nearly ten hours of light!"

"I'm sorry," he said. "I must have left them back at the fork in the tunnel."

Rowan felt tears welling up in her throat. No! It couldn't be happening! Finally, the truth burst out of her. "I can't go on," she blurted.

Alec swung around to stare at her.

"I can't go on," she repeated miserably. "I can't get enough air. The walls...the walls are shrinking. I can't stand the darkness. I don't know how I made it this far. Alec, I'm too frightened to move!" Her voice sank to a choking whisper.

Alec took the candle stub from her and pulled her into his arms. "Shh," he murmured soothingly. "It'll be all right, m'lass. I'll get us out of here."

"No, you don't understand!" she cried. "I can't stand it! I can't stand this place— I can't stand any-place that's dark and close like this. I have to get out, Alec, I have to get out right now!"

She struggled to rise, arms and hands flailing. He could feel the shaking, wire-tense muscles of her body as he held her gently against him, and he suddenly understood the full meaning of her words. He'd heard of people who lived in dread of being enclosed in a small space, but he'd never seen someone suffer that dread before his eyes. Rowan was desperate to get out, and yet too terrified to move. It pained his heart to see it. She had come down into this place to find him and Luke, despite this horrible fear. And now she was the one in need.

"Shh," he whispered. "Be calm, angel, and let me think a minute."

"Alec. I can't—"

"Yes, you can," he told her. "We'll take it one step at a time." He kissed her softly and let her feel the warmth and strength of his arms around her. "See," he said. "I'm here. I'm here, and I'm not going to leave you. You're not alone."

The candle guttered out in his hand. Rowan buried her face in his shoulder and let out a great, wracking sob. Alec tossed away the bit of wax and hugged her close. She was breathing in shallow, panting breaths.

"Now," he said, releasing her. "I'm going ahead a few feet. You come as far as you can, and then we'll stop. Understand?"

"Alec, I'm sorry, I don't mean to be such a coward—"

"I don't have time to listen to that kind of rubbish," he said firmly. "You can do this, Rowan. I know you can. Just a few feet, and then we'll stop."

Rowan gasped for air as he moved away from her. Without his strong, reassuring touch, she felt more of the fear creep in.

"Come on, angel," Alec said. His voice went velvet-soft and deep, the way it did when he took her in his arms and loved her. "Come with me. I need you."

She got to her hands and knees, all of them bruised and sore. She reached out and felt Alec's leg in front of her. He was near, near enough to touch. Then he moved away. She surged after him in panic.

"That's m'lass," he said over his shoulder. *"Trob-had, ionmhuinn."*

"What . . . does that . . . mean?" she managed to say between gasps for air.

"'Come with me, beloved.' It's Gaelic." His voice was richer and darker than the darkness around her. His words reached through the choking fog of her fear, and allowed her to come forward a few more steps.

"There," he said quickly. "Now let me hold you."

She collapsed against his chest, and shivered there in his arms. He smoothed her choppy hair and kissed her, and at last she snuggled a little against the bare heat of him.

"Mmm, so nice," he murmured. "Now a few more steps, all right?"

She protested when he pulled away, but again he let her feel that he was right there before her. Then he moved off.

On they went, making slow, small progress through the narrow passage. Alec showered her with praise each time she completed a segment of the journey, and his kisses and caresses were like soothing, warming honey poured over her tattered, terrified spirit. As he moved ahead, he coaxed her toward him with endearments in English, Gaelic, and even broken schoolboy French, promising delightful, intimate pleasures when they touched again.

She was still cold with fear, and shaking, but she was moving, and she clung to that knowledge with all her mind. She began to look forward to Alec's arousing, yet comforting, "rewards" at the end of each leg. His velvety voice became her beacon, and she was drawn forward on the strength of its lure.

At long last, they reached the end of that long stretch and stepped out into open space once more. Alec helped her to stand, and she wrapped herself around him, drawing still more strength from his powerful, rock-solid form.

"You were wonderful," he said against her temple. "You are so brave."

"I'm not," she said, shaking her head where it rested on his shoulder.

"You are," he said. "And I suspect that you're making me say and do all these wonderful things to you just so that you can have your way with me."

"I am not!" she gasped.

"Oh, no?" He pressed her bottom softly, bringing her hips even closer to his. "And what does that say to you, miss?"

She felt the hard truth of his arousal, and gave a soft chuckle. She rubbed herself against him, feeling deep wonder at the relief that such a simple, animal pleasure could bring. "Hmm," she murmured. "Perhaps there is something in what you say."

"Witch. Wanton. You can't have me until we're in my bed."

They were locked in each other's arms when a scrabbling came from the other side of the tunnel. John Samuel stepped over the edge into the passage and lifted his lantern to see the two startled lovers freeze in its light.

Rowan felt herself coloring up as she and Alec jumped apart. What must John Samuel be thinking of her, to find her, Luke's wife, in the arms of another man! They both began to speak at once.

"Luke's still down there—" Rowan began.

"I can show you where he is," Alec interjected.

"We ran out of candles. Is John Wesley all right—?"

"The explosion caught us at the—"

The other men began to pour through from the entrance. Alec and Rowan started to repeat their story as the men pressed in with questions.

"Hold, hold!" John Samuel said, waving his hand. There was silence. "First, Scotsman, 'e just tell us how to find our Luke, and we'll nip right down and bring him up."

Alec did so. John then turned to Rowan. "And 'e, 'Tom Polvethy,' what's 'e got to say to us?"

Rowan blushed furiously, then caught the twinkle in John's eyes. "I heard talk about this wedding for days now, and it didn't ring true t'me," he went on. "But I know our Luke, and I know a Cousin in love. Happen we've not heard the end of all this, leastways not according to Emily Trethewey down to the post office. You got letters waitin' on you from over 'ome, missus."

Rowan sagged with wonder and relief. The gossips in Grass Valley and Carn Rose were truly artists at their craft. But there were more pressing matters at hand than saving face. "You can find Luke by following the tappings," she told him solemnly. "The Tommyknockers will lead you to him. Just as they led me to Alec."

"'E's a rare 'un, missus—er, miss," John said, wonderingly. "We always said wimmin was bad luck below grass. But 'e's brought the luck down with 'e, it seems."

Alec and Rowan looked at each other and began to laugh.

"Well, now. 'E's got friends above, waitin' on 'e, and I daresay 'e wants a bite of croust and a dipper or two. We got the skip not far up from here. 'E knows the way out, I believe, Cousin?" John said, grinning at Rowan once more.

She crossed her arms across her chest, chin raised in pride. "Eh, lad, I could find it blindfolded."

The men went off laughing, with instructions from Alec about handling Luke's splinted leg. They left candles and matches with Rowan to light the way up.

She was looking down at them when Alec returned from guiding the men out of the chamber, carrying a lighted candle of his own.

"Shall we go?" he asked.

"I was thinking," she said slowly, her lips curving up into a small, mischievous smile.

"Yes?" he drawled.

She leaned forward and blew out his candle.

"What's this?" he asked cautiously.

"I like the way you light up the passage better."

"Temptress."

She slipped a hand up over his belly and sank her fingers into the crisp thatch of his chest hair. "I would be very good," she murmured. "I'd stop just as soon as you said."

"Would you indeed?" He caught his breath as her lips nibbled at his neck. "I'm not sure I'd like that at all...." He began to return her attentions with surprising energy.

"Alec!" His name slipped out on a delighted breath.

As it turned out, their idyll was interrupted by the sounds of more men coming through. Alec lighted a candle, smiling at Rowan in its light. They hurried up to the skip and rode on into the waiting arms of Molly, Taggart, and many others.

Most of the miners' wives were there by now, and they brought Rowan and Alec hot food and coffee, and blankets to wrap around them as they sat down with Molly and Taggart to wait for Luke. The looks they cast on the friends were openly curious, but as Rowan clasped Molly's hand and Alec reassured her again and again that Luke was fine, they shrugged at one another in wonder and amusement. Rowan caught their glances and was reminded of what Melissa Davies had said to her in Sacramento—when it came down to it, people in the West helped one another all they could, for you never knew when you were going to be the one needing help. No matter how peculiar your circumstances might look to be.

Molly's face stayed gray and pinched until the shouts from the tunnel announced the safe return of "our Luke." Then she raced for the platform and shoved everyone aside to reach him. Luke was conscious, but weak and exhausted, and still in great pain. All the same, he raised his hand to Molly's cheek and smiled when she leaned over him, laughing and crying and scolding.

She took charge of his removal to the doctor's office, ordering the big, gruff miners about with an air worthy of a general. Rowan and Alec watched with fond amusement as they left, and then turned to pour out their thanks to John Samuel, and all the others who had helped them. Their thanks were waved away.

"'Tes only what any one of us'd do for the other," John said, gratefully accepting the cup of hot tea Rowan pressed into his hand. "Th' bells ring, no man asks who's below or why."

"But it was our Luke," Rowan said softly.

John's face grew more serious. "That it was, true enough. And we's grateful to 'e for leadin' the way. 'E and th' Tommyknockers, that is."

Her eyes went wide. "You heard it, then?"

He nodded with utter solemnity. "Clear as clear they was knockin', too, all the way. How they got here from over home is one too many for me, but I guess they got their ways."

Taggart swept his arms around Rowan and Alec and leaned in between them. "Let's go home," he said. "You people need your rest and—I must say it—a long, hot bath. And I need a vital infusion of champagne."

The sun was almost blinding when Rowan stepped outside into the blessed air. Weariness flooded her, body and spirit, and she staggered against Alec's shoulder. He picked her up without a word and carried her to the waiting wagon. She barely heard the conversation as they made their way down the hill to town.

"A commission arrived from Lieutenant Parker to do a geological expedition...." she heard Alec say softly to Taggart.

"Maybe it is better that way, MacKenzie. She's going to want to go home to her mother and brother, but..."

"All the same, it'll be best for Rowan," Alec was saying stubbornly. "It'll be best for all..."

Chapter Eighteen

Taggart insisted that Rowan take a suite at the small hotel, and she was too sleepy to argue as she tumbled out of the wagon on Alec's arm. She woke the following day with every fiber in her body screaming for revenge, and was only too happy to accept the services lavished upon her there.

Alec visited briefly, with Molly, but excused himself almost as soon as he had come, saying that he had to join Taggart at the hotel. Rowan stared at the door long after he had exited through it.

"I'm so glad Luke's going to be all right," she said with a sigh, easing back against the pillows at last. "Is the whole town scandalized?"

Molly nodded vigorously. "Chins are flapping like washing in the breeze," she said. "I don't know what to make of everything they're saying. All that talk about Tommies knocking, and you and Alec coming back alone, and you takin' off down that mine with all your hair chopped off, and now all this talk about annulments and geological expeditions and what all..."

"Geological expeditions?" Rowan came to attention. "What about a geological expedition? Alec was talking about that while we were driving home."

Molly shifted uncomfortably, knowing she'd said too much. "Oh, it's just some talk those men were tossing back and forth. It doesn't signify."

"Molly."

"Well, now, that's all you're going to get out of me for now! You ask Alec if you want to know." Molly bounced up and yanked on the bellpull. "I ordered some food for you, had 'em keep it ready till you waked up."

"Molly—"

There was a knock at the door, and lunch was served. The matter was forgotten as Molly told her the rest of the news.

"They were pretty mad, all right, down at the mine, when Dewey and them heard about Alec bein' down there takin' pictures. They had Alec up before the sheriff this morning early."

"Molly, no!"

"Oh, yes. And they came to see Luke, as well, though I told 'em what I thought of 'em for pestering a man with a new-broken leg."

"But what did they— Molly, did Alec set off that explosion?"

Molly looked indignant as she poured coffee for them both. "With my Luke along with him? He'd never let any such thing happen to his mine. No, Alec never took a single picture down there. Didn't even get his stuff unpacked."

"You're joking." Rowan stared at her, a muffin growing cold in her hand.

"I surely am not. Luke got him down there and made him sit down and listen to the whole story about your pa and his brother and your money and the marriage deal and how we all went to Sacramento together. And they got to laughin' so hard, Luke said, they couldn't hardly move. Then the explosion came."

Rowan sat back, amazed and relieved. "Alec will be disappointed that he didn't get those pictures," she mused. "He thought they'd help sell his pictures from the Southwest. But they were laughing, did you say?"

"Laughin' fit to bust, my Luke said." Molly's eyes twinkled. "Seems they got to talking about all you've done since you hit America's shores, and they just couldn't help it. Luke especially liked where you went after Alec with a butter knife and near skinned him for a wolf."

Rowan colored up to the roots of her hair. "Well, there was more to it than that. I thought—" She broke off, and joined Molly in her laughter. "Oh, dear," she said, "I suppose I have been in a few scrapes along the way."

"I'll say. I don't know what I'm going to do when you go away." Molly's eyes were bright with humor and fondness.

Rowan sobered. Go away. Where would she go? What would she do? "Molly, you must tell me. Is Alec going on a geological expedition? I can't believe he'd give up his plans to go on his own."

"I honestly can't say, sweetie. Him and that Mr. Taggart fella have been all around town today, and nobody seems to know anything for sure."

Rowan smiled wryly. "That's hard to believe, in this town. It seems to me that they always know what we're doing before we do it."

Molly gave a giggle. "Lordy, what this town must think of us!"

"Pooh," Rowan said, buttering a muffin. "I don't care what they think, as long as all my friends are well and safe. To friends," she exclaimed, lifting her teacup.

"Friends and lovers," Molly said pointedly.

"Friends and lovers," Rowan repeated, but she felt a hollow place in her heart. Had all those words of love Alec had said to her in the mines been just a way to persuade her, to get her out safely? Had he been acting as a lover, or only as a friend?

The letters from Carn Rose were full of good news and startling revelations. Luke's letter from Henry was brief and to the point, but amazing, as well—he not only released the Trelarkens from their debt, but even apologized to both Luke and Rowan for the way in which he had manipulated their lives. Luke puffed on his pipe as Rowan read it to him, and sent looks of shy devotion to his Molly.

Gil's letter was much longer, and filled with news. Rowan read it with growing wonder, and then with tears both bitter and sweet.

"Rowan," he wrote, "the world is a cruel and wondrous place. I followed all the bits of information that

Father gave to me, and found that he was indeed telling the truth about the theft. There were two men seen
that night at the mine offices, and one was Father, as
he got the last of his papers before he slipped out of
town. The other, according to the witness that came
forward at last, was none other than our friend Henry
Syms. Henry had snooped around enough to know
about the extent of Father's troubles, and when he saw
him leaving the mine, he went in and took the money,
making it look as if Father took it. I found the records
of Henry's businesses and saw that his fortunes took a
great swing upward shortly after Father's disappear-
ance, though he took pains to keep his investments
away from Cornwall.

"I confronted Henry, along with a man I have made
friends with in London—more of him later. Henry saw
that his back was against the wall, and that we would
denounce him if he didn't do as we ordered. So, he tore
up the note and agreed to end the marriage bargain.
But we were not in time for you and Luke, I gather, for
your telegrams came that very day, saying that you had
been married. I'm sorry, Row. I would have spared you
this. But if you want an annulment, Henry is willing to
offer proof that he made you sign the contract under
duress and false pretenses. I'm drawing up the papers
right away, and hope they will come in time to spare
you and Luke much unpleasantness or pain."

They were free! Rowan sat back with the letter in her
hand, tears springing to her eyes. Her father was not a
thief, and he'd been as much a victim of Henry Syms's
lust for power and money as the rest of them. How
many lives had been touched by that one shameful act!

How many had nearly been destroyed. Anger boiled up in her, then quickly passed as she realized again that the long pain was ended.

She returned to the letter and read with delight that Gil had found a girl and was in love himself. "Her name is Miranda, and she is the daughter of Mr. John Edwards, the friend of mine who was so helpful to me in Carn Rose. I know that you will like her. Mother already does—she even seems to know that she's not someone out of the past, so that's progress, I should say."

Rowan smiled in happiness. It sounded as if Gil had been hiding his feelings for his Miranda from everyone, including the lady herself, and now he, too, was feeling the new freedom the truth had brought. Miranda's father was a London merchant of impeccable family and connections, he wrote, and Gil hadn't dared to speak until he had better prospects.

"She is the prettiest, best, and brightest girl ever, Row," he wrote with pride. "And she seems to like me well enough, though of course we don't speak of anything serious yet."

Rowan lowered the page in wonder. How far she had come from home, she thought. Not too long ago, she would have expected a courtship of that kind, full of attention to the fine points of manners and social custom. But here—in America!—all such customs had been left behind. From the moment she'd landed in San Francisco, everything had been turned topsy-turvy. Gil would be shocked, but he'd laugh, too, and understand her feelings and her reasons. Her mother, most likely, would doubtless refuse to understand a word of it, smile graciously, and change the subject.

"Well, Rowan Trelarken," she mused to herself. "What will *you* do next?"

She could be free and independent and live as she liked. She could pan for gold, if she wanted, or even run a hotel.

She could go home, to Cornwall. Now there was a temptation to be reckoned with. To see Gil again, and meet Miranda, to share in her mother's care—that would fill a real ache in her heart. And to see Nanstowe. That would be a sweet sight indeed.

She could stay in Grass Valley and work. People were more accepting of her now, and she had proved that she knew how to work at Alec's studio. She'd grown fond of this rough-and-tumble town, with its Cornish ties and its American independence.

But none of these tantalizing ideas filled her heart. They were lovely dreams, and some of them she would like to make come true, if she could, but none of them satisfied the way her single—and seemingly impossible—dream satisfied.

She wanted to be with Alec MacKenzie. She didn't care where or how, she just wanted to be at his side day after day, and in his arms night after night. She wanted to help him with his work, to care for him, to hear his voice and his laughter, to watch him move and hold him tight. She wanted to be with him and share his pains and sorrows. She wanted to share with him all their joys, triumphs, and even their failures. She wanted to hear him roll his *R*s when he got angry. She wanted to shower on him every pleasure and passion she could invent, and explore the limits of the magic they experienced every time their bodies were joined. She wanted to love him all the days of her life.

But he didn't seem to want her. Or did he? She had to have a plan....

Alec nailed the lid shut on the last box of darkroom supplies and made a circuit of his studio, checking for any items he might have left behind. The room rang with his footsteps; most of the furniture had been sold and carted away yesterday. All that remained was the kitchen table and his bed, both of which had come with the studio when he rented it.

He was leaving Grass Valley this morning, heading south with his cameras and his wagon and his dreams. By the end of the month, he'd be on some desert, or climbing a rocky canyon to take photographs that would not merely record the wonders of the American lands, but would also fill and satisfy his soul-deep need to accomplish this one great task. Yet there was one more thing he had to do, and he wasn't feeling at all confident about it.

He hefted a couple of boxes and pulled open the front door. He was halfway down the steps to the street before he saw her standing in the middle of his path, a shawl wrapped about her in the early morning chill.

"Rowan?"

"Good morning. Are there more things to be loaded up?" She nodded down to where his wagon waited on the street.

"Well, yes, but—"

He didn't get the chance to finish. She mounted the stairs two at a time and soon returned, minus her shawl and carrying a box of supplies.

"Rowan, you don't have to do that. I can—"

"I do have to," she said airily. "I intend to pull my weight on this trip."

"Your weight?" He stared as she passed him, heading for the wagon below. "This trip?"

"Yes."

He caught up with her at the back of the wagon. She was studying the layout of the interior with serious intent. "Now, where is the best place for these to go?" she asked. "Are they things we'll need now, or when we get where we're going?"

"Rowan, you aren't coming with me to Arizona. You can't." He set his burdens down and turned her to face him.

"Why can't I? I still owe you money. And Taggart. I want to work to pay off my debt. I can't work for you if I don't go with you."

He ran a hand over his face and groaned. "You don't owe me anything. You saved my life in the mine, remember? That was payment enough. And I have plenty of money now to make my way."

"What about the geological expedition?"

"I turned it down. I thought it would be all right at first, but then I realized that what I wanted was to make this trip myself, and not take any orders from anyone else. But that's not the point. The point is that you must either stay here or go home to your family in Cornwall. I want you to be happy, Rowan. I want you to be safe. You won't be safe or happy rattling through the wilderness with me.''

"Who says I won't?'' she asked, chin tilting upward. "How do you know that I'll be happy here, with Molly and Luke wrapped up in their own lives, and you and Taggart gone?''

"Then what about Cornwall? What about your mother and brother?''

She sighed. "I do love them. I hope to see them someday, but they don't really need me anymore. I have debts here. I won't leave America with anyone saying that I took advantage of everyone I met. You aren't the only one that I owe, you know. I owe Taggart, as well.''

She hopped up into the wagon and reached out her arms. "Hand one of those cartons to me. I think I recall where they belong.''

"Rowan!'' he cried. "You *cannot* come. Get down out of there and let me talk sensibly to you.''

"I won't.'' She crossed her arms over her chest. "If you try to leave without me, I'll go to the minister and the sheriff and every gossip in town and tell them you took advantage of me and left me ruined.''

"But I'm not leaving you ruined, you silly—'' He leapt up into the wagon and grabbed her by the shoulders. "If you'd only be still a moment and stop trying to railroad one of your mad plans through, you'd understand that I love you and that I'm not going away forever and that I want you for my wife!''

She gazed at him, startled. "What?''

"Which words should I explain? I love you. I don't want to lose you. I want you waiting for me when I come back." He dug into his waistcoat pocket and pulled out a small box. "I was going to give this to you tonight, over dinner at the hotel. I had a perfectly respectable—and, I think, rather winning—proposal all prepared. I had hoped for once that you wouldn't do something patently Rowanish, but here I am, in the middle of the street, with mules as my witnesses, asking you to marry me. I can't believe it."

He sank back against the cabinet, shaking his head. Rowan stared at him for a long moment, myriad emotions flickering across her face. Finally she touched his sleeve. "Do you want my answer?" she asked softly.

He looked up, his eyes hopeful. "Yes."

"Well, it's no!" she shouted. "If you think that you can pack me off with a pretty little ring and a pat on the head, saying 'Be a good girl and wait for me,' then you'd better think again, Alec MacKenzie! Of all the nerve, promising me all those wonderful things down there in the mine and then never making good on any of them! You said you'd make love to me on the kitchen table! You said you weren't going to let me out of your bed for a solid week! And now you want to—to patronize me with an engagement ring, and more hollow promises!"

She was in full fury now. Alec could only watch her in stunned surprise and growing amusement as she fumed at him. He opened the little box and held it out toward her.

"And don't you tell me it's too dangerous! I came all the way over to America on board a ship crowded with people, and I faced dangers all the way, and I— Oh, my God, Alec, it's gorgeous!" She put her hand out toward the glowing pearl-and-ruby ring nestled in black velvet. "Oh, no," she said, yanking her hand back. "I won't take it. You can't trick me with that. Either I go with you now, or I wake up this whole town and tell them how you've led me astray."

He grabbed her hand and pushed the ring onto her finger. "They'll never believe you. I'll just show them this and tell them I'm fully prepared to make an honest woman of you. And after all the fantastic stories you and Luke and Molly have been circulating around here, who do you think they'll believe?"

"I don't want to be an honest woman! Can't you see what I need?" She slipped her arms around his neck. "I don't care about being married or being respectable. I just want to be at your side, to share your life." She raised wide, crystal-rimmed eyes to his. "I love you, Alec. I'd be your mistress just to be with you."

"You will do no such thing." He embraced her tightly. "Angel, I want to be with you, too. I love you, more than my miserable tongue can speak. But I want to protect you, care for you." He moved away from her, to stand near the door and look out at the gathering day.

"You've shown me things as I've never seen them before," he continued. "These past few weeks, being with you and Luke and Molly, I've seen what it is to have friends around and to care for them, the way you do. After the war, I never thought I'd love anyone or care for anyone again. All happiness seemed a mockery to me after all the pain I'd seen. But you... you came along, and you messed up my life royally." He gave her a sudden grin. "You breathed life into me with all your insane plans and your irresistible illogic. You showed me the world that existed beyond my camera lens. You carry more light in your blue eyes than I can find in the whole of the sky." He came and embraced her again. "You're precious to me. I want to keep you safe."

She pulled back to look at him. "But you can't do that if you're nowhere around, can you?"

"Maybe not, but—"

"And I won't let you give up your dream." She peered at him intently. "I've watched you work. I've helped you work. Your photography is too much a part of you. I know what this trip means to you. I understand about the war and what you need to do. You need something to take the place of all those awful pictures in your mind, and you need to make a name for yourself as the great photographer you truly are. I'd never ask you to give this up."

She took a deep breath. "I've learned a great deal these past weeks, too. I've learned that no matter how much I love them and how much I do for them, bad things can happen to the people I love. I've learned that I can't give everything I have to others—there has to be something left for me. I have dreams, too, Alec. And right now, you and Arizona are my dreams."

"Love, it's dangerous out there. And dirty." He paused. "There'd be raccoons."

She laughed and wound herself around him, pressing herself against him from shoulder to thigh. "And you would miss this, wouldn't you?" she murmured against his cheek. "And this?" She kissed him deeply, her tongue making a delicate outline of his lips before it thrust gently inside to raise his body heat until it was rapidly approaching a boil.

"Oh, God," he moaned, capitulating to her tantalizing, shameless explorations with hands and lips. "What am I going to do with you?"

"Love me," she demanded, writhing in his arms. "Take me with you, and love me every step of the way."

He pushed her gently away. "All right. I will. But only on two conditions."

"And those are?"

"First, that we're married tonight."

"Done. Oh, Alec!" She hugged him tightly. "I can't think of anything more wonderful!" She pulled back to look at him, happiness radiant in her face. "And the second condition?"

He pulled her down out of the wagon and hurried her up the stairs, protesting and squealing at his insistence. He ushered her through the door, banged it shut, locked it, and yanked down the shade. She was wide-eyed with wonder and apprehension as he turned and faced her.

"The kitchen table is over there," he said. He moved toward her with a warm, determined glint in his eyes. "I'll not have my wife saying I don't keep my promises."

By the time they left the following morning, all their promises had been fulfilled.

* * * * *

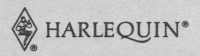

HARLEQUIN®

THE TAGGARTS OF TEXAS!

Harlequin's Ruth Jean Dale brings you
THE TAGGARTS OF TEXAS!

Those Taggart men—strong, sexy and hard to resist...

You've met Jesse James Taggart in FIREWORKS!
Harlequin Romance #3205 (July 1992)

And Trey Smith—he's THE RED-BLOODED YANKEE!
Harlequin Temptation #413 (October 1992)

And the unforgettable Daniel Boone Taggart in SHOWDOWN!
Harlequin Romance #3242 (January 1993)

Now meet Boone Smith and the Taggarts who started it all—
in LEGEND!
Harlequin Historical #168 (April 1993)

Read all the Taggart romances!
Meet all the Taggart men!

Available wherever Harlequin Books are sold.

Harlequin® Historical

WARRIOR SERIES

The WARRIOR SERIES from author
Margaret Moore

It began with A WARRIOR'S HEART (HH #118, March 1992)—the unforgettable story of Emryss Delanyea, a wounded Welsh nobleman who returns from the crusades with all thoughts of love put aside forever . . . until he meets the Lady Roanna.

Now, in A WARRIOR'S QUEST (HH #175, June 1993), healer Fritha Kendrick teaches mercenary Urien Fitzroy to live by his heart rather than his sword.

And, coming in early 1994, look for A WARRIOR'S PRIDE, the third title of this medieval trilogy.

WIN-A-FORTUNE
OFFICIAL RULES • MILLION DOLLAR SWEEPSTAKES
NO PURCHASE OR OBLIGATION NECESSARY TO ENTER

To enter, follow the directions published. **ALTERNATE MEANS OF ENTRY:** Hand-print your name and address on a 3″×5″ card and mail to either: Harlequin Win-A-Fortune, 3010 Walden Ave., P.O. Box 1867, Buffalo, NY 14269-1867, or Harlequin Win A Fortune, P.O. Box 609, Fort Erie, Ontario L2A 5X3, and we will assign your Sweepstakes numbers (Limit: one entry per envelope). For eligibility, entries must be received no later than March 31, 1994 and be sent via 1st-class mail. No liability is assumed for printing errors or lost, late or misdirected entries.

To determine winners, the sweepstakes numbers on submitted entries will be compared against a list of randomly preselected prizewinning numbers. In the event all prizes are not claimed via the return of prizewinning numbers, random drawings will be held from among all other entries received to award unclaimed prizes.

Prizewinners will be determined no later than May 30, 1994. Selection of winning numbers and random drawings are under the supervision of D.L. Blair, Inc., an independent judging organization whose decisions are final. One prize to a family or organization. No substitution will be made for any prize, except as offered. Taxes and duties on all prizes are the sole responsibility of winners. Winners will be notified by mail. Chances of winning are determined by the number of entries distributed and received.

Sweepstakes open to persons 18 years of age or older, except employees and immediate family members of Torstar Corporation, D.L. Blair, Inc., their affiliates, subsidiaries and all other agencies, entities and persons connected with the use, marketing or conduct of this Sweepstakes. All applicable laws and regulations apply. Sweepstakes offer void wherever prohibited by law. Any litigation within the province of Quebec respecting the conduct and awarding of a prize in this Sweepstakes must be submitted to the Régies des Loteries et Courses du Quebec. In order to win a prize, residents of Canada will be required to correctly answer a time-limited arithmetical skill-testing question. Values of all prizes are in U.S. currency.

Winners of major prizes will be obligated to sign and return an affidavit of eligibility and release of liability within 30 days of notification. In the event of non-compliance within this time period, prize may be awarded to an alternate winner. Any prize or prize notification returned as undeliverable will result in the awarding of the prize to an alternate winner. By acceptance of their prize, winners consent to use of their names, photographs or other likenesses for purposes of advertising, trade and promotion on behalf of Torstar Corporation without further compensation, unless prohibited by law.

This Sweepstakes is presented by Torstar Corporation, its subsidiaries and affiliates in conjunction with book, merchandise and/or product offerings. Prizes are as follows: Grand Prize—$1,000,000 (payable at $33,333.33 a year for 30 years). First through Sixth Prizes may be presented in different creative executions, each with the following approximate values: First Prize—$35,000; Second Prize—$10,000; 2 Third Prizes—$5,000 each; 5 Fourth Prizes—$1,000 each; 10 Fifth Prizes—$250 each; 1,000 Sixth Prizes—$100 each. Prizewinners will have the opportunity of selecting any prize offered for that level. A travel-prize option if offered and selected by winner, must be completed within 12 months of selection and is subject to hotel and flight accommodations availability. Torstar Corporation may present this sweepstakes utilizing names other than Million Dollar Sweepstakes. For a current list of all prize options offered within prize levels and all names the Sweepstakes may utilize, send a self-addressed stamped envelope (WA residents need not affix return postage) to: Million Dollar Sweepstakes Prize Options/Names, P.O. Box 7410, Blair, NE 68009.

For a list of prizewinners (available after July 31, 1994) send a separate, stamped self-addressed envelope to: Million Dollar Sweepstakes Winners, P.O. Box 4728, Blair NE 68009.

SWP-H493

Where do you find hot Texas nights, smooth Texas charm and dangerously sexy cowboys?

AMARILLO BY MORNING

Show time—Texas style!

Everybody loves a cowboy, and Cal McKinney is one of the best. So when designer Serena Davis approaches this handsome rodeo star, the last thing Cal expects is a business proposition!

CRYSTAL CREEK reverberates with the exciting rhythm of Texas. Each story features the rugged individuals who live and love in the Lone Star State. And each one ends with the same invitation...

Y'ALL COME BACK...REAL SOON!

Don't miss **AMARILLO BY MORNING** by Bethany Campbell. Available in May wherever Harlequin books are sold.

Following the success of WITH THIS RING and
TO HAVE AND TO HOLD, Harlequin brings you

JUST MARRIED

SANDRA CANFIELD
MURIEL JENSEN
ELISE TITLE
REBECCA WINTERS

just in time for the 1993 wedding season!

Written by four of Harlequin's most popular authors, this
four-story collection celebrates the joy, excitement and
adjustment that comes with being "just married."

You won't want to miss this spring tradition, whether
you're just married or not!

**AVAILABLE IN APRIL WHEREVER HARLEQUIN
BOOKS ARE SOLD**